RED IN THE MORNING

BY THE SAME AUTHOR

Published by
WARD, LOCK & CO., LTD.

THE "BERRY" BOOKS
THE BROTHER OF DAPHNE
THE COURTS OF IDLENESS
BERRY AND CO.
JONAH AND CO.
ADÈLE AND CO.
AND BERRY CAME TOO
THE HOUSE THAT BERRY
  BUILT

THE "CHANDOS" BOOKS
BLIND CORNER
PERISHABLE GOODS
BLOOD ROYAL
FIRE BELOW
SHE FELL AMONG THIEVES
AN EYE FOR A TOOTH
RED IN THE MORNING

OTHER VOLUMES
THE STOLEN MARCH
THIS PUBLICAN
ANTHONY LYVEDEN
VALERIE FRENCH
SAFE CUSTODY
STORM MUSIC
AND FIVE WERE FOOLISH
AS OTHER MEN ARE
MAIDEN STAKES
SHE PAINTED HER FACE
GALE WARNING
SHOAL WATER
PERIOD STUFF

RED IN
THE MORNING

BY

DORNFORD YATES

Red in the morning,
Shepherd's warning.

WARD, LOCK & CO., LIMITED
LONDON AND MELBOURNE

First published . . 1946

BOOK
PRODUCTION
WAR ECONOMY
STANDARD

THE TYPOGRAPHY OF THIS BOOK
CONFORMS TO THE
AUTHORIZED ECONOMY STANDARD

MADE IN ENGLAND
Printed in Great Britain by Butler & Tanner Ltd., Frome and London

CONTENTS

To

JILL

for her great heart

RED IN THE MORNING

CHAPTER I

WE MAKE AN ENEMY

IT was, I remember, in the summer of 193— that Jenny (my wife) and I had taken a villa at Freilles and that Jonathan Mansel was spending some days with us. Freilles was a little resort some thirty miles north of Bayonne on the Bay of Biscay. It was simple and quite unspoiled, but its sands were the finest for bathing I ever knew: they were broad and firm and they sloped very gently seaward without any ' steps,' thus making smooth the path of the great Atlantic rollers, that came prepared to do battle and played a pageant, instead.

How we three came to be there, I need not say ; but Mansel and I were both tired and were glad to take it easy and, so to speak, put up our feet. Carson and Bell, our servants, were taking their ease with us, and, indeed, our quiet establishment was more like a rest-camp in warfare than anything else.

And then, one summer evening, without the slightest warning, we found ourselves involved in a matter of life and death.

This was the way of it.

Some friends of ours in Biarritz had learned that we were at Freilles, and nothing would satisfy them but that we should drive over one evening, to dine and dance. And so we did—and, against all expectation, enjoyed our-selves very much. We finished the evening at the Casino —in fact, in the Baccarat Room, for, though Mansel cared little for playing, he liked to observe the company gathered about the board. We stayed for about an hour, and

Jenny, because she knew nothing, won seventeen thousand francs—to her own great confusion and everyone else's delight. The party then broke up, but, since somebody staying at Bidart was short of a car, we sent them back with Jenny and asked the latter to meet us a little way off; for, after the airless card-room, Mansel and I were glad of a chance to walk.

Mansel spoke to the servants.

"Drive to the light-house," he said, "and wait for us there. It's under a mile and a half, so we ought to be there very nearly as soon as you."

So the Rolls went off with Jenny, who would, I fear, have preferred to walk with us, while Mansel and I set out for our rendezvous.

To reach the *Phare* or light-house, we had to walk the length of the *plage* and then up a fairly long hill : at the top of this we should have to turn to the left and on to the spur or headland on which the light-house stood.

There was nobody by the *plage*, but Biarritz keeps late hours and, when we came to the hill, more than one villa was lighted and cars were moving or were waiting by the side of the way.

We were half-way up the hill and were almost abreast of a car which was facing us and had been drawn close to our kerb, when its driver struck a match and lighted a cigarette. And so we both saw his face . . .

I had not seen him for years, but I knew him at once—and so did Mansel. He was a man called Punter, a common thief; and twice we had come up against him in days gone by. He had not worked alone, but had made one of a gang which knew no law. And since the fellow was incorrigible, I had no doubt at all that he was at this moment subscribing to some iniquity.

As we moved clear of the car, I felt Mansel's hand on my arm.

"Did you see who that was?" he breathed.

" I did," I whispered. " He's going a little gray."

" But he's just the same," murmured Mansel ; " let's loiter here for a moment."

The wall which we had been skirting had come to a sudden end, or, rather, had turned at right angles away from the road. We left the pavement and stood behind the corner it made.

Mansel continued quietly.

" Just the same wash-out. Must have his cigarette— so he gives a first-class close-up to a couple of passers-by. I wonder who he's working for now. And when I say ' now,' I mean it. I'll lay there's something doing within those walls." He glanced at the villa, standing within its garden, right upon the edge of the cliff. " No lights to be seen : but Punter is sitting, waiting, outside its door. And the engine of his car is running. . . ."

With his words, came the sound of a shot—the roar of an automatic : it came from within the villa, by which we stood. We heard it, Mansel and I ; and Punter heard it, too—for, as we leaned out of our cover, to glance at the car, his cigarette came flying out of his window, to lie and glow where it fell in front of the door in the wall.

Now I had fully expected that the shot would herald the departure of Punter's friends : and so, I imagine, had he : but thirty seconds went by, yet no one appeared.

Again Mansel spoke in my ear.

" Big business, this, I fancy. I don't propose to intrude, but, just for old times' sake, we might put a spoke in his wheel. Literally. I mean, those rods are waiting."

I had but to follow his gaze, to see what he meant.

A street-lamp was lighting the spot by which we stood— by the garden-wall of the villa in which the shot had been fired. Here building was being done, and a number of soft-steel rods—to be used in ferro-concrete—were lying by the side of the pavement, three paces from where we were. In a flash I had picked one up . . .

(In that instant, I well remember, the Rolls went by— on her way, of course, to the light-house, a quarter of a mile ahead.)

I glanced up and down the hill, but no other car was moving, and the nearest that I could see was a hundred yards off. I moved out into the road, holding the rod in my hands, as a tight-rope dancer holds his balancing-pole. I stopped when I was abreast of Punter's near hind wheel. Then I ' fed ' the rod to Mansel, who took its end and passed this between the spokes—or, to be more precise, through one of the gaps in the disc of the modern wheel. So for, perhaps, five seconds . . . Then Mansel lifted his hand, as a signal to stop, and whipped like a shadow itself to the opposite side of the car. Almost at once his hand went up again, and again I ' fed ' the steel to his capable hands. When he gave me the signal to stop, some seven feet were protruding from either side of the car.

I bent the steel at right angles and stepped behind the boot, and Mansel did the same and handed his end to me. I twisted the two together and laid them down. Then I followed him back to our corner, beside the wall.

We waited, I suppose, ninety seconds—it may have been less. Then the door in the wall was opened, and I saw the flash of a torch.

Three figures whipped out of that door, over the pavement and into the waiting car ; and from the villa behind them came shouts and cries.

As a door of the car was slammed, the car seemed to jar and shudder ; and that was all.

" Your hand-brake, you ——— ! " screeched someone.

Punter used his self-starter and opened his throttle wide, but the car only jarred again, and its engine stopped.

With a frightful oath—

" Out and break," snapped the man who had spoken before.

The uproar in the villa was growing.

As Punter made to get out, some object flew out of the villa and struck his door—I afterwards found that this was a log of wood—and we heard the man yelp with pain, because, I suppose, the door had returned upon him and had jammed his hand or his leg.

The next moment the car was empty.

Where the other two went, I did not see, but Punter went down the hill and one man flung up past us with a case in his hand. He never saw us in the shadows, but he saw the half-finished building and whipped inside. A moment later he emerged, but without his case, and turned up the hill again, running on the tips of his toes. Twice I had seen his face clearly, thanks to the street-lamp's light. To my great surprise, it looked the face of an idiot—at any rate, that of a very foolish man: only, the eyes were burning.

Logs were being hurled at the standing car. Then a man in dress clothes appeared, with a log in his hand.

"Come back, Toby, you madman!" cried someone in French.

The man slammed his log through a window and peered inside.

"They're gone," he roared, in English. "This car's a decoy. They left it here, to fool us: and now they're two miles off."

Thus reassured, the others came pouring out—men and women and servants, English and French. Some ran, I think, for the police, and others to telephone; but Mansel stepped out of the shadows and up to the man called Toby, still standing with his log in his hand.

"Well, Toby," I heard him say.

"By ——, Jonah," said the other. "And here's a go."

"I know," said Mansel. "Come over here, will you? I want to say a word in your ear."

They came to where I was standing, and Mansel introduced him as Captain Toby Rage.

"Now get this, Toby," said Mansel, "I am not on in this scene. French police investigation is bad for my heart. But we two saw some of what happened, and if you look in that building, I think you will find 'the swag.'"

"Go on," said Toby, incredulously.

"I think so. I think it's been parked there—something certainly has. Now if I am right, the wallah that parked it there is going to come back : so if you play your cards carefully, you'll not only get 'the swag,' but you'll get him, too."

"But they had two cars," cried Toby.

"No, they didn't," said Mansel. "That was their car. But they couldn't drive it away, for we put it out of action as soon as we heard the shot. Was anyone hurt ? "

"Butler shot dead," said Toby. "I saw it done."

Mansel shrugged his shoulders.

"It's up to you," he said. "The stuff is in that building. The—big shot put it there, before he retired. And if it's at all worth having, he'll come back to pick it up."

Toby set a hand on his arm.

"Help us to get him, Jonah. I mean, this is right down your street."

Mansel shook his head.

"Sorry. The police are too tiresome. I don't want to be involved. Remember that. Toby. You're not to let me in. Damn it all—if you're careful, you can't go wrong." He turned to me. "Come, William."

We bade Toby Rage good night and turned up the hill.

"Did you see the—big shot ? " said Mansel.

"Clearly," said I.

"Queer-looking cove, isn't he ? "

"You know him ? " said I.

"I know who he is," said Mansel. "I thought it was

he the moment I heard his voice. I got in his way once
—a few years back. My cousins and I, between us,
prevented him from acquiring some eighty thousand
pounds."

I swallowed before replying, for exaggeration is not
among Mansel's faults.

"I don't suppose," said I, "he remembers you in his
prayers."

"That," said Mansel, gravely, "would be too much to
expect. Still, it was nice to see him again—and nicer
still to have put a spoke in his wheel. And if Toby
Rage does his stuff, he ought to go down the drain. And
it's just about time he did—he's a devilish dangerous
man. You see, he's one of those felons—happily, very
few—who are ready to go all lengths. That is why he
has lasted so long. Audacity always pays. It was
almost certainly he who shot the butler dead. If death
will assist such a man, then somebody dies."

"And he looks," said I, "he looks a full-marks fool."

"I know," said Mansel. "A most extraordinary
thing. Yet, he's right at the top of his calling, and always
was. Thieves call him ' Auntie Emma '—of all strange
sobriquets. His real name is Daniel Gedge, and he must
be about forty-five."

"Just as well he didn't see you," said I. "I mean,
he'd have known at once that he had you to thank for
his failure to get away. And his eyes betrayed his
emotion—you can't get away from that."

"Just as well," said Mansel, and left it there.

At the top of the hill we turned to go down to the
light-house, and two or three minutes later we rounded
a bend to see the lights of the Rolls.

I must make two things clear. First, in front of the
light-house there was an open space in which, despite
the trees, there could have been parked some fifteen or
twenty cars: the spot was in fact a public belvedere,

from which a man could survey the whole of the Biarritz *plage*. Secondly, the lantern of the light-house had been at work since dusk, and every so many seconds its beam swept round, to search the neighbourhood. (The beam had hardly illumined the hill up which we had come, for the buildings upon our left hand had stood in its way.)

We were, perhaps, eighty yards off, when the lantern's beam came round, to show the Rolls facing our way and Carson standing beside her—with his arms not folded but crossed, his right wrist over his left.

Mansel and I stopped dead. Though we could not see the pistol, we knew it was in Carson's right hand.

"And here's trouble," breathed Mansel. "Gedge has come by this way." His hand went up to his chin. "He must have recognized Carson, and Carson has recognized him. And he knows that where Carson is, I shall very soon be."

"And he knows," said I, "he knows why his car wouldn't move."

"More," said Mansel. "He knows that to return for his plunder would be the act of a fool."

I bit my lip.

"He's waiting for you," I said.

"I imagine so," said Mansel. "I mean, his emotions apart, he'd be very well advised to put me out. You see, inside the villa he was almost certainly masked: but I can identify him." He sighed. "And Jenny sitting there waiting . . . I hope to God she's asleep."

Mercifully, though we could see, we could not be seen, for some trees which were growing beside us were thick with leaves, and the beam could not pierce the cover their branches gave. But ten paces farther on this came to an end.

I tried to think what we could do.

We always carried a pistol within the Rolls; but Carson would never have drawn it, unless some considerable danger had lifted its head. He, of course, knew nothing of what we had seen and done : but he knew that Gedge was at hand, and that was enough for him. That he did not know where he was was perfectly clear, for whenever the beam came round, I saw his head slowly turning, as though to miss no movement which might give his man away.

" You go back," said I, " and let me go up to the car." But as I spoke, I knew what the answer would be.

" Not on your life," said Mansel. " He is expecting me—and he hasn't seen me for years. Remember, this light is tricky. And though he mayn't be quite certain, he'll play for safety—and shoot. And Carson is in very great danger. Gedge can, of course, see him ; but he can't see Gedge."

That we were badly placed was painfully clear.

Gedge had done one murder some twenty minutes ago : and, since he had but one neck, the fellow had nothing to lose by doing two more : but he had much to gain, for Mansel and Carson *alive* could both identify him. Then, again, to kill Mansel must be his heart's desire, for this was the second time that Mansel had spoiled his game. And he was there in the shadows, behind a bush or a tree ; but the Rolls was out in the fairway, which, every so many seconds, was lighted up. And Jenny, my wife, the gentlest creature, I think, I ever knew, was actually on the stage which was set for battle and murder and sudden death.

" It goes without saying," said Mansel, " that Bell has the wheel of the Rolls and his eyes on this road. We could, therefore, move clear of these trees and sign to him to come on. But I daren't do that because of Carson : for the moment Gedge sees the car move, he'll open fire. At least, he very well may : and that's a risk I can't take. And Jenny in the front line ! There must be some way out, but I can't see it yet."

B

"I believe I can," said I. "I've just remembered something. I stayed here years ago, and I've never been back. But now I remember . . . This isn't the only road that leads to the *Phare*. There's another one— to the right : less than a road—a lane. We can't see it from here, but, as she is standing now, the Rolls must be opposite its mouth. Broadside on, of course."

"Where," said Mansel, "where does that lane come out ? "

"Into the road we left six minutes ago. It's the second turning on the left : we took the first : I don't think they're more than three hundred yards apart."

"What then ? " said Mansel.

"I leave you here," I said, "and I take that lane. I shall find the car before me, broadside on. I shall be on her near side : but Carson is on her off side and is looking away from the car. The car will, therefore, be standing between me and Gedge. And if I watch that beam, I can get to a door unseen."

"So far, so good. And then ? "

"I whisper to Bell to call Carson. That's natural enough. He tells him to wait thirty seconds and then to move round the car and, once it's between him and Gedge, to sprint up the lane. There he will find Bell and me—with Jenny safe in my arms. And when Gedge gets tired of waiting, he's free to have a look at the Rolls : with her switch and her bonnet locked, she won't help him much."

After, perhaps, one minute—

"I don't like it much," said Mansel : "but, as I live, I can't see a better way out. I don't like your going alone, but I daren't leave here. That Carson should speak to Bell is natural enough, but he simply must play up when he moves round the car . . . behave as though he had heard a suspicious sound . . . prowl, rather than move—you see what I mean. For Gedge is no damned fool. And for God's sake watch that beam. I can't think of anything else."

"You'll leave with Carson," I said.

"Yes," said Mansel. "The Hotel Regina's at hand: we'd better meet there."

"In twenty minutes," said I, and, with that, I ran like a hare the way we had come. . . .

My memory had not failed me. The Rolls was presenting her side to the little lane. But there was no cover there, and I had to lie flat on my face, when the beam came round, and then get up and advance when the light was gone. This for some sixty yards: and I had to step warily, for the surface was rough. And, curiously enough, that fact contributed to our deliverance.

I was ten paces from the car, when my foot struck a stone. Carson heard the sound and 'prowled' round the back of the Rolls, to see what it meant. And, as we met, two cars full of joyous revellers came sliding down past Mansel, to come to rest on the other side of the Rolls.

In a flash I had the doors open.

"Let her go, Bell," I cried. . . .

Carson and I were inside, Jenny was in my arms, and the Rolls was clear of the *place* in a moment of time.

"Stand by for Captain Mansel: he's just on your right."

"I see him, sir," said Bell, and slowed for an instant, while Mansel whipped into the car.

As we swung to the left for Chiberta, *en route* for Freilles—

"You have been a long time," said Jenny.

"I know, we have, my beauty. You see, we saw some-one we knew."

"I said you had," said Jenny. "Didn't I say so, Bell?"

"You did, madam."

"Is that the truth?" said Jenny. "Because, although I said it, I wasn't sure?"

"Why weren't you sure, my darling?"

"I had a feeling that you were up against it—and Jonathan, too. It was—very strong, Richard."

(My names are Richard, William. When Jenny calls me Richard, I know she is very grave.)

"We did have a brush," said I. "But it's over now."

"I don't think it is," said Jenny. "So please be very careful in all you do."

And there we left the business, to talk of other things. But Jenny has an instinct such as I never encountered in anyone else. For this faculty, Mansel and I had a deep respect : and I knew that he, as was I, was thinking of Daniel Gedge and was wondering whether indeed we had seen the last of him.

It was, perhaps, an hour later, when Jenny had gone to bed, that we summoned Bell and Carson, to hear what they had to tell.

"It was like this, sir," said Carson. "Bell had the wheel, and I was, of course, by his side. We'd been waiting about ten minutes—it may have been more—waiting just where you saw us, with just the parking lights on. When we'd stopped, I'd let my window down, for you know that Madam can't never have too much air. I hadn't seen no one about, but I thought I heard a foot-step behind the car. So I put out my head to see. At that moment the beam comes round an' lights everything up. And there I see Gedge standing—not twelve feet off. Of course I knew him at once, an' I saw him recognize me. There was no mistaking that, for I saw him start. Then he shot a look up the road—and the beam went out. I strained my ears an' waited : but when the beam came back, there he still was where he'd been, staring up the road. The light seemed to wake him up, for he turned his head very sharp, to look back at me. Glare, rather than look, sir. That made me think. Then the beam went out again, and I heard him run very lightly behind the car. An' then Bell heard him moving the other side.

" So I tipped Bell off, drew the pistol and then slipped out of the car. Gedge was mischievous, sir : I was sure of that. And with Madam sitting behind . . . But once I was out of the car, it gave me a chance. Of course he was not to be seen, when the beam came round : but I knew he was there somewhere ; and, sure enough, when the beam came round again, I saw him move. An' then I lost him again."

He addressed himself to Mansel.

" I made sure something had happened to make him mad. An' then I realized that it must be something you'd done. I mean, sir, he'd come your way an', knowing that I was your servant, he'd showed his hate. And I didn't half like the idea of your walking up to the car : but I daren't tell Bell to move, because you'd said to wait there, an', for all I knew, as things were, you'd had some good reason for that. An' then I remembered you'd see me, as you came down the road, an' directly you saw me, sir, you'd know there was something wrong."

" As I did," said Mansel, and set a match to his pipe. " You couldn't have done any more, and I certainly owe you my life. And now you shall hear our tale."

With that, he related what I have already set down.

" And there we are," he concluded. " I hardly think our friend will pursue the matter. Thieves have their living to earn : and they wouldn't earn their living if they spent their time destroying the people who'd cramped their style. All the same, Gedge is sore—for this is the second time that I've helped to get in his way. And so he may turn nasty. If he does—well, he doesn't know where we are, but he'll soon find out : he has the number of the car, and there aren't so many Rolls on the Silver Coast. So let us keep our eyes open—and carry arms."

* * * * *

In the paper of the following morning, the violent affair at Biarritz took pride of place. As Mansel had surmised, the men had been masked : the jewels which had been taken were said to be worth some seventy thousand pounds : (this may have been true, for the party had been attended by two immensely rich women, both well known for the rarity of their gems) : the butler had been shot dead, because, though told to stand still, he had made to set on a table a tray which he had in his hands—a very barbarous thing, for the tray was heavy-laden and the butler was not a young man. All the jewels had been recovered : they had been found, through the vigilance of the police (*sic*), in the half-finished building of which I have spoken before ; but, though a strict watch had been kept, the thieves had not returned to collect their spoil when the workmen engaged on the building began to arrive.

Then came ' the mystery.'

' An examination of the car which had been used by the bandits at once revealed the reason for its abandonment.' (Here followed a description of the method which we had applied.) ' The question is—who did the rogues this ill turn ? Was it a rival gang ? Or was it some mischievous idler, who had no idea that he was assisting Justice, but only meant to embarrass some innocent motorist ? If it was a rival gang . . . In any event it is clear that to this action is due the so prompt recovery of the jewels. That they would have been recovered eventually goes without saying, just as the arrest of the bandits is but a matter of time. The police are pursuing their inquiries with their customary efficiency.'

It was, at least, clear that Captain Toby Rage had kept his counsel and ours.

When I showed Mansel the paper, he covered his eyes.

"The last sentence," he said, "is pathetic. It really is. Gedge has been 'working' the Continent for certainly fifteen years. He frequents *The Wet Flag* at Rouen and *The Red Nose* at Montmartre—taverns which the police never raid, for reasons best known to themselves. So that, if they show no more than their 'customary efficiency,' Gedge is about as safe as a man in an iron lung."

"They don't know that Gedge was involved."

"They damned well ought to," said Mansel. "And I think they probably do. In England, five times out of six, the Yard know at once who's committed a crime like this. I don't say they always get him—they mayn't be able to crack his alibi. But they see him all right. And they ask him where he was on the twenty-second day of July. But I'll lay any money you like that the French police never see Gedge. He's out of the top drawer. Add to that that they concentrate on their ports. But Gedge never tries to get out. The continent of Europe is quite good enough for him."

"And us? Will he turn on us?"

Mansel shrugged his shoulders.

"We shall know," he said, "before the end of this week."

In fact we knew that morning—at about a quarter to twelve.

The three of us were bathing as usual, for it was a lovely day. Whilst Bell remained in the house, Carson had brought us to the *plage* and was coming to fetch us again at a quarter to one. All Freilles was in the water or on the sand, that is to say, some hundred and fifty souls: but since there was room for five thousand, every party was very well able to keep to itself. In fact, our bathing-tent was the last of the line and was pitched about thirty yards from the one on its right. We seldom entered the tent, for we drove from the villa in *peignoirs*, all ready to bathe ; but we left our things before it, or sometimes inside. On this particular morning, Mansel had folded his gown and had laid it within the tent, for a pistol was in its pocket in case of accidents.

We usually left the water about mid-day, to bask for forty-five minutes, before we left the *plage* ; upon this morning, however, Jenny came out before we did and made her way to the tent. Five minutes later, perhaps, I looked towards where she would be, to see her in conversation with a man who was actually seated inside our tent. At once I hailed Mansel, some twenty yards farther out, and when I saw that he heard me, I swam for the shore. . . .

I waded out of the water and hastened over the sand. As I reached Jenny's side—

" Pray be seated, Mr. Chandos," said the stranger. " Quite close to Mrs. Chandos. And please don't interfere with Captain Mansel's approach. I'm not going to kill him—here."

The fellow was sitting cross-legged, as tailors do. His wrists were upon his thighs, and in either hand was a pistol, their muzzles drooping together into his lap. But his wrists looked very supple . . .

All things considered, it seemed best to do as he said.

" So provoking," he continued, " so odious to embarrass Mrs. Chandos like this. If there is one thing I hate doing, it is revealing to a lady my cloven hoof. Yes, this is Captain Mansel's pistol. So very thoughtful of him to have left it here. . . . Ah, here he is." A flick of his wrists, and one pistol was covering Mansel and the other was covering me. " Charmed to meet you, Captain

Mansel. I trust you will see the wisdom of sitting down. Force my hand if you must ; but I'd rather not startle the *plage*."

Mansel regarded him straitly. Then he sat down by my side. Slowly the two muzzles turned, to droop into the stranger's lap.

He continued easily.

"I was just telling Mr. Chandos how deeply I regretted——"

"No doubt," said Mansel, shortly. "What do you want ? "

The other nodded.

"I know just how you feel," he said. "Never mind. You ask what I want. The answer is the great pleasure of ten minutes' talk with you."

"Kindly allow Mrs. Chandos to take her leave."

The stranger shook his head.

"For reasons which you will appreciate, your request is refused."

"She will go to the edge of the water and stay within sight."

"No."

The fellow rapped out the word, as a sergeant upon the square.

Mansel raised his eyebrows.

"Come to the point," he said.

It was a most curious experience. But seventy paces away, men and women and children were frolicking in the surf. We could hear their laughter and we were full in their sight. Yet we could not move nor cry out— because there was death in the tent. Death wore the shape of a well-bred, clean-shaven man of, perhaps, forty-five, and as I presently learned that he was known as Brevet, from this time on I will venture to use his name. His features were good but his gray eyes were set too close. His voice was soft and cultured ; his manner, nonchalant ; and he wore a look of the most profound resignation from first to last.

" So unfortunate," drawled Brevet, " that you should have, er, intruded the other night. If there's one thing more than another which my, er, colleague detests, it is intrusion upon his private affairs : and when such intrusion impairs his enterprise, his, er, impatience of the intruder is very marked. This is understandable. You'd be surprised if you knew how much time and money went to the preparation of the ground for the exercise which you, er, embarrassed the other night. And what, if you will forgive the phrase, tends to aggravate your offence—of course, in my colleague's eyes—is the unfortunate fact that this is not the first time that you have, er, inconvenienced him. On the other occasion, also, a considerable amount of money—and money's worth was, I believe, involved. In these circumstances, it must be, I think, most clear that if my colleague is to pursue his, er, calling with any degree of confidence, he must receive some assurance that this interference will cease. The most satisfactory assurance would take the form of your death—upon which, I may say, my colleague had set his heart. Had. But, after two hours' hard work, I managed to bring him round. He's a difficult fellow, Gedge. A brilliant felon—quite brilliant : but, strictly between you and me, a very vulgar blackguard. His language, for instance, is sometimes incredibly coarse. And a master of blasphemy ! But, as I say, I hauled the swine out of his wallow and made him see sense. And so he agreed that I should call upon you and tell you the price at which we value your health. That price is, shortly, thirty-five thousand pounds. If you like to pay me that money within three weeks, the incident will be closed. If you don't, then your life will be closed—of that, you need have no doubt. Gedge is in the slips. And, to be perfectly frank, offered your life or your

money, he'd choose your life. But I am more mer-
cenary. Besides, of course, you've only embarrassed me
once. Well, there we are, Captain Mansel. How do you
feel?"

"There's only one answer," said Mansel.

"Pray let me have it," said the other, "for what it is
worth. Such language as Gedge understands must be
painfully clear."

Mansel regarded him sternly.

"You have demanded with menaces thirty-five thousand pounds. If you had asked thirty-five shillings, you
would have gone empty away. You see, I'm one of
those people who don't subscribe to blackmail."

The other sighed.

"You know," he said, "I felt it would be like that.
From Gedge's strictures upon your outlook—strictures,
I may say, which were tinctured with every shade of
obscenity—there emerged the clear impression that you
would have nothing to do with dirty work. And so,
when I set out, I had a definite feeling that I was wasting
my time. When I saw you, that feeling was, so to speak,
fortified. And I am by no means surprised that you
prefer to die, rather than to render to Caesar the things
that are God's. You must forgive my flights—I was once
a gentleman. Years ago, of course. And I took a first
class in Honour Moderations. Unfortunately, shortly
afterwards, I took twenty-seven pounds from the monies
entrusted to my care. *Facilis descensus Averni*. And I
have never looked back." In one astonishing movement, he rose to his feet and slid his hands into the
pockets of the good-looking jacket he wore. "Well,
Captain Mansel, that's over. There'll be no holding my
colleague, when he hears what you have to say. And he
can do his stuff, you know. That's why I work with
him. A poisonous bounder, of course: but he can do
his stuff. Frankly, I shouldn't like him to, er, earmark

me. And, of course, he will have my support in all that he does."

" You've had my answer," said Mansel.

" I have," said Brevet. " *Te moriturum saluto*." He took out Mansel's pistol and laid it down on his gown. " I had to impound it," he said, " but I'm not here to steal. You may need it to kill me with. One never knows."

With that, he bowed to Jenny and nodded to Mansel and me. Then he walked out of the tent and up to the road.

" That was Latin," said Jenny. " What does it mean ? "

" ' See you later,' " said Mansel. " I'm so awfully sorry, my sweet."

" I didn't mind," said Jenny. " And it might have been very much worse. He spoke so nicely to me, before William came. I said it was such a pity that he should have come to this : and he said he never would have, if he had had the honour of knowing people like us. His father was a clergyman, he said, with only two articles of faith : one was the elevation of the birth-rate—What are you laughing at ? "

" My beauty," said I, " you'd get off with the devil himself."

" Oh, of course he's hopeless," said Jenny. " And dangerous, too. I felt that all the time. But he was like us once, you know, and he can throw back to those days."

I looked at Mansel.

" What do we do ? " I said.

Mansel got to his feet and strolled round the back of the tent. Then he returned and sat down.

" Leave Freilles," he said quietly. " At once. What a mercy we have the two cars ! " Jenny and I had a Rolls, and Mansel had brought his with him, when he had come to stay. "We must give no sign of departure, for the villa is certainly watched. To all appearances, we must behave as usual. When Carson comes for us, we shall go back to lunch : and we shall return to the *plage* at half-past three—wearing *peignoirs* and bathing-things. And Carson will come to get us at half past five. But he won't come here, because we shall not be here. We shall have left the *plage* and strolled into the woods. He'll pick us up at the cross-roads, four miles north of this place. In the car he will have a suit-case, containing our clothes.

"Now before Carson leaves the villa at twenty past five, he and Bell will have packed and have loaded the other car. There's a door from the house to the garage, and so that operation will not be observed. At exactly half-past five, Bell will leave the garage and drive for Bayonne. That will make any watcher think, but he can't do much. You see, he is bound to wait until Carson is overdue. At Bayonne Bell will turn East, without going into the town : and later he will turn North, to join us somewhere near Dax. And that's as far as I've got."

I thought, and still think, that it was a very long way, for Brevet had left us less than five minutes before. But Jonathan Mansel's brain was unearthly swift ; and, what is more to the point, so far from being troubled by any sudden pass, the more instant the peril, the clearer it seemed to grow.

Mansel was addressing Jenny.

"I'm terribly sorry, my darling, to rope you and William in. But, as things are, I cannot possibly go and leave you here. It's me they want, of course : but if I alone cleared out, they'd turn upon you and William the moment they found I'd gone."

The great, blue eyes surveyed him, and a little hand came out, to rest on my knee.

" D'you think," said Jenny, slowly, " that we would have let you go ? That we could have gone on bathing, day after day, while those two men were trying to take your life ? "

" My sweet———"

" You know as well as I do that Richard will never leave you, until this danger's past. And I will never leave him, unless, because I'm a girl, I'm in the way."

So simple a declaration upset both Mansel and me, for Jenny is wholly artless and the words which she had spoken were those her heart bade her say. That those words were perfectly true, I need hardly say, for Mansel's quarrel was mine, as, had the case been reversed, my quarrel would have been his.

Since forty minutes must pass before Carson was due, we all went back to the rollers and bathed again. This at Mansel's suggestion : " for," said he, " to dwell upon this business is idle—and heaven knows when we'll get such bathing again."

*   *   *   *   *

By three o'clock that day I had done what I had to do. I had paid our rent in advance, so, except for the current bills, I owed no money in Freilles : but the house-agent was a nice man, so I wrote him a note, enclosing five thousand francs and a list of the tradesmen we used and begging him to pay their accounts and to keep what remained. Then I gave Bell the maid-servants' wages, and told him to pay them off ten minutes before he left. And then I walked upstairs, where Jenny was calling for Bell—for he had been doing her packing, to the delight of them both.

As I passed Mansel's door, he called me into his room.

" I fear that friend Brevet," he said, " was not all he seemed to be. His gesture of returning my pistol was very fine. I can't say that I felt at the time that it was

too good to be true ; but Brevet's affection for Virgil is
one which I share and I have an immense respect for a
proverb which the Mantuan has adorned. *Timeo Danaos
et dona ferentes.* And he did have the tent to himself,
before Jenny arrived. So I took a look at my pistol, as
soon as we'd finished lunch. And it's just as well that
I did, for that was what I discovered . . . rammed
down the barrel, until it was touching the round."

' That ' was an ordinary pipe-cleaner—that is to say,
a furred wire—which had been tied and twisted into a
ball. For ram-rod, an ordinary pencil had probably
served very well.

Had Mansel fired his pistol, when such an obstruction
was resting against the round, the weapon must have
burst in his grasp, blowing his hand to pieces, if doing
nothing worse.

I looked up to meet Mansel's eyes.

"And that reptile," said I, "had the nerve to call
Gedge a blackguard."

Mansel nodded.

"I frankly admit that he had me on," he said. "He
set out to satisfy me that he wasn't too bad : and he
damned well did it, William. Of course I've no excuse,
for what of a well-bred man who works with a wallah like
Gedge ? "

"So clear when one sees it," I said. "And I quite
liked the swine, while Jenny——"

"Steady," said Mansel. "Do you remember her
words. ' He's dangerous, too. I felt that all the time.'
Her instinct, William, is worth many parcels of jewels."

Twenty minutes later, we left the house for the
plage. . . .

Keeping our sand-shoes on, we left our bathing-gowns
in front of our tent and strolled together down to the
edge of the waves. Mansel and I were knee-deep, when
Jenny called and pointed along the shore. (The gesture

had been rehearsed, for Mansel left nothing to chance.) At once we turned and joined her, to stroll, three abreast, northwards, beside the tumbling surf.

So, for nearly a mile, when the sand took the shape of dunes and the forest drew close to the sea. And there we took a path which led into the woods.

I shall always remember that walk—indeed, I remember wishing that we had taken it before. The day was immensely hot, but the forest was pleasantly cool ; the bracken all about us was dappled with light and shade ; the steady hum of the insects and the murmur of the sea we had left made up a comfortable harmony, giving the lie to apprehension and preaching Herrick's doctrine with all their might ; and Jenny, walking before me along the narrow path, looked like some hamadryad, taking the way she had taken for half a century.

We moved very slowly, for we had plenty of time, and, as we expected, we had the woods to ourselves. When once we had seen the road, we kept it in sight, but we did not leave the forest, till Carson came.

We reached a spot above the cross-roads ten minutes before he arrived, and I was thankful to see him, because, for some stupid reason, I longed for a cigarette.

Jenny, of course, was dressed before either Mansel or I ; but within ten minutes of time we had taken our seats in the car.

Mansel spoke over his shoulder—he had the wheel.

"What about Bergerac? We ought to be there by nine, and they do you uncommonly well at *The Lion of Gold*."

"Every time," said Jenny.

"Bergerac has it," said Mansel, and let in his clutch. He spoke to Carson. "Where are we picking up Bell ?"

"Five miles east of Dax, sir. We know the place."

"Right," said Mansel. And then, "I never asked you —anything to report ?"

"Nothing at all, sir," said Carson. "That doesn't mean, of course, there was nobody there : for I took good care to keep my eyes to myself."

"Quite right," said Mansel, and put down his foot. "I don't want to pass through Dax, so tell me when to turn off."

Bell had fifty miles to cover, while we had but twenty-five, for he was to go by Bayonne, clean out of his way : we had therefore expected to wait for thirty-five minutes or so at the rendezvous : but when an hour had gone by, but Bell had not come, we were none of us very easy, and that is putting it low. But when another hour had gone by, but Bell had not come, we were, to say the least, most deeply concerned.

What was so trying was that we could do nothing but wait. We could not go to meet him, because we did not know which way he would come : to go to seek him was futile, so long as a chance remained that he was no more than late.

I looked at Mansel.

"If he's not here by nine," said I, "Jenny must stay here with Carson, and we must go out on patrol."

Mansel nodded.

"I think so. I decline to believe that he's met it, but that he is up against something is painfully clear. So much for my blasted plan."

"Be fair to yourself," said I. "Short of leaving one of the cars, what more could we have done ? "

"This," said Mansel. "Bell should have left to-morrow, instead of this afternoon. By then the coast would have been clear. I made a bad mistake, when I said that whoever was watching was bound to wait until Carson was overdue. Nine men out of ten would have waited : but Gedge is the tenth. I'll lay you any money that he was watching himself."

" Why should he go for Bell ? He doesn't even know him by sight."

" I hope he hasn't," said Mansel. " But I think that he's followed him—because he is perfectly certain that Bell will lead him to us. A bird in the hand, you know. . . ."

" It was," said I, " a big decision to take. And Bell's damned quick off the mark, so he had no time to think."

" Ah, but that's Gedge," said Mansel. " Brevet called him ' quite brilliant,' and so he is. Of course I may be quite wrong. Bell may have had a smash. But that does not alter the fact that I made a bad mistake."

Five minutes later, to our immense relief, the Rolls slid round a turning and up to our side.

With my hand on the door—

" By God, Bell, I'm glad to see you."

" Thank you, sir," said Bell. " I'm sorry I'm late."

" Are you all right ? " said Jenny. " Your eyes look tired."

" Quite all right, thank you, Madam."

" Before you report," said Mansel, " d'you think that we can wait here ? "

" I think, sir," said Bell, " that the cars should be off the road."

It was easy to find a track which ran into a wood ; and there, some five minutes later, Bell told his tale.

" I was out pretty quick, sir, but not, I'm afraid, quick enough. Five miles from Freilles I noticed a Lowland behind. I was slipping along then, so I lifted my foot a little, to see if he'd like to go by. But he only came a bit closer, before lifting his. That looked very much as though he was after me : but I couldn't be sure, so I gave him another test. Just short of Bayonne, I turned East, as you said—and so did he. Well, that might

only have meant that he wasn't bound for Bayonne : so
I took the next turning South, whipped into and out of
the town and up to where I'd turned East five minutes
before. Then I looked in the mirror again, and there he
was. Well, that left no doubt at all—the only thing to
do was to shake him off." He paused there, and a hand
went up to his head. " That Lowland can shift, sir, and
it isn't the first time the driver has trailed a car. Do
what I would, I couldn't get away from the man. I
doubled in Peyrehorade and I tried to lose him in Orthez
—in fact, I thought I had lost him ; but when I was clear
of the town, there he was on my tail. I had to go right
into Pau, to shake him off. I knew Pau, but he didn't ;
and after a minute or two, I'd tied him up."

" Well done, indeed," said Mansel. He glanced at
his wrist. " Have we got any food in the car ? "

" Chicken and beef," said Jenny, " and bread and
butter and eggs. Is that right, Bell ? "

" And cheese and beer, Madam ; and water for you."

" Good for you, Jenny," said Mansel.

" Bell's idea," said Jenny. " He said it seemed a pity
to leave so much behind."

" Well, let's eat now," said Mansel. " Bell's pretty
tired, and we shan't get in till late."

We broke our fast there and then, while the dusk came
in ; and not until after nine did we take the road.

As we ran into Bergerac, I heard some clock tell the
time. A quarter-past twelve.

CHAPTER II

RIPOSTE

THE LION OF GOLD has a garden, very old and peaceful, and sheltered by nine-foot walls. Jenny was still asleep, but Mansel and I were breakfasting under the limes.

"The thing is this," said Mansel. "I don't have to tell you that I am not running away : but I do not want them to find me where I do not want to be found. Find me they will—before long : and if they don't, I shall find them. Gedge has got to be dealt with, because he is out for blood. I can go back to England—he won't come there. But I'm not prepared to give the Continent up, and I've no desire whatever to be bumped off in Paris in two years' time."

"Do you put it as high as that ? "

"Yes," said Mansel, "I do. Twice I've hit Gedge damned hard, and Gedge is no ordinary man. He'll never rest till he gets me, or I get him. Brevet was telling the truth, when he said he was in the slips. And Gedge will stick at nothing—to gain his heart's desire." He paused, to refill his cup. "Will you take Jenny back to England ? "

"No, I won't," said I. "Jenny must go to Anise. John Bagot and Audrey are there, and they will look after her."

(John Bagot and Audrey Nuneham had been our guests at Freilles : and now they were married and had gone to stay at Anise. Anise was a tiny village, seventy miles from Bordeaux, and terribly hard to discover, unless you knew where it lay.)

"Very well," said Mansel. "We'll take her there this morning and stay to lunch."

When I broke the news to Jenny, she bit her lip.

" I'd like to be with you," she said. " You see, we're all three in danger—not only Jonathan."

" Why d'you say that, my darling ? "

" I—know it, Richard."

" All three of us ? "

" Yes, Richard."

I put my arms about her and held her close.

" This is very worrying, Jenny."

" I know. I'm dreadfully sorry. I don't want to cramp your style."

" I tell you what," I said, " I'll leave you at Anise with Bell. If after twenty-four hours, you still know that you are in danger, then Bell shall bring you to me wherever I am. But, if at the end of that tnme you know that the danger is past, then you must leit Bell go and stay with Audrey and John."

Jenny nodded her head. Then she threw her arms round my neck and burst into tears. . . .

To say that I was concerned means nothing at all. Jenny had spent her girlhood at Nature's knee. Birds and beasts were the only friends she had, and meadows, mountains and forests were all the world she knew. Now Jenny's understanding was very quick : and she had learned of Nature much of her lovely lore. With her, the most shy animals were at their ease ; birds would come at her call ; things that would grow for no gardener grew for her ; and of the poor, dumb creatures she knew so well, she had acquired that instinct of which I have spoken before. And though I dare say that the pundits would laugh it to scorn, I had seen it at work too often not to accord it a very deep regard. And now that faculty warned me that she was in danger, too. And Jenny was all that I had . . . far more than I deserved —but all that I had.

We ran into Anise a little before mid-day—to the very

great surprise of John and Audrey Bagot, for, after all, they were on their honeymoon. Still, I honestly think that they were glad to see us, and, after all, they were no ordinary friends. Being such, they at once agreed to play their part, that is to say, to keep Jenny as safe as a jewel in its drawer; and they actually wrote out a wire, to send to their man, summoning him to Anise, for he knew Punter by sight and could stand by the side of John Bagot, if trouble came. But, though this was reassuring, I was not reassured. Jenny was happy and smiling, as though the word 'apprehension' was one that she did not know: but then she had a great heart and was in all things a most obedient wife; and I found it hard to believe that forty odd miles had put to rout the danger in which she stood.

It was about half-past three that I bade her goodbye and took my seat beside Mansel, with Carson behind. Our plan was, so to speak, fluid, depending on what we found. But we hoped to locate the rogues and, having done that, to let one of their number see us and see the way we took. If we could do this, we could draw them on to the ground upon which we proposed to meet them and have things out; "for we can't have a scandal," said Mansel, "and so we must do our stuff in the country-side." Since Bell had 'lost' them in Pau, that was the region for which we proposed to make; and, with or without Jenny, Bell was to meet us by Orthez the following night.

We had covered some ninety miles and had spoken hardly a word, when I came to a sudden decision and touched Mansel on the arm.

"Yes, William?"

"Please go back to Anise," was all I said.

Mansel looked at me sharply.

Then, seeing a turning ahead, he set a foot on the brake . . .

A moment later we were flying the way we had come.
Anise was no more than a hamlet, but it boasted a
fine, old inn, with an archway which would have accepted
a coach and four : this gave to a cobbled yard, on one
side of which was a coach-house, now used for cars.
The most agreeable rooms were at the back of the inn :
they were on the first floor and faced South, commanding
a charming prospect of woods and meadows and water,
in the shape of a lazy stream.   Though, on three of its
sides, the meadows ran up to the house, you could not
enter them without passing under the archway and into
the road ; but this was a small price to pay for the
privacy of the apartments in which, when we were at
Anise, we ate and slept.   They were, indeed, as secluded
as Anise itself, and that was why Mansel and I had
frequently stayed at the inn : I am sure that our host
never talked and that many a passer-by has broken his
fast at the inn and has never dreamed that he was not
its only guest.   Still, unless you cared to keep house,
you were bound to use the highway for fifty or sixty
yards : then you came to an aged gate which made you
free of the meadows, the stream and the forest beyond.

When we were nearing the hamlet, I began to feel more
at ease.   I remember turning to Mansel and telling him
so.   " But I can't say I'm sorry," I added, " because it
wouldn't be true.   What we're to do with Jenny, I
really don't know : but I should have been useless to
you, if we'd left her behind."

" Don't worry, William," said Mansel.   " As like as
not, you've done us a very good turn.   If your apprehension is sound, it can only mean that one or more of our
friends are coming to Anise to-night.   What in the world
could be better ?   We see them ; but we take care that
they don't see us—until they have left the place : we
can put the cars in a meadow and lie very close ourselves.
We follow and overtake them and pass them by, and then

we let them chase us . . . on to the ground we have chosen . . . We'll talk that over this evening, but there is some attractive country not far from Lannemezan."

So we came back to Anise, at exactly a quarter-past seven, for Mansel had let the car go.

As the inn came into our view, I saw that something was wrong, and I think that my heart stood still.

A figure was lying by the archway, and beside it the hostess was kneeling, with one of her hands to her head. Then her husband came running out, with water and towels. An instant later I saw that the figure was Bell's.

Mansel brought up the Rolls, all standing, and Carson and I leaped out. . . .

Bell was unconscious—no worse: I judged that he had been hit on the b.ack of the head. Sending the woman for more, I poured the cold water steadily on to his brow. Mansel was questioning the man, but I did not hear what he said. I heard Mansel speak to Carson.

" Try the rooms, Carson, and see if the cars are there." He soused a towel in the pitcher the woman had brought, gave the pitcher to me and set the towel under Bell's head. " The people know nothing," he said. " They found Bell lying here a moment before we arrived. Audrey had cried out for them, but when they got here she was gone." He turned to the host. " Another pitcher of water, and bring some ice."

As the man ran under the archway, Carson returned.

" The rooms are empty, sir, and the Lowland's out." (John and Audrey Bagot were using a Lowland car.) I looked at Mansel.

" If he doesn't come round in two minutes . . ."

" I agree," said Mansel ; " we can't wait longer than that. Give Carson your keys, will you ? He'll start your car."

As the landlord returned with the ice, Bell opened his eyes.

For a moment he stared upon me. Then he let out a cry and made to get up.

" Where's Madam, sir ? "

" We'll talk in a minute," I said. " Lie back and shut your eyes and try to concentrate. What was about to happen when you went out ? "

Mansel wrapped some ice in a towel and held it across Bell's brow, and I poured water upon the compress this made.

Bell was speaking again.

" I've got it straight now, sir. We were going up to the meadow, where Mr. and Mrs. Bagot were going to try for a trout. When they were just about ready, I went down to the yard, and as soon as I heard them coming I walked out under the archway, to see that the road was clear." He hesitated there, and a hand went up to his head. " Wait a minute, sir . . . Yes, that's right. We were going to take the Lowland. Mr. Bagot had been to Jois, to buy cigarettes, and he said he'd left her outside, so that Madam could drive, an' not walk. He'd left her across the entrance, so I couldn't see the road without going out. Very close to the archway, he'd left her : I'd only just room to get by. I turned to pass behind her, an' then . . . There was something strange, I know, just before I went out."

" Let it go for the moment," said I. " You can't say where Madam was ? "

" Ahead of the others, I think, sir. I heard her call out ' Come on.' But I know there was something important—something that shook me up." He sat up there, and the compress fell into his lap. " I'm all right now, sir. But Madam ! My God, sir, don't say they've— Ah ! I've got it. . . . As I turned to pass behind her, *I saw another Lowland ten paces away.* And *that* was Mr. Bagot's—I saw the number-plate."

He made to rise and I helped him up to his feet.

Mansel's voice rang out.

" Bring out the car, Carson, and follow us."

Before ten seconds had passed, Bell was sitting with Carson and I was sitting with Mansel, as I had sat before. And both cars were on the road.

* * * * *

I will not set out my feelings, except to say this—that, had Gedge been able to divine them, hard and black as it was, his heart would have failed him for fear. As for Brevet, had there been any question of mercy, I would have shown him less ; for he had spoken with Jenny and had seen for himself that she was ingenuous.

For a moment I let my brain browse on the vengeance which I would take : then I pulled myself together and considered our present duty and how it could best be done. This was, of course, to overtake Gedge.

How the man had traced us to Anise, I could not think : but once he had brought that off, he had his reward. That the Bagots were using a standard Lowland car—a car which resembled his own in every particular—was one of those precious presents which Fortune is apt to bestow upon just and unjust alike. And Gedge had been quick to seize this valuable gift. He had seen John Bagot leave his Lowland without the inn : that meant that the car was going to be used again. At once Gedge had laid *his* Lowland across the archway's mouth : so placed, it would seem to be Bagot's—to any-one other than Bagot, for he alone would know where he left his car. The rest was easy. The first person down was Bell—and Gedge put him out. The second was Jenny, for whom he had laid the trap : but had Audrey or John come before her, they would have been simply silenced, for, sooner or later, Jenny was bound to come.

So much for the abduction.

There could, happily, be no doubt that Audrey or John or both had seen something of what had occurred and that they had at once given chase, without waiting to care for Bell. Since Audrey was a beautiful driver, I hoped very hard that they were on Gedge's heels. What was less fortunate was that they could have no idea that we were coming behind and so would take no action to indicate to us the way they had gone—a scarf let fall at a turning, and things like that. All that we knew for certain was that they must have gone West; for only one road serves Anise, and we had come from the East. Still, anyone of us four could have mapped the neighbourhood for twenty or thirty miles; and that, I was sure, was more than the rogues could do.

Mansel was speaking.

" Gedge knows where he's going, of course; but unless it's just round the corner—and that I do not believe—he will probably use the main roads. This for three reasons; first, he can get along quicker; secondly, because of the traffic, his passage will not be remarked; thirdly, to lose his way is the last thing he wants to do. Now, if I'm right, he turned when he got to Jois: but did he turn North or South ? "

" There's a service station there, and they may know the Bagots' car."

" That's right. It's worth stopping to ask if they saw them go by. If they didn't . . ."

" We go South," said I, " and Carson and Bell go North."

Mansel nodded.

" Communications ? " he said.

" God knows. They'd better report by wire to Agen and Pau : and we to Ruffec."

That was a poor enough plan, but Mansel could think of none better and said as much. But then we were both of us frantic—and the Rolls was moving at eighty-five miles an hour.

The village of Jois flung towards us . . .

As we swept to the service station, a car was pulling away from the petrol-pump.

Mansel put the question.

" Five minutes ago," came the answer. " Believe me, there is something afoot."

" Why d'you say that ? " snapped Mansel.

" Monsieur, I know the car which the lady usually drives. Myself, I have changed its oil. And I saw it come up from Anise and then turn South."

" That'll do," said I.

" Have patience, Monsieur," said the other, and Mansel set a hand on my arm. " I saw it go by very fast, but neither Monsieur nor Madame was at its wheel. ' The car has been stolen,' I cry, and run for the telephone. But while I am demanding the police, I hear the Englishman's voice. And when I come out, there is the car I have seen, with Madame in the driver's seat. ' A car like this ? ' she cries. ' Which way did it go ? ' ' South,' I cry. ' I have seen it . . .' "

And that was as much as we heard of the good man's tale. But it was worth waiting for, because it told us plainly that the Bagots were close to Gedge. He might have the faster car, for Bell had suggested that it must have been ' specially tuned ' : but that any one of the four could drive a car as could Audrey, I simply did not believe.

Mansel rounded a bend at eighty, passed a car which was passing a char-à-banc, ' cut in ' between two waggons of six wheels each and put the Rolls at a hill at ninety-six. There were nine cars using that hill : three were coming towards us, and six were going our way. Mansel went by in the middle, as though they were, none of them, there. As we swung to the right, at the top, I turned to look back for Carson : there were then ten cars on that hill, of which Carson's made one. And the French do not drive slowly . . .

" I hope you feel better," said Mansel. " I know I do. That fellow's report was a tonic. And unless that Lowland's a winner, we must be coming up."

" I do feel better," I said. " And my brain's more clear. And now listen. Ahead of us is Libourne—some forty miles off. If I were Gedge, I'd avoid a town of that size."

" So," said Mansel, " should I. If he knows where he is, the fellow will turn at Mielle. To the left, of course. He's obviously driving South."

" I agree. But we can't be sure. If he has perceived that the Bagots are on his tail, he may do anything."

" Except turn North," said Mansel. " Twist and double, perhaps : but he'll always bear South."

I thought this was sound, and said so : but when we had covered another three miles in two minutes, only to be checked in a village and lose the time we had won, my desperation came back, as clouds return after the rain.

Check or no, we must have gained on the others : with ordinary luck, we should sight them before they could reach Mielle—*provided that they did not turn off before they came to that place* : but Mielle was twenty miles distant, and in those twenty miles there were at least three cross roads running East and West.

As though he had read my thoughts—

" Unless," said Mansel, " unless we are checked again, I think that we ought to turn off before we get to Mielle. I decline to believe that they're moving as fast as we— they're meeting checks, too, you know. There are cross roads at Balet : that's nine—no eight miles ahead. If we haven't caught them by Balet, I'll swear they're not on this road." He cornered perfectly—not skirting the side of the road, but skirting the side of a swift-moving limousine, flashed between two lorries and raced for a level-crossing on which a furniture-van was bearing down. As we whipped across the bows of the van and over the rails, " I suggest," he went on, " that we should turn East at Balet. What do you think ? "

" I think so. And Carson, too. It's no good his going on ; and if Gedge is Southward bound, he's sure to turn East ; otherwise he'd find himself faced with threading Libourne or Bordeaux."

" True," said Mansel. " And then ? "

" Look at it this way," I said. " If we haven't caught up by Balet, they've either turned at Balet or turned before."

" At Poule," said Mansel. " That's just about two miles on. If we go on to Balet, but Carson——"

" I think that's them," I cried. " Them, or the Bagots. Steady. They're slowing down. . . . Petrol. They're stopping for petrol. My God, if it's . . ."

Before the Lowland had stopped, I saw John Bagot fling out and rush to the back of the car. Before he had the cap off the tank, we had drawn alongside.

Mansel addressed Audrey Bagot, white as a sheet.

" Were they in your view ? " he said.

" Jonah ! Thank God ! Yes, yes. They've only just rounded that bend."

" Their number ? "

" Six two four two."

" Carson's behind," said Mansel. " Tell him to turn East at Poule. Report by wire to Orthez and Auch. You go on to Libourne."

And then we were gone.

We had lost twenty seconds, perhaps—no more than that. But that is a lot to make up in a mile and a half. You see, we wanted to know if Gedge turned at Poule . . . We could, of course, leave him to Carson—Carson

was as 'safe as a house,' and Bell would be sound by
now. But we naturally wished to deal with the matter
ourselves.

"He'll turn at Poule," I said. "If they could see him,
it follows that he could see them. And now that he
thinks he's lost them, he'll turn at once."

Mansel said nothing. But he drove as even that day
he had never driven before. And that noble car responded
—like the thoroughbred that she was. Mercifully, the
road was open. . . .

Poule is a very long village, as villages go ; and the
main road runs straight through it, as a river between
its banks. The moment I saw it, I remembered that the
cross roads of which I have spoken lay right at its farther
end.

It was half a mile off when I sighted the streak of gray
which it made. With the speed of a Disney drawing,
the streak took shape. Always increasing in stature,
I watched Poule tear towards us, exactly as though
it belonged to some motion-picture and we to the
audience.

"I can see two cars," I said. "No—three. One's
coming our way. I think one's standing still. There's a
fourth . . . and a fifth—right ahead. And now a 'bus
coming— Oh, blast his neck, he's right in my line of
view. . . . That's better, but where's the fifth ? By
God, he's turned off ! He must have—the road's dead
straight."

Ahead of us people were straggling, and standing and
talking, too. Mansel sounded his high-pitched horn—
and kept the button pressed down. Discretion beat
Assertion—the figures fled.

"Did he turn left ?" said Mansel.

"I couldn't say. As you turn, I'll look to the right.
But I'll swear it was he that turned : there's nothing
ahead."

This was a fact; and we could see the road for a third of a mile.

As we swept past the waiting 'bus, Mansel lifted his foot and clapped on his brakes.

A volley of indignation just flicked my ears, as a flash of summer lightning will flick the sight.

I slewed myself round in my seat, and as Mansel swung to the left, I looked behind—to see some three hundred yards of an empty road.

"Go on," I said. "We must risk it. If they're not in view in two minutes, we must come back."

Our new road curled like a serpent, defying a very high speed. But it ran down into a valley that opened out to the West, and, knowing the way of the country hereabouts, I was ready to swear that it climbed up out of the valley upon the opposite side. I tried my best to pick up the line that it took.

And then, below where I was looking, the tail of my eye reported the tiniest flash. The screen of a car that was moving had rendered the brilliant light of the sinking sun.

"They're down there," I said somehow. "God send it's Gedge."

"Amen," breathed Mansel. "And now we've got to be careful: but, first of all, we must see their number-plate."

"Stop," I cried. "There's their road. For God's sake, give me the glasses—I daren't look away."

It was but a glimpse of the road some twenty yards of its length: to anyone where we were, anything moving upon it would be completely exposed: but it lay too far away for the naked eye to determine the make of a car. I should not, of course, be able to see the number-plates; but, if it was a Lowland . . .

Mansel thrust a binocular into my hand . . .

He need not have hurried to do so: thirty seconds

dragged by, while we listened to the drone of the engine, not turning as fast as it could.

"I think," breathed Mansel, "I think that's a Lowland's note."

With his words, a Lowland slid into and out of my view.

"Good for you," said I, and put the binocular down.

As he let in his clutch—

"We must close up a bit," said Mansel. "We mustn't lose them now."

(Here, perhaps, I should say that had the rogues chosen to do as we had done, that is to say, to look across the valley, they must, I think, have seen us, for we were much more exposed : that they did not was, I am sure, because they were not used to the countryside and so thought of nothing more than of looking directly behind : for this reason, time and again, we had the advantage of them, for we were at home in country of any kind ; but they were at home in a city, as felons usually are.)

The road, which was still serpentine, now stood us in stead. We were able to draw very close, without being seen. Indeed, as we rounded one of the last of the bends, we saw the tail of the Lowland flick out of view round the next.

"If," said Mansel, "we can avoid being seen . . . for the moment, of course. I mean, we must have no shooting, till Jenny is out of the way."

"We're nearly up," said I. "Stop at the last of the bends, and I'll have a look round."

Once we stopped in vain, for another bend lay ahead. But that was the last of the turnings ; and when I peered cautiously round it, I saw the Lowland at rest a hundred yards off. She was out of the valley and up on the top of a hill, just short of a fork in the road ; and a slice of an opened map was sticking out of a window, to show that someone was seeking to settle which way to go. So for ten seconds or so. Then the map was withdrawn, and the Lowland began to move.

I waited until I saw her enter the road that bore to the right. As I turned to beckon to Mansel, Carson whipped round the last but one of the bends.

The eagles were gathering . . .

I returned to the Lowland, to see her slide out of sight.

As I took my seat beside Mansel—

" Go on gently," I said, " and then bear right. They don't know where they are ; for they've just been using the map. And they've taken the road to Stère. Can you picture Stère ? I remember it very well."

" I can," said Mansel. " A most inconvenient townlet. Streets about twelve feet wide, and police all over the place."

I cannot better that description. Stère was not built for these days : and its Mayor was determined that accidents should not occur : for a motorist in a hurry, the place was a nightmare.

" More," I said. " There are two ways into Stère."

" That's right : they start at the same point : they then diverge—and return, to meet at the bottle-neck— an idle and offensive performance, for which there is no excuse."

" They may help us this evening. Carson follows the Lowland ; but we take the way which the Lowland does not take : so we are in front of Gedge when he comes to the bottle-neck : and Carson is just behind."

" Very good indeed," said Mansel. " Ah, here we are, STERE—7 MILES. And there they go round that bend. Summon Carson, will you ? We'll put him wise."

At a sign from me, Carson drew alongside.

" Are you better, Bell ? " I cried.

" All right now, sir, thank you."

" Listen, Carson. The Lowland is just ahead. If and

when you see us leave her, you will close up to her tail. We are going to by-pass her, so that when she enters Stère, she will be directly between us. At least, we shall try to do that. But, whatever happens, don't lose her."

" I won't do that, sir."

" If it comes off, they won't be looking round—they'll be watching us : but I shouldn't like them to miss you, so, the moment my hand comes out, close right up to their bumper and then you and Bell get out and open their doors."

" Very good, sir."

I nodded, and he fell in behind.

" William," said Mansel, " you have my sympathy."

I knew what he meant. Violence could hardly be done in the main street of Stère. In such a place, with no chance of getting away, even Gedge would see the wisdom of holding his hand. So I must postpone my vengeance. Still, once Jenny was out of the Lowland, I promised myself a word or two with the swine. Of course, had she been ill used . . .

Stère was some seven miles off ; but the road was in our favour and alive with just enough traffic to mask our policy. Besides, I was later to learn that Gedge and his companions were sure they were out of the wood and hardly looked behind them, when once they had left the valley and borne to the right. As though to seal their doom, they did not drive fast, so that when the time came for us to overtake them, using the second road which ran into Stère, we did so comfortably.

Of course, their luck was dead out, and ours was in : had they known Stère as we did, and had they dreamed that we were upon their heels, they would have gone fifty miles to avoid the place. As it was, they tooled into the trap, to find us directly before them—and not a side street for more than a hundred yards.

Mansel was driving very slowly. Then he stopped

altogether and started to back. As he did so, my hand went out . . .

I had hardly left my seat, before Carson and Bell were opening the Lowland's rear doors.

"Richard, Richard!"

"Come, my darling," I said. "We're holding the traffic up."

In the most pregnant silence that I have ever known, I handed my wife from the Lowland into the cobbled street.

"Has anyone touched you?" I said.

"They put a coat over my head when they put me into the car: but that was all."

"Except for that, have they been rough with you by word or deed?"

"No, Richard. I can't say they have."

"Just as well," said I, and gave her over to Bell. Then I turned to regard the occupants of that car.

All three were sitting so still that they might have been images. On the back seat was sitting Brevet, staring ahead. Looking upon him, I saw a bead of sweat roll down the side of his face. Gedge was beside the driver—a man I had never seen: he was short and very thickset, and his forehead was very low. From his hands, which were on the wheel, I judged him to have been a mechanic. (In fact, I was not far out: the fellow had been a tester—and so could play with a car.)

Since I could do them no violence, I would have given much to lash the three with my tongue, but, now that they were before me, I had no words.

Feebly enough—

"Punter should have warned you," I said.

I can only suppose that Punter had said something, for the driver sniggered and Gedge made as though to turn.

"Sit still," snapped Mansel. "You can't fire, but I

can—on the men who are wanted at Biarritz. If I wasn't a fool, I should : but, as you have reason to know, I have a certain weakness for dealing direct. That is how I shall deal with you, Gedge."

" That goes for me," I said. " But let me include you all. You three have laid hands on my wife. And the punishment for that is death. Make no mistake about that. As sure as I live, I'll get you, go where you will." I glanced up at the street. " Here's a policeman coming now, to tell us to move. I've only to say one word, to send the three of you down. But I wouldn't say it for worlds. . . . You see, you're *our* meat."

With that, I slammed the door with a violence that rocked the car, and Mansel turned to deal with the policeman, who looked very cross. I could not hear all he said, but I know he declared that we had pursued the Lowland, to remonstrate with those within it for driving so fast : that he had read them a lesson and they had expressed their regret—which must have been gall and wormwood to Gedge and his friends. Then he went off to move his Rolls, while the policeman vented his anger upon the rogues, demanding to see their papers and breathing out threatenings against them for their iniquity.

I withdrew to join Jenny, who was sitting still in my car, with Bell at the door : and Mansel drove on and round to come up in our rear. This he did as a precaution, for once Gedge had a clear run, out of sheer rage he might well have fired upon Mansel, as he went by. And just as Mansel came up, the policeman released the Lowland and I saw it move out of our sight.

I was sorry to see it go, for the three had been under my hand and God only knew when and where I should find them again : but to trail them forthwith was hopeless, for night was coming on and they would have been on the look-out.

First of all, we drove out of the street and into a little

place. There we decided three things—that we should return to Anise to dine and sleep at its inn : that Carson should drive to Libourne, to try and arrest the Bagots and tell them that all was well : and that Bell should wire to them at Orthez and Auch—for neither Audrey nor John would have slept or sought to sleep until they knew from us that Jenny was safe.

When Carson had left for Libourne and Bell had gone off to wire, Jenny and Mansel and I repaired to a little café and drank some beer. Then we got into my car, and, picking up Bell at the Post Office, drove to Anise.

And there, when we had had dinner, my darling told us her tale.

" I thought, of course, it was John and Audrey's car. As I opened the door, a coat came over my head and I was pushed in. I did cry out to Audrey—I don't suppose she heard. Not being able to see, I went down on the floor ; and before I was up, we were off. I tore the coat away, and there was Brevet beside me, and two other men in front. The one by the driver gave orders, and so I knew it was Gedge. They called the driver ' Lousy.' He certainly knows how to drive—it was that more than anything else that shook me up. I knew that Audrey was good and I was sure that she must have seen us leave—I mean, she was just behind me—but I couldn't believe that she could drive like Lousy. He really was terribly good, and she deserves full marks for hanging on to his tail.

" Of course I knew you'd get me—you and Jonathan. But I believed, of course, you were miles away and that you would know nothing till Bell reported at Orthez to-morrow night. And then you would have to find me. . . . And I knew that Gedge wouldn't leave me lying about. Still, I thought the best thing to do was to watch the road, not only to see which way we seemed to be heading, but also to give the idea that I wasn't hearing or caring what they might say. Brevet started to talk in a slimy way; but I said when I wanted to talk I'd let him know. So then he was quiet. And I stared out of the window and listened with all my might.

"Soon after leaving Jois, Lousy said we were being trailed, and Gedge and Brevet looked round.

"'It's a Lowland all right,' said Lousy.

"'Well, run away,' said Gedge.

"'Perhaps,' said Lousy. 'There's someone sitting there that knows how to drive.'

"Then Gedge asked what he was paid for: and Lousy said he'd only one neck and that, if Gedge liked, he'd get out and Gedge could try for himself to 'run away.'

"Of course I was so excited that I could hardly sit still, and I thought it best to look round. But Gedge said, 'Don't do that. We'll tell you when your friends overtake us.' And Brevet laughed.

"Nobody spoke after that, except to announce that Audrey was still behind. Sometimes they thought they'd lost her, but always she reappeared until, just before they turned off, they swore she was out of sight. You can imagine my feelings . . .

"Well, we went down into a valley, and Lousy eased up. And when we came up and out on the other side, Gedge told him to stop. Then he got out the map and found where we were. And then he said this: 'If we turn left at Stère, in six or eight miles we'll strike the Agen road. And from Agen to the château is, I know, a hundred and one.'

"Then Brevet laughed.

"'I'm not at all sure,' he said, 'that our beloved Horace will welcome this particular guest to the Sabine Hills.'

"'He won't,' said Gedge. 'He'll do as he's damned well told, and The Stoat will look after her. The Baron is where he belongs, and if you don't know that, he does.'

"Then nobody spoke again till we were approaching Stère.

"And then Brevet spoke to me.

"'We appear to be nearing what is sometimes called a "built-up area." I can hardly say how distressing it would be for us both——'

"'Speak English,' said Gedge. Then he turned round and looked at me. 'Give your word to stay put, or down you go on the floor, with Brevet's feet on your back and this in your mouth.' And he threw to Brevet a handful of cotton waste.

"I knew he meant what he said, so it seemed best to give my word.

"I saw the Rolls before they did, and nearly cried out with joy.

"And then——

"'My God, that's Mansel,' cried Gedge; and Lousy laughed, and Gedge hit him on the side of the head.

"And then you started to back . . .

"Back, you ——,' screamed Gedge. 'Back and get out, you ——.'

"And Lousy said, 'Look behind.'

"And, as Gedge turned to look, the doors of the Lowland were opened by Carson and Bell."

There was a little silence.

Then——

"Jenny," said Mansel, "you're a marvel. I know no other being that, placed as you were, would contrive to pull their weight. And now for the riddle. Happily, Brevet can't forget that he was once a gentleman. And a scholar. So he calls 'the Baron' Horace, and he places his retreat in 'the Sabine Hills.' Why? I mean, he is a scholar—no doubt about that. And the Roman poet Horace did have a little farm in the Sabine

Hills. But why should Brevet compare the Baron to him ? "

I was out of my depth and said so. But Mansel insisted that there was something there.

" If we can read it," he said, " we shall know where they are. ' The Sabine Hills,' I assume, are the Pyrenees. A hundred miles from Agen would take you right into the range. And what was Horace's farm called ? I don't think it had a name. And yet—he called it something . . . Give me the *Michelin Guide*."

Could I have helped him, I would have sat up all night ; but my intimacy with the Classics is very slight and does not include the pet names by which the Roman poets were accustomed to call their farms. So Jenny and I went to bed and left him reading the map—and wishing that Carson would come, for he had in his Rolls some maps of a larger scale.

*   *   *   *   *

The next morning I learned two things. The first was that Carson was back, and John and Audrey with him. This was a great piece of luck, for he had encountered them as he was approaching and they were leaving Libourne. The second was that Mansel had left for Jois— and would be back for breakfast at half-past eight.

And so he was.

" I've solved the riddle," he said. " At a quarter to one this morning I found in the large-scale map of the Pyrenees a little village called Arx. That was what Horace called his homestead. Arx is the Latin for a stronghold, or, if you translate it freely, in this case an ivory tower. Well, I knew I was right ; but, just to assure assurance, I've been to Jois to look at the tele-phone-book. Sure enough, the Baron Horace de Parol inhabits the *Château d'Arx*."

" I give you best," said I.

" To Brevet the glory," said Mansel.   " He never took his degree, but to how many Masters of Arts would those two names have remembered the Sabine Hills ? "

CHAPTER III

ENTER THE STOAT

SOME thirty-four hours had gone by.

Jenny and Audrey were in Wiltshire—I had a wire in my pocket, saying that they had reached Maintenance, which is the name of my home.   Myself, I had driven the two of them up to Dieppe, had put them aboard the night-packet and watched it sail.   And my Rolls, with them.   After that, I had taken the boat-train to Paris, to spend the next few hours at a quiet hotel.   And then I had travelled to Dax, where John Bagot was on the platform and the Lowland, with Bell at its wheel, in the station yard.

As we took our seats in the car—

" How far have you got ? " said I.

" We've got a fine base," said John, " in some of the prettiest country I ever saw.   It's a farm which is owned by a butler, now upon holiday.   His parents run it for him : but he's modernized the first floor and made it into a really excellent flat.   Here he and his wife repair, whenever they can.   When they are not there, it stands empty : but, after a word with Mansel, he saw the wisdom of letting the flat to us.   He's returning to duty to-morrow, so we can go in the next day.   His mother will feed us, and Carson and Bell and Rowley will do the rest.   The flat has a separate entrance, and the cars can go in the barn."

" Splendid," said I.   " Where is this—sanctuary ? "

" Thirty-one miles from Arx and eleven from Ray."

" Ray, I know. Which way do you go from Ray ? "

" South and by West."

" That's off my map," said I.

" It gives the impression of being off most people's maps."

" So much the better," said I. " And how about Arx ? "

" Mansel and Carson are having a peep this evening."

I nodded. Then—

" Where are we bound for now ? "

" Only a barn, I'm afraid : but Rowley's cooking some food, and we've got some beer upon ice."

" What more can anyone ask ? When shall we be there ? "

" Under the hour. It's not very far from Pau."

Sure enough, we reached the barn before it was half-past eight, and a quarter of an hour later Mansel and Carson arrived. As we ate a most excellent supper, the former made his report.

This was disappointing.

" Arx lies in a valley, and it is served by one road : this road runs right through it from East to West. So much the map told me. You won't be surprised to hear that I avoided that road. I chose a parallel road about three miles South, and when I was level with Arx, I left the Rolls with Carson and took to my feet. The idea was to gain the top of the intervening ridge and then look down upon Arx in the valley below. . . . I looked down on the valley all right, but not upon Arx. I could see the road which serves it on either side ; but then the woods closed in. I was directly above it, for I could hear its cascade, which is marked on the map : but neither château nor village can be surveyed from the South. So to-morrow we must try from the North. There aren't any woods that side, so we ought to have a clear view."

" Early," said I. " I'll lay Gedge doesn't get up before nine o'clock."

" I doubt if he's there," said Mansel. " Unless I'm much mistaken, he's looking for me. Which brings me to something we've never had time to discuss. How did he trace us to Anise ? "

" I'm damned if I know," said I.

" Nor I. It's got me beat. But I think I've told you that Gedge is no ordinary man. Brevet has, any way. All of his kidney regard him with great respect. They'd rather go to jug than get across Gedge. So we must be on the tips of our toes. He's caught me bending twice : once, two days ago, and once a year or so back. On each of those occasions I had good reason to think that he could not know where I was. But he did. So Carson is watching now. A sentinel is something which we must always have." He looked at John Bagot. " I've told you plainly, John, that you should not be on in this scene. Your place is with Audrey. This affair is ours and has nothing to do with you."

" Yes, it has," said John Bagot. " Jenny was left in our charge, and we let her go."

" That is not being fair to yourself."

" Then put it like this," said John. " If you were placed as I am, would you retire to Wiltshire and hope for the best ? "

" I might if I were just married."

" To Audrey Nuneham ? "

We all of us laughed at that, for Audrey's one regret was that she had been born a woman and not a man.

" Well, so be it," said Mansel. " But no funny business, John. You've got to do as we say."

Then we strolled for half an hour, before we went to our beds in some sweet-smelling hay.

* * * * *

At half-past six the next morning I saw the sun strike the roof of the Château of Arx.

The house was more of a castle than châteaux usually are and was hanging above the village upon the side of the hill. It was as big as the village, which was a tiny place. By its side fell down the cascade which Mansel had heard, to swell the blue-and-white torrent which neighboured the road. Above and on either hand the woods came down, and the house was wholly screened from every side but the North. A drive slanted out of the village and curled through terraced meadows up to the *porte-cochère* : the great doors of this were shut, but it clearly gave to a court of considerable size. And that was all, except that three rows of beehives stood near the waterfall. The village was huddled on either side of the road, and it showed no sign of life, because, as is often the case, the villagers paid no attention to summer time. To the left or East of the château, miniature railway lines ran out of a little cutting and crossed the road : they skirted the north of the village and then turned South, to cross the road again and disappear in a wood. They might have been serving some quarry, out of our sight.

" A level crossing," said Mansel, " on either side. That's very convenient, you know. You'll observe that the poles are down."

This was a fact. No car could have entered that village ; because upon either hand the road was barred.

" It's mediaeval," I said.

Mansel nodded.

" The idea is mediaeval ; but ' our beloved Horace ' has moved with the times. The portcullis is *demodé*. The level crossing is very much more to the point. A car can be held at arm's length."

" And the Departmental surveyor ? "

" Is deeply appreciative," said Mansel. " Light railways need not be guarded. But the Baron shows a fine sense of duty towards his fellow men. What I really want to see is how and when those good-looking poles are raised."

His desire was granted precisely at seven o'clock.

At that hour, as though by magic, the barriers rose—first one pair and then the other. Somewhere two levers had been pulled or two wheels had been turned. . . . And very soon after this, château and village alike showed signs of life. Shutters and doors were opened, and smoke began to rise—and a servant came out of the wicket which hung in one of the doors of the *porte-cochère*. But, though we waited till ten, no car came in or went out and all that we saw were peasants delivering bread and things like that. Had the great doors been opened, we could, we were sure, have seen well into the court, for we had binoculars with us, which showed us everything. Still, we had now surveyed the enemy's lair: we had seen some of its features; and, if we had occasion to approach it, we should not be all at sea. And since, in a case like this, the first thing to do, if we could, was to get to know the country which lay between us and our foes, we wasted no more time, but made our way back to our barn. There we broke our fast, and then we set out with both cars for the farm at which we should sleep on the following night. We proved the country about this on every side, gradually producing our radius until the circle it commanded swept very close to Arx: and, since our maps were good and the roads were few, by the evening we were familiar with all the neighbourhood. On the following day, taking Arx as our centre, we did the same, proving the country about it for twenty miles. When, therefore, we sat down to supper in our most excellent flat, we all of us knew the ground over which we might have to move—and knew it thoroughly.

*   *   *   *   *

Mansel rose from the table and took out a pipe.

"By rights," he said, "our friends should have found us by now. But—well, I'm not going to say they haven't, because I know Gedge : but I do not think they have. In which case, they're looking for us. Whether they are yet back at Arx I have no idea. We'll keep some observation tomorrow. . . .

"Now Gedge is out to get me, so I am out to get Gedge : and William has scores to settle. Gedge and Co. know these things, and, after what happened at Stère, I have no doubt at all that any one of those four is ready to shoot at sight any one of us six. Perhaps I should except Rowley, for Punter's the only one who has seen him before : but Punter knows Rowley as well as Carson and Bell. And let us remember this—that if one of them should get killed, the others will cover it up ; for, however good their case, they simply cannot afford to get involved with the police. That's the worst of not having clean hands. Now if Brevet or Lousy or Punter meets his doom, Gedge will have him buried and carry straight on : but the moment Gedge is killed the others will fade away." He looked at me. "Perhaps that would be a good thing."

"I'm going to kill Brevet," I said. "Lousy can live if he likes, but he won't be the same."

Mansel nodded.

"Right. We can't very well say ' Gedge last,' because that mightn't suit Gedge. But Brevet and Lousy shall be preferred to him.

"Now I think it would be a mistake to carry the fight to them. Unless I am much mistaken, Arx is very much more than an ivory tower : and if we attacked such a place, I think it more than likely that we should play into their hands. It would be very much better to let them see us near Arx, draw them into the uplands and let them have it there. With luck, we might bring that off. But such a move would have to be perfectly made, for Gedge is well aware that we don't run away. Otherwise, we must watch them go out and then follow them. The snag there is that they may not go where we want. I mean, we've got to be careful. Much of this country is suited to sudden death : but you cannot bump a man off at noon on a main highway. Gedge would—don't forget that. But I don't want to lie low for the next three months. Neither do you, William—cub-hunting's coming on. Still, I think we must look to one of these lines for success. Either we lead them along, or we let them lead us : and when they are where we want them, we do our worst.

" And now for Arx. That château interests me and I think it must interest you. And if I were Gedge, once I knew that mine enemy was at hand, I'd do my level best to lead him to Arx. What is de Parol's business, I've no idea : but it's something pretty hot to warrant a place like that. But, whatever it is I don't want to get involved. I'm not a thief-taker. So let us agree upon this—that we never approach that village, however desirable such an approach may appear.

" Finally, let me say this. Gedge isn't downstairs at this moment, for Bell, who is watching the road, would have let us know if he was. But there aren't any street-lamps here and in twenty minutes or so Bell won't be able to see. And ten minutes after that Gedge may be downstairs. That's the sort of fellow he is. We'll get him all right, but I do think he'll give us a run.

" And now let's forget the blackguard—for half an hour. What about wires, William ? "

" Wires are delivered with letters, once a day ; that is to say in the morning about ten o'clock : but the postman passes this house when he's on his way home, so if a wire or a letter should arrive in the course of the day, he'll leave it here in the evening, as he goes by. And he'll take any wires for us—I've left a thousand francs at the Post Office on which they are going to draw."

" He'll take a letter ? " said John.

" Of course," said I. " But if you're going to write one, you'll have to be quick. If he's coming to-night, he'll be here any minute now."

John sat down there and then and began to write, but before he had covered a page Rowley entered the room, bearing a letter for Mansel and a telegram from me.

I opened and read my wire.

Friday all very well Jenny.

I opened my note-book and checked it : all was well.

(False wires can be sent. So my wife was always to name the day of the week and to vary her way of saying that all was well.)

I looked up to meet Mansel's eyes. He was holding an envelope up.

" You must admit," he said, " that Brevet writes a very nice hand."

> *Captain Jonathan Mansel D.S.O.*
> *c/o Monsieur et Madame Caillau,*
> *par Izard.*

" Well I'm damned," said I.

" What did I say ? " said Mansel.

He slit the envelope and read the letter aloud.

DEAR CAPTAIN MANSEL,

It is so nice to know that we are neighbours. And, from what I hear of Madame Caillau, you will be well looked after for the rest of your life. What glorious weather ! I have just asked Gedge if he has any message for you.

E

His reply has been typically downright, but hardly, shall we say, in tune with the Infinite.

> *Pray remember me to Mr. Chandos, and*
> > *Believe me,*
> > > *Yours very sincerely,*
> > > > *MAURICE BREVET.*

" No man can deny," said Mansel, " that Brevet has an excellent wit : but, as before, he must show it : he would have been so much wiser to keep to himself the fact that they knew we were here."

" How did they know ? " said John.

" I've no idea," said Mansel. " If de Parol is breaking the law—and I think he is—the presence of strangers may be reported to him. Or Caillau may have run into some servant from Arx. Any way, it doesn't matter. I don't think they will come here : but I'll lay any money they try and get us to Arx."

I got to my feet.

" I'm tired of the swine," I said. " Let's take the evening air."

The valley in which our farm stood was as rich as any I know in the Pyrenees. It lay beyond the foot-hills and under the mountains themselves, and it seemed all pasture and orchards, with a tiny village or two, to serve its husbandmen. It was by no means flat, and the pretty road which served it was rising and falling and twisting for all its length : had a man walked those six miles, I think they would have seemed three, so varied and so rare were the prospects which would have filled his eye. Below the hanging forests, the writ of Husbandry ran : but Nature had not been ousted : the merry waters sang in their ancient beds ; the sweet, rich grass arrayed outlines beyond the reach of art ; grove and orchard and paddock were rendering unto their Mother the things that were hers.

Dusk was in, when we entered this pretty pleasance, and night came down before we turned to come back. There was, I remember, no moon, and the air was still.

We were not very far from our farm, when I heard the sound of a car.

We all stood still and listened. Then—

"Behind us," I said.

As a rule in the Pyrenees the meadows are kept by stone walls, but one of the pleasantest virtues our valley had was that the English hedgerow bordered the fields. These hedges were beautifully tended—a very rare thing in France ; but now they stood against us, for the car was upon our road and we should be caught by its headlights unless we could take to the fields. And a sudden, much louder drawl declared that the car was close—it is an astonishing thing how wood and spur and hillock can baffle sound.

"Gate on the left," said Mansel, and led the way.

We vaulted the gate with just a few seconds to spare, to see an American car go blandly by. But almost at once we heard it begin to lose speed, and then it slowed right down and stopped at our farm.

We ran down the road behind it, making no noise.

As we approached, an off-side door was opened, and someone got out.

"Take the car, William," said Mansel. "John Bagot with you."

The car was a sportsman's coupé that could have held four. Bent double, I passed its near side until I was close to its door : then I lifted my head, to see that the window was down. As I was listening for a movement, I heard Mansel speaking French.

"Have you lost your way ? "

There was a moment's silence. Then—

"Who's that ? " said a girl, in English.

" I'm staying near here," said Mansel. " If you want to get to ——, I can tell you the way."

" I don't want to get to ——. Do you happen to be Captain Mansel ? "

" I do. May I ask what you want ? "

" Half an hour's talk. Where are you ? "

" Please stand very still," said Mansel, " and tell me from where you come."

" I should think you could guess."

" I prefer to be told."

" From a place beginning with A."

" I see. Please get into your car and switch on the ceiling-light."

" I'm all alone."

" I know. Please do as I say."

There was another silence. Then the girl gave a short laugh and turned to the car. I heard her flounce into her seat. A moment later the ceiling-light went up.

At once I lifted my head. She was alone in the car.

" All clear, Mansel," I said.

The girl started violently.

" My God," she said. And then, " You don't take any risks."

" Not with places like Arx," I said.

" You're wise. How's Mrs. Chandos ? "

" None the worse."

" You're rather abrupt, Mr. Chandos."

" Yes."

Mansel took up the running.

" Do you still wish to talk ? " he said.

" That's what I came for," said the girl.

" Very well. I will talk in this car. But not here. If you will allow me to drive it, I'll move a little way off. Mr. Chandos will sit behind."

" I can hardly help myself."

" Oh, yes, you can," said Mansel. " You can turn my conditions down and drive on your way."

" Damn your soul," said the girl : " you can do as you please."

" I will in a moment," said Mansel : and then, " I want you, John."

He moved away from the car and I knew he was giving orders. After perhaps a minute I heard the Lowland start. . . .

The girl was extremely handsome—not to say, beautiful. She might have been twenty-six. Her face was oval, and her cheek-bones were rather high. She was very dark, and she had a beautiful skin. Her blue-black hair was so sleek that it looked like a cap. She was wearing an elegant house-coat of flowered silk and a very fine emerald bracelet upon her right arm : this was matched by earrings which must have been worth a great deal. On her left wrist, a watch was set in the same rare stones. She was using a strong make-up, and she looked theatrical.

When Mansel appeared again, I opened my door of the car and took my seat behind : the girl moved across to the left, and Mansel took the wheel. He switched off the ceiling- and head-lights, but left the parking-lights on. Then he started the engine and let in the clutch.

We drove for three miles in silence, before turning up a track and into a wood. As we came to rest, I heard the Lowland behind us turn off the road.

It was then that I saw the girl's wrist-watch, which had a luminous dial. It moved from beneath her skirt and up to the door : there it seemed to hover for a moment and then returned to her lap. I switched on the ceiling-light, to see that the pocket on the door was showing a very slight bulge.

" And now," said Mansel.

" I don't come from Gedge," said the girl.

" No ? "

" I come from my Uncle Horace, who owns the Château of Arx."

" I see."

" He—doesn't like Gedge very much."

" Not everyone does."

" Oh, for God's sake be human," snapped the girl. " I'm here as a friend."

" But we are not," said Mansel. " We are here at your invitation—no more and no less."

" Guilty, until I'm proved innocent ? "

" Yes," said Mansel. " Anyone must be that who comes out of Arx."

The girl bit her lip. Then—

" My Uncle Horace knows that you are up against Gedge. He, too, is up against Gedge. He thinks, if you worked together, it would be rather more easy to put Gedge out."

" I see," said Mansel. " Why is he up against Gedge ? "

" Blackmail. Certain letters of his fell into Gedge's hands. That was two years ago. Gedge doesn't ask for money. Instead, he uses the château as though it were his. And that is intolerable."

" I can think of few things more unpleasant. Why doesn't the Baron de Parol go to the police ? "

The girl shrugged her elegant shoulders.

" People who are blackmailed very seldom do."

" I don't agree. In any event, to submit to blackmail is madness. The price is always too high."

" Aren't we running away from the point ? "

" I don't think so. Gedge cumbers your uncle's earth. Your uncle desires to uproot him. Well, he can do so to-morrow—he's only to go to the police. Instead——"

" Why don't you go to the police ? "

" Why should I ? "

" You know what Gedge is."

" I know this—that some years ago he tried his best to possess some jewels that were mine."

" Why didn't you go to the police ? "

" Because he had committed no crime. He was trying to rob the fellow who had robbed me."

" You know that Gedge is one of the very big shots."

" I think that is very likely. He doesn't happen to have practised his art against me."

" He kidnapped Mrs. Chandos. Why don't you jug him for that ? "

" That's surely Chandos' affair."

The girl expired.

" What the devil are you here for ? " she said.

" I am here because Gedge has declared his intention of taking my life. I always think it best to settle a thing like that. And so I have come to this region to give him his chance : and if he tries to take it, I shall kill him in self-defence."

" My uncle offers to assist you."

" To defend myself ? I'm much obliged, but I think it would be a mistake to rope him in."

" You mean you don't trust him."

" I neither trust nor distrust him. But Gedge has thrown down the glove and I've picked it up. Seconds out of the ring, in a show like that."

The girl raised her eyebrows.

" You'd be well advised," she said, " to accept my uncle's help. Gedge's eyes—when your name is mentioned . . ."

" Who mentions my name ? " said Mansel.

" If you have to know, it's seldom off somebody's lips. Gedge's crowd, I mean."

" Why do you have to do with people like them ? "

" *Force majeure*, I suppose."

" Forgive me for pointing out that you have their confidence."

" Which is absurd."

" You knew my name. You knew where I was staying. You knew why I was there. You knew that Mrs. Chandos had been kidnapped. You know that Gedge is ' one of the very big shots.' "

" When Brevet has had a couple, he can't keep quiet."

" I see. D'you know Gedge's nickname ? "

For a split second the girl hesitated. Then—

" Yes, I know that. Auntie Emma."

As she spoke, she moved in her seat, and I saw her left hand go out to the pocket on the door of the car.

" Have you got a sobriquet ? "

The explosion the question provoked was shocking enough. As the girl whipped out a pistol, I caught her wrist and took the weapon away. Her face distorted with passion, she turned to stare upon me. Then she swung round upon Mansel and started to fight. Mansel seized her ankles and I caught her other wrist ; but it was not easy to hold her, for fury had lent her a strength few women possess. And then, all at once, she went slack.

" I'm through," she said. " Let me go."

We did as she said, and she put her head in her hands and sank her hands to her lap. So she stayed for a minute, and then she began to weep . . .

Perhaps five minutes went by—a painful interval. Then the girl lifted her head and sat back in her seat.

" Yes, I'm The Stoat," she said. " And, as I have shown you, I'm not as nice as I look."

" I'm not so sure," said Mansel.

The girl turned and looked upon him.

" What do you mean ? " she said.

" That the company you keep is against you."

" That may be true," said the girl. A hand went up to her head. " You're the first decent men I've met for nearly three years."

" There you are," said Mansel. He pressed the self-starter button. " Come on : let's be getting back."

In silence we gained the road, and a moment later we were stealing the way we had come.

" I suppose you know," said the girl, " that I've told you a pack of lies."

" That's all right," said Mansel. " We'll wash this evening out."

" I shan't—ever," said The Stoat.

Her voice was none too steady, and Mansel began at once to commend her car, quietly comparing her manners with those of other makes and remembering other models which were not so good.

We had covered perhaps two miles when the girl burst out.

" I can't let you go like this. Listen. When my uncle heard you were here, there was the most frightful scene . . . Gedge has a pull with him—that's perfectly true— and so can use the château from time to time. But— honour among thieves : and to lead anybody to Arx was a hideous breach of faith. Any way, the damage was done, and the only way to repair it was to eliminate you. My uncle wouldn't mourn Gedge : but until you are dead, he won't rest—and that *is* the truth."

There was a little silence. Then—

" Thank you very much," said Mansel.

No more was said until we had reached the farm, where Mansel and I got out, and the girl took the driving seat. I slid her pistol into the pocket beside her and shut the door. Then I stood back beside Mansel.

The girl leaned out of her window as though she had something to say.

We moved to her side.

" I'm soppy enough," she said, " to hope that you two will think of me by another name. I'm not going to give you my own, for my father commanded his Regiment and died by Ypres. But I had a stage name once. It was Mona Lelong."

" Good night, Miss Lelong."

The girl caught her breath.

Then she smiled and nodded, and let in her clutch. . . .

As her tail light flicked out of sight—

" We shall see her again," said I.

" I hope so," said Mansel. " Nothing like having a friend in the enemy's camp."

" You handled her devilish well."

" It wasn't so very hard. I was almost sure she was lying : and then she put a foot wrong. She said Brevet talked in his cups. . . . And I will lay any money that Brevet can carry his wine. So I fired my big gun at once—as you and I know, the only gun that I'd got. I let her see that I knew that she was The Stoat. She at once assumed that I knew all about her and had been playing with her from first to last. And so she went off the deep end and then broke down." Here the Lowland came up and he waved her into the yard. " We're on to something, William. I wish I knew what. But it must be of some importance if ' our beloved Horace ' regards us as trespassers."

*   *   *   *   *

The next morning I drove to Sarrat, a neighbouring town, while Mansel kept observation upon the Château of Arx. And John Bagot with him.

I was taking the Lowland to a garage, for she had a fault in her wiring we could not find. With me was Bell.

It was market day at Sarrat, and the old-fashioned streets were full. As we were picking our way, I saw Gedge's Lowland some thirty paces ahead. But I could not see who was in her, and, since the traffic was checked, I told Bell to take the wheel and whipped out of the car.

Under cover of vehicles, I was able to draw pretty

close, to see that Lousy was driving, with Punter sitting beside. The back of the car was empty. At that moment the line of traffic began to move again, but slowly enough for me to follow on foot. Then, twenty yards farther on, Lousy drew in to the kerb and Punter prepared to alight. This meant that he would look back before he opened his door, so I drew back behind a lorry and out of his sight. And as I did so, the lorry began to move.

If I was not to be seen, there was only one thing to be done, and that was to board the lorry, whose tailboard was down. This I accordingly did, and flung myself down on some sacks which, I think, contained meal. What such as observed me would think, I did not care, but I hoped very much that no one would take any action until I was away from the car. Almost at once the lorry was checked again, and whilst I was lying there, jerking like any puppet to the tune of an engine which must have been twenty years old, almost directly beside me I heard Punter's voice.

"All right. In a quarter of an hour."

"Yes," said Lousy, "I know your quarter of an hours. I'm leaving this —— town at half-past ten. 'Back at eleven sharp,' was wot he said. An' from here to the —— shatter's just over twenty miles. If you——"

"All right, all right," said Punter. "I'll be there."

I heard the slam of his door.

Now, thanks to the work we had done, I knew the road they must take to bring them from Sarrat to Arx, and since it was now exactly a quarter-past ten, I had only to rejoin Bell, take that road before them and choose the spot at which we would hold them up. I, therefore, began to move backwards without delay; but hardly had I begun, when the lorry's clutch was let in with a jolt that shook the teeth in my head. I can only suppose that the traffic had opened before it. Be that as it may, before I knew where I was, the lorry was pounding along at ten or twelve miles an hour : then its driver swung to the left and changed into top . . .

I scrambled up to the cab—leaned out and round to the window and called upon the fellow to stop. So far from expressing surprise to see me there, he merely shouted back that he was already late and would be fined twenty francs if he did not get back to ' the depot ' by half-past ten. I replied that I'd give him a hundred, if he would let me get down.

" Show me the money," he roared—and actually put down his foot.

Between the speed and vibration, at least a mile had gone by, before I could pull out the money and thrust the note under his nose. And then he applied his brakes and brought his conveyance to rest by the side of the road.

But of course my cake was dough. I was fully two miles from Sarrat, and the time was twenty minutes past ten. As I made my way back on foot, I could not help reflecting that the adjective ' fickle ' suits Fortune down to the ground. At a quarter past ten that morning she had delivered the enemy into my hands : precisely five minutes later I was myself in balk.

At eleven o'clock I found Bell, who had carefully ' covered ' Lousy, seen him joined by Punter and watched them drive out of the town. By twelve, the fault in the wiring had been found out and repaired. And just before one o'clock, I threw myself down beside Mansel in the hollow from which we observed the Château of Arx.

I related what had occurred.

" And there you are," I concluded. " If I had been quick off that lorry, you wouldn't have had the pleasure of seeing Lousy return."

John Bagot was bubbling, but Mansel lifted a hand.

" William," he said, " you have a most remarkable trait. You take your reverses so gently that Fortune relents."

I raised my eyebrows.

"I don't understand," I said.

"I know," said Mansel. "How should you? The point is this. We've never had our eyes off that château, *but Lousy has never returned.* So unless he is two hours late—and that I find hard to believe—you have proved that there is another way into the Château of Arx."

CHAPTER IV

AN AFTERNOON CALL

NOW though we had decided that we must give Arx a wide berth, I do not think we should have been human if we had not desired to find out where this second entrance might be ; and as soon as we reached our farm, we began to study the map.

This proved that it lay to the West, as did the town of Sarrat ; for, had it lain to the East, the distance must have been more than Lousy had said. More. There was only one road, so far as we could make out, upon which such an entrance could lie, and that was the road which served the village of Arx. But this we had not surveyed, except from our post to the North ; and from there we could only see the last of its run.

What kind of entrance there was we could not conceive, for the château was standing upon a mountainside ; and when you are facing a mountain, as we had been, there can be nothing hidden if only you use your eyes. Add to that that it was to the West that the fall of water came down . . .

That same afternoon we drove to the south of Arx and climbed to the spot to which Mansel had made his way : but though we stood directly above the fall, we could see next to nothing except a reach of the road in the valley below. And between that and where we stood the cliffs were precipitous. It seemed there was nothing for it, but to approach from the West, and at dawn the next day we made a reconnaissance in force.

There were two parallel roads, running East and West. One was the road which served the valley of Arx; the other lay three miles South. The six of us set out to prove the country which lay between.

At five o'clock that morning we took up a ragged line, some three miles west of Arx, and, as the dawn came up, we moved, as beaters do, from West to East. Of such was the country we could not be all in touch, but Carson and Bell were in the middle, John Bagot and Rowley to the South, while Mansel and I took care of the northern side. In fact, Mansel used the road which served the valley of Arx; but I made my way through the forest a quarter of a mile higher up. (I say 'a quarter of a mile,' but sometimes it was very much more; for the going was far from easy and simply did not allow me to hold my course.)

I had been moving for an hour and had covered perhaps a mile when I heard the sound of water somewhere at hand. It was not very loud, but had a more vigorous note than the voice of a rill; and yet I could see no fall nor any sign of one. This seemed phenomenal, for water can run but one way on a mountainside; and though it had nothing to do with the matter in hand, I felt I must find out the reason for such a remarkable thing. I, therefore, listened as carefully as I could and, judging the sound to be coming from directly above me, I made for a little recess about forty feet higher up. I call it a 'recess' for lack of a better term, but it looked like the very rough step which some giant had made and used when climbing the mountainside. As I went up, it was clear that the sound was coming from there, yet even above the recess the ground was dry. It took me five or six minutes to reach the spot, but there was the answer to the riddle as clear as day.

The recess had been made by the caving in of the soil, and the soil had at this point caved in because it was only a crust : beneath this crust was a grotto, down in whose depths was running the stream that had made it when Earth was young. Several such grottoes exist in the Pyrenees : possibly there are hundreds, but only a few are known. This seemed to be one of those which had not been found, for the hole into which I was peering had certainly never been entered for many years : yet the grotto to which it admitted was of a considerable size. Not that I could see it, for I could see nothing at all ; but the torrent which I could hear running was some little distance off.

Having solved my mystery, I turned again to my duty of searching the ground to the East, but half a mile farther on a cliff rose out of the mountain, to block my way. I could have gone down and round the base of the cliff : but, so far as I could judge, Mansel would be able to answer for the ground that ran up to its foot : and so I turned up the mountain to gain its head.

This proved a much harder task than I had supposed, for the farther I climbed, the steeper the ground became, until this, too, rose into a cliff or cornice, up which I could not go. To skirt this, I turned again, until I was facing West, but I had to move for nearly a quarter of a mile before the cornice gave way and let me come up.

That is the way of mountains : indeed, I know no country which may be so hard to cross as mountain, thick clad with forest, in summer time. Again and again you are forced to compass some feature of which, if you could have seen it, you might have steered clear : and when at last you are round, as like as not you will find you have lost your bearings and have but a poor idea which way you should turn. Since I had a compass with me, I was not so badly placed, but the lie of the land surprised me, for, when I turned East again, the mountainside was before me when it should have lain on my right.

However, steep as it was, I could make my way up, and after a while I saw a very small plateau directly ahead. Of this I was very glad, for it meant that I could sit down and take some rest; and two minutes later I hauled myself on to it, panting, and threw myself down on its turf.

It was a true mountain lawn. How it came to be there, whether Nature or man had made it, I could not tell. But the beeches stood back about it, as though they recognized its right to be there.

After resting for five or six minutes, I got to my feet and looked round, and then at once I saw the remains of a path. It had not been trodden, I think, for a number of years, and on the plateau itself all trace was gone: but it ran down off the plateau towards the East, that is to say, the way I was trying to go.

Such a path was natural enough. With the approach of summer, shepherds lead their flocks to the mountain-tops: the way is long and hard, and the sheep are glad of a lawn upon which they can rest and feed, before they go on: this lawn had been found or made for the sheep to use, and the path led down to the valleys and up to the pastures above. And since in this kind of country a path was above all price, I was hastening down its zig-zag before a minute was out.

At first it ran down a gorge: then it curled to the right, to slope down the side of a mountain quite bare of trees. I did not like the look of this reach, for I have a poor head for heights, and the ground below it fell sharply for ten or twelve feet and then disappeared. Still, two hundred yards farther on the forest again took charge, so I started along the reach, keeping my eyes on the path and away from the edge.

I had gone much more than half-way, when, rounding a curve of the mountain, I saw before me a stile which I could not climb. As the result of some landslide, the path was gone. And more than the path. Thousands of tons of soil had fallen away, to fix, between me and the trees for which I was bound, a gulf full forty feet wide and God knows how deep.

This was, of course, why the path had been abandoned, for the fall was by no means recent—already Nature had painted most of the scar.

After a long look, I turned to retrace my steps.

Till now I had been very careful to look away from the brink ; but, as I turned, I glanced down, and what I saw far below me wiped all fear of falling out of my mind.

I was looking into a dingle of a considerable size. It might have been the head of a valley, whose exit was out of my view. To the left, built into the hill, was a decent, two-storied house : to the right, in the shade of some trees, were a table and chairs : facing me was a garage which could have accepted six cars : and just in front of the garage a Lowland was being washed.

At once I looked round for cover, but, except upon the edge of the gulf, there was none to be seen. I, therefore, lay down on the path, to find I could still see the car and the farther end of the house. I then took my binocular out, and, though I was badly placed, for I could not lie square, I was able to see that the man who was washing was Lousy and the Lowland was Gedge's car.

The garage was stoutly built of good-looking, uncut stone ; but the house, which was very much older, was built of stones which had come from some river's bed. Indeed, it seemed to me that the house had been a farm-house, but had been partly rebuilt : certainly its shutters had been added, for these were of steel.

Now if Lousy had raised his eyes, he might or might not have observed that someone or something was lying

F

upon the path : but I was perfectly sure that if Gedge or Brevet were to appear on the scene, he would look up and round and would at once remark that someone or something was there. And since it was now past eight, I made up my mind to withdraw as soon as I could. But, though I did nothing else, I must take a bearing first. I, therefore, put up my glasses and got my compass out.

This showed me that the house was facing roughly South-West, that the entrance to the dingle must lie between North and West, and that, from where I was lying, a peak with a broken tooth was rising South-East and by South. With that very meagre information, I felt I must be content : so I put my compass away and began to crawl back to the gorge.

In half an hour I was back again on the plateau from which I had taken the path ; and there once more I sat down—this time less to rest than to consider my discovery.

The rogues were not staying at Arx—at least not the Arx that we knew. From the château to the dingle must be at least two miles. That the dingle was no more than a garage, I simply did not believe ; for Gedge would never sleep a mile from his car. The entrance to the dingle was the entrance we had to find, for that was where Lousy had driven the day before. Yet he had spoken of the 'shatter,' as being some twenty miles off . . . at which he had to be back by eleven o'clock. And Mona Lelong had said that Gedge used the château . . . had made it perfectly clear that she and her uncle were living cheek by jowl with Brevet and Gedge.

I remembered the light-railway cuttings. The one to the West of the château might possibly lead to the dingle. . . . No, that was wrong, for in that case I must have crossed it, and no one could ever have tunnelled under those hills.

After twenty minutes' hard thinking, I gave the thing

up. The hour was now nine o'clock, and I must be getting back. So I ate two sandwiches and wished that I had brought six—and then set out for the point at which I had parted from Mansel four hours before.

This time I did lose my bearings. Of course, my compass helped me, but not very much, for cliff and ravine and thicket conspired to stand in my way. For two hours I fought and struggled, always perceiving too late the line which I should have taken, the path which I should have trod. And when at last in desperation I made to come down to the road and chance being seen, I was not allowed to do that without very near breaking my neck, for I blundered on to the very brink of a quarry, to see the road beyond and below it, some eighty yards off.

I was walking round the brink and wiping the sweat from my face, when a sound came up to me from the floor of the quarry below. It was a very slight sound, but I parted the bushes beside me, to see, if I could, what had made it and who was there.

I think that Brevet had made it, for Brevet was there. I shall always think he had tripped, for he was nursing his foot. Any way, after a minute, he limped to the road. He looked up and down and then listened, as though for the sound of a car. Then he stooped and picked up a pebble, and turning, threw it behind him into the quarry itself. This must have been a signal, for almost at once the car I had seen—the Lowland—pulled quietly out of the quarry and on to the road. There it stopped for Brevet to take his seat: and then it slid out of my sight and away from Arx.

As fast as I could, I made my way down to the road, and there I found Mansel waiting, with a hand to his chin.

"Did you see that?" he said.

"I did."

"Then the entrance is here—somewhere. And yet I

inspected this quarry three hours ago. I admit there's a shed or garage—it must be through that."

We walked back into the quarry.

To the left, out of sight of the road, I saw the end of the cutting which ran to the level-crossing, west of the village of Arx. Opposite this, again out of sight of the road, a shelter of galvanized iron was projecting from the welter of rock—a thing to house a lorry against the snows. This housing was shut by a curtain—and when we sought to raise it, the curtain was locked.

"Very ingenious," said Mansel. "This is the entrance, of course. Observe, if you please, the causeway of baulks of wood : that might be no more than a runway : in fact it is there to prevent a tire leaving a print. So simple, so very obvious—when demonstrated by facts. You know, I'm losing my cunning—and that's the truth. You'll have to help me, William . . . And now please resolve this riddle. This, we know, is the entrance, because we've seen them come out. But this quarry is more than a mile from the Château of Arx. About a mile and three quarters. Well, what about that ? "

"This," said I. "It's about a drive and a chip from where they garage the car."

*   *   *   *   *

The others had little to report.

Carson had reached the head of my avalanche or landslide, but had seen nothing from there : Bell had gained the trees which grew on its farther side, but a persistent cornice had stopped him from going down : John Bagot and Rowley had searched the southern slopes and found nothing at all.

Still, we had much to digest, and when we were back at the farm, we sat down to draw our conclusions and see where they led.

We had located the second entrance to Arx.

There could be no doubt that the quarry belonged to Arx, and had been used by the Baron to serve his special requirements and mask them, too. It was an incomparable cloak—an honest, uninteresting feature, whose use or disuse would attract no attention at all.

The quarry warranted the railway : the railway warranted the crossings : and the crossings warranted the barriers across the road. The quarry made an admirable entrance—comparatively easy to construct and unobtrusive to use. The dingle into which I had peered was certainly the head of a valley whose tail I could not see : that tail approached the quarry from the opposite side, and a tunnel had been driven, connecting the two : if proof of this were needed, the blue-brown stone of the quarry was that of which the garage had been built.

So much for the second entrance which we had set out to find. What troubled us was that it was not the entrance to Arx.

So far as we could judge, the château and the house in the dingle stood more or less back to back ; but between the two there was a mountain, and this, at its base, must have been six hundred yards thick. That this had been pierced was more than we could believe. The cost would have been gigantic : the work would have been the talk of the countryside : spring after spring of water would have very soon turned the tunnel into an aqueduct : finally, where was the earth that had been displaced ? Yet château and house were connected—of that we were sure : tradesmen called at the château—only the day before six crates of beer had been driven up to its door : what was still more to the point, a petrol-waggon had entered the *porte-cochère*.

"It doesn't really matter," said Mansel. "We know that there is some connection, and that is enough. And the dingle is simply ideal as a bumping-off place."

John Bagot's face was a study, but I began to shake

with laughter. The thing was so true. As ' a place of execution ' the dingle was incomparable.

" But what a show ! " Mansel continued. " Arx and Petit Arx—of which no one has any idea. My respect for Horace is rising very high. But what ever is his profession—his special line ? It's got to be pretty good to be worthy of a lay-out like this. No one would ever dream that the château was just a façade. There, to all appearance, the Baron de Parol is leading a normal life. Even if it was searched, I don't suppose for a moment that anything would be found. And all the time he's doing his stuff from the dingle . . .

" Well, William, as always, you have delivered the goods. We know of the dingle, but they don't know that we do. More. We know the way in. So now we must watch the quarry and learn how to open the door." He stopped short there, and a hand went up to his mouth. " No, that's not right. It's too easy."

" Yes," said I. " That's right. We learn how to open the door. But we don't open it—just like that. Because, when that door is opened a signal is transmitted to Petit Arx."

" Quite right," said Mansel. " We'll have to be careful there. There's sure to be a signal of some sort, whenever that curtain's raised. I mean, it's just common sense."

" There may," said John Bagot, " there may be another way in."

We both of us looked at him. Then—

" Spill it, John," said Mansel. " What do you know ? " John Bagot moistened his lips.

" I'm thinking of the grotto," he said. " The grotto that Chandos found. We might have a look at that. They sometimes run for miles. And I think there's probably one between Arx and Petit Arx."

There was a long silence. Then—

"I give you best, John," said Mansel. "Of course you're right."

*   *   *   *   *

Now, nearly three days had gone by since Brevet had posted his note, and we could not help feeling that Gedge and his host must both be growing impatient to come to grips with us. No doubt, as Mansel had said, they were hoping, by taking no action, to lure us to Arx : but time was money to Gedge and, according to Mona Lelong, the Baron was losing weight. And though, three days ago, we were ready and willing to meet them anywhere else, our outlook was now reversed : not only was Petit Arx a highly suitable spot, but it was, of course, the last place to which they would expect us to come. "So, if we can," said Mansel, "we must avoid a brush until we can enter the dingle and have things out there. But Gedge may force our hand. I need hardly say that if he had the faintest idea that we know what we do, the fellow would be outside now—and Horace with him."

"He can't know yet," said I. "But he does seem to find things out."

"I know he does," said Mansel. "But he—must—not—find—this—out, until we tell him ourselves. That is why this afternoon John Bagot and I are going to drive ninety miles to purchase gear we could certainly purchase at Sarrat and probably nearer than that. Rope and torches and such. I think we'll take Rowley with us. And you and Bell and Carson shall hold the fort. How wide was the hole, William ? The hole admitting to the grotto. And what were its edges like ? "

"Less than four feet across," said I. "And its edges were sound."

Mansel nodded and got to his feet.

Five minutes later, he and John Bagot and Rowley had left the farm.

I had no mind to sit indoors, for the weather was very fine, so I summoned Carson and Bell and the three of us made for a meadow above and behind the farm. Here was a pleasant spot, where the downward slope of the meadow was stayed for ten or twelve feet, and the little lap thus formed was shaded by chestnut trees. A man lying here in the shade could see the whole of the farm as well as some of the road upon either side.

I take no shame to say that I slept for an hour and more, whilst the servants watched. Then I rubbed the sleep from my eyes and told them to take their ease while I did my turn. And whilst I was watching, I wrote a few lines to Jenny—a poor, disjointed letter, for I am no master of the art of doing two things at once.

I had just made an end and had sealed my envelope, when a car came into my view on the road to the east of the farm. I heard Bell rousing Carson, which meant he had seen it, too.

Now the road was a public road, and cars did sometimes go by: but those that did were few, for, as a thoroughfare, the road was valueless, while, as a promenade, it was, as they say, off the map. And so the chances were that the car now approaching the farm had something to do with Arx.

It was moving slowly enough, and it was a limousine. With my glasses I saw the chauffeur—a man I had never seen. But, because they were sitting back, I could see no one else.

For a moment it passed out of sight; but, when it reappeared, it was moving more slowly still. Whoever was there was proposing either to stop at or to crawl past the farm.

Again it passed out of view—this time behind the farm. Then it appeared again, on the opposite side. And then it stopped.

Now because of the hedgerow which bordered the side

of the road, I could see but little more than the top of
the car : but its front door was opened and closed, and
this suggested that the chauffeur had been told to alight.
Sure enough, a moment later I saw the man appear at
the gate of the farm. In his hand he carried a basket,
which might have held fruit.

He threw a look round as might have done anyone who
wanted to ask his way or had some message to give.
Then he passed through the gateway and into the yard.
I saw him look at the barn, the doors of which were shut :
then he turned to the right and up to the door of the
house. To reach this, he passed the stairway which led
to our flat.

I saw him knock on the door and, after a moment or
two, Madame Caillau appear. There was a little conversation : then the fellow presented the basket, which
Madame Caillau received with the traditional rapture
which the French in such cases observe. Then Madame
Caillau retired, basket in hand—no doubt to empty the
thing, before handing it back.

Directly she disappeared, I saw the chauffeur lean forward, inclining his head, as though to be sure that he was
out of her sight. Then he put a hand in his pocket and,
taking something out, threw it well and truly into the
road.

That was enough for me.

" Get down to that car," I said. " Hold up whoever is
there, until I come."

" Both of us, sir ? " said Bell.

" Yes."

As Madame Caillau returned, Punter appeared in the
gateway. He stood there in view of the chauffeur, now
talking with Madame Caillau. The chauffeur received
the basket, leaned against the jamb of the doorway and
pushed back his hat. This was clearly another signal, for
Punter lifted an arm. Thirty seconds later, another man

appeared, bearing what seemed a dispatch-case, rather thick through. Punter and this man waited, their eyes fast on the chauffeur, still deep in talk. So for perhaps one minute. Then the chauffeur's hand went behind him and moved up and down. When it stopped moving, Punter stepped into the road and looked either way. Then I saw his lips move, and the third man whipped up the stairway which led to our flat. . . .

And that was as much as I saw, for there I got to my feet and ran for the car. . . .

As I peered over the hedgerow—

" Empty, sir," said Carson, who was standing in front of the car. " No key in the switch."

" Can you see Punter ? " I said.

" He's not looking, sir," said Bell, who was lying by the side of the way.

" Into the car, Carson, and shut the door."

Carson was in in a flash.

" Did Punter see him ? " I said.

" No, sir."

Six paces ahead of the car the road fell sharp to a culvert some seventy yards away : there it curled to the left, to climb again to the level which it had left. The meadow in which I was standing fell with the road ; so I turned and ran for a gate a few paces down the hill.

Well out of Punter's sight, I gained the road : there I turned and ran back, keeping the car between us, so that I could not be seen.

" Has Punter moved ? " I said.

" No, sir," said Bell.

" Listen, Carson," I said. " The car is on the down grade—but only just : if you were to take off the hand-brake, she wouldn't move. But I'm going to damned well move her. . . . Once I can get her going, she'll make the dip. That is the moment at which you get out on the step : and, as she gathers speed, you hold her steady, so that she fouls the bend and goes clean through the hedgerow and into the dell. You jump as she meets the hedgerow. Is that quite clear?"

"Quite clear, sir," said Carson.

"Then take the hand-brake off. Is Punter looking, Bell?"

"Not at the moment, sir."

I laid hold of the bumper bar . . .

For a moment I thought I should have to call upon Bell, for the car was very heavy and her tire-pressure something low. And then I found she was moving . . . I pressed this slight advantage with all my might, for, had I once let her stop, I do not think I could have moved her again. But, as though she knew what was coming, that car seemed reluctant to move, and for five out of six of the paces that lay between her and the dip, she really might be said to have stuck in her toes. And then she seemed to throw in her hand. . . .

As I leaped clear—

"Punter's signalling, sir, but he hasn't looked this way yet."

"Too good to be true," said I, and fell flat on my face. "Make your way into the dip and into the field on the other side of the road."

As I spoke, the limousine left the road at thirty-five miles an hour, put her nose over the culvert and then did an elegant somersault into the dell.

As Carson looked round, I jerked my head to the left and crawled into the dip. . . .

Now exactly when Punter perceived that the car was gone, I cannot honestly say. I had made my way into the dip and so out of his view : I had climbed the gate on my left, and had run back beside the hedgerow which covered me from the road. Carson was just behind me, and Bell was out of sight on the opposite side. It was then that Punter came pelting along the midst of the way. . . .

Grimly, I watched him go by—to the head of the dip. There he stopped and stared. Then he began to go down. After, perhaps, ten paces, he clapped both hands to his mouth. . . . Subduing an impulse to laugh, I turned my head to the farm.

Almost at once the man with the dispatch-case appeared, whipping out of the gateway and down the road. At first he failed to observe that the car was gone : and, when he saw, he put a foot wrong and stumbled and very nearly fell down. And, as he was standing there, gaping, the chauffeur appeared . . .

The thing was as good as a play, and that is the honest truth.

The chauffeur at once perceived that his charge had been moved. As he came up at a run, the other let go.

" You left the brake off, *canaille*. She's run away."

That this was the Baron de Parol, I had no doubt. He was very plainly a Frenchman—his looks, his manner, his speech declared this fact. His face, which was very much lined, was as gray as his hair, and he had the squarest jaw I have ever seen. And as he looked upon the chauffeur his eyes burned in his head.

The latter was plainly frightened.

" No, I never, Baron—so 'elp me Gawd."

" Then where is the car ? Did Punter give the alarm ? "

" No, 'e didn't give no alarm, but——"

" Filth ! " screamed the other. " Do you deny——"

" Filf to you ! " roared the chauffeur, cut, I suppose, to the quick. " Look at the —— road. That's where I lef' the car. An', —— brake on or off, are you goin' to tell me she moved ? "

The Baron regarded the road.

" The slope is down," he said.

" Yes. One in a nundred," said the chauffeur. He

leaned forward, poking his head. "An' if she moved on 'er own, why didn't she start to move before you got out an' left 'er? Wot about that?"

The other frowned at this excellent argument. Then he looked over his shoulder and round about.

"Eg-zacly," said the chauffeur.

"But Punter," mouthed the Baron. "Punter was on the watch."

"I know," said the chauffeur. "I know. I—wonder —where—Punter—is."

The man was an artist. His delivery of the sinister statement left nothing to be desired; and the Baron started with a violence that caused him to drop his case.

At once, a strange thing happened.

The chauffeur let out the screech of a terrified man and cowered away from the other, shielding his face.

Furiously the baron regarded him.

"Dam fool!" he spat. "Dam fool!"

The chauffeur let fall his hands. Then he wrung the sweat from his brow.

"My mistake," he said. "But you didn't 'alf give me a turn. It's natural enough, you know. Wot with the car not 'ere, an'——"

"Had Punter a key of the switch?"

"No," said the chauffeur, "'e 'adn't. I've got them both here."

"Then the car has run down the hill."

"Not unless she was moved—an' that'd take four strong men."

The Baron looked slowly round, with a hand to his chin.

"Perhaps it did."

That the Baron was also an artist was very plain.

The chauffeur jumped at his words, stared at the sturdy hedgerows and back the way he had come.

Then, without much conviction—

" No, no," he said. " She said they was all of them out. That's why I give the signal, like wot you tole me to do. Besides . . ." He broke off there and moved forward, exactly as Punter had done. " You see, if she 'ad run forward, she'd never 'ave managed that bend. She'd a 'eld straight on, she would ; jumped that culvert an'— Oh my Gawd, she done it . . . just as I said."

With that, he rushed down the hill, like a man possessed, while the other, who had missed the apostrophe, because he was looking away, stood staring after his servant with a hand half-way to his mouth. Then he began to follow, muttering under his breath, until he made the third to arrive at that point in the road from which his automobile could be identified.

For a moment he stood as though spellbound. Then his French nature came out. He raised his two hands to heaven screaming and yelling curses with all his voice : then he flung his hat on the ground and belaboured it with his dispatch-case until the handle came off. He then endeavoured to throw the case over the hedge, but such was his nervous exhaustion that twice he failed. These failures enraged him so much, that I made sure he was going to fall in a fit : however he picked up the case and tried again and, having at last succeeded, spat violently in the direction in which it had disappeared.

Behaviour so much out of reason would, I think, have made a mute smile ; and we were half dead with laughter before the man picked up his hat and, raging at its horrid condition, shambled down the hill in the wake of his men.

Wiping the tears from my face, I tried to decide what to do. The three men were at our disposal. Was it better to deal with them, or to stay out of sight ? After a little, I decided that we should lie low. Except, perhaps, for Punter, I bore them no personal grudge : if this was indeed the Baron, Mansel was far more fitted to talk to a man of his kind : thirdly, as I have shown, they did not know what to think—a condition of mind I had no desire to relieve : finally, I was most anxious to have a good look at our flat. And so I told Carson to stay—or, rather, to make for the dell and to draw as near as he could, without being seen ; for it goes, I think, without saying that while observation is good, overhearing is better still. Then I called to Bell, and the two of us made for the farm.

I now gave all my mind to the mischief de Parol had done or was hoping to do in our flat, for he had not gone such lengths just to see if our beds were made. To enter another man's house, like a common thief, was a serious step for a man of his standing to take : and the rank incompetence with which he had gone to work showed that he was not accustomed to such activities. Why, then, had he come himself ? The answer seemed to be this. Either because he proposed to do something which he was not ready to trust another to do ; or because he proposed to do something which nobody else would do.

Now Gedge was not scrupulous, and I was about to dismiss the second alternative, when I remembered the terror the chauffeur had shown when the Baron had dropped his dispatch-case into the road. And then I perceived the truth, which, I must confess, I should have perceived before.

That the case had contained an explosive, I now had no doubt.

The fellow had come himself, not only because he alone could place and set the bomb, but also because the others fought shy of its energy. The chauffeur had plainly been frightened to death of the thing—had driven in fear and trembling, because it was on the back seat : and then, when he saw the case fall, apprehension overrode reason and made him cry out. And the pressure of the tires had been lowered, out of respect, of course, for this captious passenger.

Now of bombs and explosives, I had no knowledge at all : but Bell, who was older than I, had been through the Great War : so I told him my conclusions and waited to see what he said.

"That's right, sir," said Bell. "A time bomb. Or it might be a booby-trap. They're easy enough to set. And, if I may say so, we'll have to be careful here. Three of my squadron were killed that way—in 1918. The Germans had hung up a cat by one of its legs. Alive, of course. And as soon as our fellows saw it they ran to cut it down. An' then the whole cottage went up."

"We'll go in by the house," I said, "instead of the outside stair. And we might have a word with Madame. What was he asking her ? And why was he moving his hand ? "

"Moving his hand, sir ? " said Bell.

"Behind his back," I said. "He was moving it up and down."

"An' the Baron waited for that, sir ? "

"Yes."

There was a little silence. Then—

"I think you're right, sir, to have a word with Madame. But if she can't give us a line, I think we'd be wise to wait till the Captain comes in. You see, it's this way, sir. We're out to discover the trap which the Baron has set : well, we can't do that without moving about the flat : and, if he's done his stuff well, the very first movement we make may set that trap off."

I frowned.

"D'you put it as high as that ? "

"I do, indeed, sir," said Bell. "We've got electricity there : and the things a sapper can do with a couple of lengths of wire . . ."

"Well, we'll see Madame Caillau," I said.

The interview was trying and yielded little enough. The poor woman had found the chauffeur the most delightful of men—a friend, of course, of her son—who had come on his afternoon out to bring her the finest peaches she ever had seen. Her son had told him of us, and, since he was English, too, he had wished to know all about us and how we did. And so she had told him how pleasant and easy were our habits, how we were abroad all day and how helpful the servants were, how we went for a stroll at night and were up at dawn and a dozen other trifles not one of which shed light on the movements the chauffeur had made when his hand was out of her view.

I led the way out of the gate and into the road.

"As I see it, Bell," I said, "there's only one thing to be done. You must stay here, to warn Captain Mansel off in case he gets back before me. And I must collect the Baron. He set the blasted trap : and he can damned well spring it—or take it off."

"That's the best way, sir," said Bell, solemnly.

As fast as I could, I made my way to the dell. This took some time, for I had to fetch a compass lest I should be seen, and I was much afraid that the Baron would have withdrawn. I mean, to do so was ordinary common sense. To stay on the scene was folly, for he could do no good. But when I had found and joined Carson—with infinite care, he showed me de Parol sitting some thirty yards off, malevolently staring upon Punter who seemed to be fast asleep.

The chauffeur, it seemed, had gone to the nearest village, to telephone to the château and ask for another car. Punter had urged that to stay on the spot was madness ; but de Parol had pointed out that none of us knew him by sight and had added with dignity that we could hardly object to an accident's having occurred so close to our farm. This point of view had made Punter laugh so immoderately that the other had charged him with throwing the car away and had sworn to denounce him to Gedge before the sun went down. But Punter had had the last word.

"A lot's going to happen," he said, "before the sun goes down. You see what Auntie says when he hears you're waitin' here for another car. Talk about a ——."

Here perhaps I should say that the car, close to which they were sitting, looked hardly worth while taking up. I think she had turned over twice. Be that as it may, she was now the right way up : but the height of her body had been reduced by half, the two wheels that I could see, though still attached to the axle, were resting upon their sides instead of their rims, and her engine seemed to be flowing out of a battered grotto which bore no resemblance at all to the front of a car.

Under the murmur of the water, I made Carson free of my plan.

"We'll have to take Punter," I said. "Not that I want the swine, but to cover our tracks. Then, when the chauffeur gets back, he won't know what to think. How long has he been gone ? "

Carson glanced at his wrist.

"Just twenty minutes, sir. He's a mile to go each way, and then he'll have to wait for his telephone call. I can't believe he'll be back before half-past five."

"That'll do very well. If we need him, you can come back and fetch him along. He'll tell us quick enough what he meant when he waggled his hand."

Carson smiled.

"It seems it's our day out, sir."

"Don't speak too soon," said I. "But I must admit they have played into our hands."

With that, I rose out of my lair and, walking up to de Parol, desired him to get to his feet.

"To-day," I said, "uninvited, you entered my flat. Now you are invited to do so. Should you decline, you will be ordered to do so. Get up and march."

Without a word, the fellow did as I said.

Punter was still asleep, so I kicked his ribs.

He awoke with a howl, to see Carson, pistol in hand.

"Put them up, Punter," said Carson, and when the fellow obeyed, he took his pistol away.

So the procession took shape.

After some fifty paces, the Baron turned to protest: but, seeing the look on my face, he thought better of his proposal and, with a muttered apology, held on his way. Ten minutes later, perhaps, we came to the farm.

As Bell stepped out of the gateway—

"Tie this man's wrists," I said.

Bell ran for a piece of cord.

"This is an outrage," said de Parol. "Misfortune has made me your prisoner. I expect to receive from you the honours of war."

I turned the man about, took him by the nape of the neck, and approached his face to the wall.

"You're a filthy blackguard," I said. "And filthy blackguards are treated as they deserve."

With that, I rubbed his nose on the wall, till he screamed again.

Then I let him go.

"Now answer me back," I said.

Tears mingled with the blood on his face, but the man had nothing to say.

I turned to look at Punter, whose eyes were wide.

"The gloves are off, Punter," I said. "I'm not as soft as I was."

Punter swallowed and blinked, but he never opened his mouth.

A minute later, the Baron's wrists were fastened behind his back.

"Into the flat," I said. "You know the way."

The fellow went up the stairway quickly enough.

"Turn round and open the door."

By my order, he led the way to our sitting-room.

"And now," I said, "now show me the trap you set."

The fellow drew himself up.

"I do not know what you mean . . ."

"Think again," said I. "You have put something here, which, if it is not removed, will do us no good. Kindly show me how to remove it—without delay."

"I have done no such thing."

I took out my cigarette lighter and struck the thing into flame.

"Turn him round, Bell," I said. "I'll start on his finger-tips."

The statement was more than enough.

Under his tearful direction, we followed the stricken nobleman into our dining-room. Punter accompanied us, sweating : the fellow was frightened to death : but for Carson's pistol, he would, I am sure, have endeavoured to leave the flat.

De Parol looked round the room with bolting eyes. Then—

"Unless you unfasten my hands——"

"Not yet. Show me what you have done."

There was a painful silence. Then—

"It was a prank," said de Parol, "a foolish prank. I extracted one of the fuses "—he nodded towards a fuse-box, high up on the wall— "and put in one of my own. Had that remained in place, as soon as the light was switched on, there would have been—a little explosion . . ."

"I see," said I, slowly. "How did you reach the fuse-box ? "

"I stood on a chair."

I looked at Bell.

"Put a chair under that fuse-box."

The Baron started forward.

" It would be better," he mouthed, " that no one should touch."

" No one will touch," said I. " I'll show you why."

With that, I mounted the chair and put up my hand. The fuse-box was fully six inches out of my reach.

" You see ? " I said. " And I'm very much taller than you."

The man began to tremble.

As I stepped down—

" And now," I said, " I'll give you one more chance. If you lie again, you and Punter will be tied back to back and will be left in this room for twenty-four hours."

This threat, as I had expected, was more than Punter could bear.

" For ——'s sake, show 'im," he cried. " 'E means wot 'e says. I'd —— well show 'im meself, but I don't know wot you done."

The other drew himself up. Then he turned to me.

" If I do so," he said, " I assume I may rely upon your good taste to——"

" No."

" In that case, I regret——"

That was as far as he got, for Punter lost his temper and hit him full on the mouth.

" How's that for good taste ? " he blared. " You —— shover, you——"

With a scream of rage, the other turned upon Punter, wrenching his arms like a madman to free his wrists ; and when he could not do this, baring his teeth and spitting like any beast. Indeed, he had in a moment put off the semblance of man, for his face was a mask of hatred—a wild demoniac malice, shocking to see.

If we were taken aback, Punter himself was shaken, for he cowered and put up an arm, as though to ward off the flame of the other's wrath.

So the five of us stood for perhaps ten seconds of time.

Then I called the Baron to order, because such bestial behaviour was really not fit to be seen.

Very slowly he turned to face me.

" Yes ? "

" Pull yourself together," I said. " And do what you're here to do."

The distorted features relaxed.

" Who are you to command me ? " he said.

This was too much.

Already Gedge must have heard of the loss of the car, yet no watch was being kept, for Bell and Carson and I were all in the flat. There was here some infernal machine, which should have been discovered five minutes ago, which, for all I knew, might any moment go off. And the man who had set it here—the only man who could put it out of action, had worked himself into a frenzy which still obsessed him so much that he could not give his mind to anything else.

Something had to be done.

When I stepped behind him, he never moved, but stood staring straight before him, as though he were under some spell.

I lit my cigarette-lighter and set the flame to his palm.

With an awful shriek, he bounded into the air : then he swung round to face me and fell on his knees.

" What do you wish ? " he wailed.

" To be shown this machine."

" Ah, the machine ! Of course."

From that moment we had no more trouble.

Bell helped him up to his feet, and the fellow showed us a plug—an electric-light plug in the wainscot, into which he had inserted two leads. These he had jammed into place by pushing back the loose plug which he had withdrawn. These leads were, therefore, alive. They led to the sideboard, passing beneath the carpet and through a hole which a gimlet had made in the wood.

Within the sideboard was the infernal machine. This was controlled by a clock, the dial of which was ringed with small holes, every hour and half-hour. A pin had been set in the hole beside nine o'clock. And the clock was going : it was five minutes fast by my wrist-watch. . . . Had we sat down to dinner, as usual, at half-past eight, we should, I suppose, have died at exactly five minutes to nine.

Myself, I drew the leads from the plug, and at once the clock stopped.

The Baron had become the expert.

" Now it is safe," he declared. " It should not, of course, be lifted and then let fall."

" Gawd 'ave mercy," said Punter.

" Silence, *canaille*," spat the Baron. Then he returned to me. " So long as it is not mishandled——"

" You will remove it," I said. " Untie him, Bell."

The Baron swallowed.

" Unhappily, its valise——"

" You will remove it," I said.

And so he did.

The contraption was plainly heavy, and I must confess I was thankful to follow him out of the building and into the yard. There by my order Punter took off his coat. Upon this the machine was laid down, and, after an agony of protest, the two malefactors took each one end of the garment and started to bear it away.

Never was co-operation more vital or more reluctantly subscribed : indeed, their progress was richer than any low-comedy film. They dared not lay down their burden, for I, who was walking behind, had sworn to shoot if they did : but each was deadly afraid that the other would let fall his end of the improvised bier, and the frantic commands and threats which both continually issued, yet could not enforce, made me shake so much with laughter that, had I had occasion to fire, I cannot believe that I should have done any harm. Happily, however, the two were too much engrossed in their common apprehension and hate to spare any time for my demeanour.

While this was going on, Bell was watching the farm and Carson was fetching a compass to reach the dell; and when the Baron and Punter had reached the top of the hill, I told them to go to the devil and made my way back.

Carson returned at six, to make his report.

The Baron and Punter had staggered into the field at the head of the dell and had laid their burden under the culvert, and so to rest out of sight. They had then come down to the car and there they had sat in silence until the chauffeur returned. Punter had seemed uneasy, narrowly watching de Parol, as though the man might attack him, if ever his back were turned : the Baron showed every sign of being deeply perturbed, now nursing his nose and now inspecting his palm and now forgetting them both in some mental agony ; then he would hold his head and rock himself to and fro and clap a hand over his mouth as though to hold back some scream. After about half an hour the chauffeur returned, to offer an insolence which a conversation with Brevet had clearly inspired. De Parol, it seemed, had been warned, before he set forth. Gedge and Brevet had laughed his proposal to scorn—not because it was not convenient, but because he was not the man to carry it out : and they would not carry it out because they would not touch the infernal machine. And when the chauffeur reported that all had gone very well, but the car was destroyed, Brevet had yelled with laughter and had asked where the others were ; and when he had said "With the car," "So are Mansel and Chandos," said Brevet : "you go back and die." For this reason the chauffeur had returned by a round-about way, using what caution he might, until he could see that the two were where he had left them two hours before. This had, of course, assured him that all was well, and when Punter had undeceived him, his dismay—not to say, stupefaction—was ludicrous to behold.

" Well, where are they now ? " he said.

" Listenin' in," said Punter, " as like as not. I tell you, I know the ——. They'd lie down be'ind a matchbox, an' you'd never know they was there."

As the result of his statement, the rest of the talk was too low for Carson to hear, but he gathered that a car would be waiting a few miles off, and a very few minutes later the three climbed up to the road and passed out of his sight.

I had more than enough to consider till Mansel returned, so I left the servants on guard and made my way to the orchard which lay at the back of the farm. But I have so often observed that ' it never rains, but it pours,' that I was not at all surprised when Bell arrived at a run, to say that someone was coming up from the East, moving over the meadows just out of sight of the road.

Together we ran for the loft, where Carson was keeping watch.

As I stepped off the ladder—

" It's Miss Lelong, sir," said Carson.

* * * * *

The Stoat regarded me over the rim of her glass.

" I shan't try any more," she said. " I'm out of my depth. I decide to betray my uncle, in order to save your lives. I arrive to find that, while you are perfectly safe, my uncle is down the drain."

" We happened to be in," I said. " If we had been out, he would have had it all his own way. In which case, you see, you *would* have saved all our lives. If you were me, wouldn't you value that ? "

The lady shrugged her shoulders.

"Perhaps. I don't know. Any way, I've wasted my time. And yours. And the car's lying down, is it?"

"Right down. He'll have to remove it, of course. But it isn't worth taking up."

Miss Lelong shook her head.

"He'll report it stolen," she said. "The police will find it and the Insurance Company will do the rest. And until the tumult is over, you will be left in peace, for the dell will become the cynosure of neighbouring eyes."

"Oh, hell," said I. "That hadn't occurred to me."

"My dear, such a crash as this will not pass unobserved. The local press will attend." She emptied her glass of beer and got to her feet. "And now I must be going."

I did not desire her to stay, for though the servants were gone to stop and warn Mansel that I was not alone at the farm, in view of all that had happened I did not want him delayed.

Together we left the flat and made our way into the fields.

Suddenly—

"I suppose you know," she said, "that they want to get you to Arx."

"It had entered our heads," I said.

"Well, don't you come," said The Stoat. "And I'll tell you another thing. They're playing with the idea of using me as a decoy. They think you might not ignore an urgent call for assistance from Mona Lelong."

"More pretty ways."

"Exactly. That was Brevet's idea. So if I should make some appeal, you'll know what it's worth."

"Thank you very much," I said quietly.

"Not that I flatter myself . . ."

"We always try," I said, "not to let our friends down."

The Stoat looked away. After a moment or two—

" Don't come any farther," she said. " The car's just over that ridge."

" Mansel's due," I said, " so I think I ought to get back."

" Of course. Goodbye."

I took her hand.

" Goodbye," I said. " And thank you so very much. That we don't owe you our lives is not your fault."

" Don't mention it," said The Stoat. " ' _Her_ honour rooted in dishonour stood.' "

" You silence me," I said.

" No. Mother Nature did that. But you know how to act."

" We do our best."

" I'll say your best is damned good. Goodbye, again, Mr. Chandos."

" Goodbye, Miss Lelong."

I watched her pass over the ridge.

Twenty minutes later Mansel drove into the yard.

* * * * *

As I made an end of my tale—

" Fun and games," said Mansel. " I wish I'd been here."

" It strongly resembled," said I, " a harlequinade. If you could have seen the Baron belabour his hat . . . There was only one ugly moment, and that I've told you about."

" You mean, the Baron's outburst ? "

" Yes. Punter had certainly hit him—and hit him hard : he also called him a chauffeur, which may have been a reflection upon his birth : well, that sort of thing can very well make a man mad, but it shouldn't transform a being into a beast. Honestly, it was revolting."

" Inexcusable ? "

" To my mind." I spread out my hands. " Frankly,

I don't understand it. There was, of course, no question of any betrayal, because there was nothing to betray : but de Parol's demeanour was that of a man whose accomplice has betrayed him—I mean, such a thing might push a man over the edge."

Mansel clapped me upon the shoulder.

" Your observation, William, is very sound. You see, Punter *did* betray him. He told you and Carson and Bell what de Parol's profession is. Punter called him ' a shover '—' a —— shover,' you said. And ' a shover ' is thieves' argot for a man who utters counterfeit coin."

CHAPTER V

THE WATER UNDER THE EARTH

AT six o'clock the next morning, Mansel, John Bagot and I were sitting by the edge of the sink-hole which I had found in the forest the day before. Carson and Bell had come with us, less to carry the gear than to mark the place : then they had gone back to the farm with orders not to return till eleven that night. This meant, of course, that if the grotto were to prove impenetrable, we should pass a wasted day : but that could not be helped, for one thing we dared not risk—and that was discovery. And when they did return, they were not to return to the hole, but to a track in the forest a mile and a half away.

Our gear was slight enough, but of good quality. We had two short lengths of oak joist, a quantity of very strong cord, three pairs of hedging gloves and three powerful, leather-cased torches which we could sling. But though there were gloves and a torch for each of us, it was by no means certain that all of us could go down : indeed, the most we hoped for was that two would be able to prove the grotto's depths, while the third could stay at its mouth, if possible just underground and so out of sight. It was, of course, unlikely that the enemy's eyes would be turned to such a place : but, if they were and if any movement was seen, it might go hard indeed with whoever was down below.

Whilst John Bagot was keeping watch, Mansel fastened a cord about me and laid the lengths of timber across the aperture. A moment later, I was some ten feet down.

Finding a rest for my foot, I used my torch, to see before me a chasm some four feet wide. From this was rising the song of the underground stream, now very much more distinct and, to my ear, clearly enriched by some natural sounding-board. And this could only mean that the stream was running in a cavern of a considerable size. Looking behind me, I saw that the grotto ran straight for some fifteen or twenty feet and then came to an end, thus making a little chamber, which seemed to be sound. I trod it carefully and threw my beam on its roof. Then I summoned Mansel, that he might see for himself.

" I can see no snag," I said. " I stand beneath the hole, and John steps on to my shoulders. He picks up the wood and hands it to you. Then he comes down himself. To-night we reverse the procedure, which lets us out."

" And John stays here ? " said Mansel.

" That depends," said I. " The wood will span that chasm. If the quarters below are better, he may as well come on down."

Two minutes later, we were, all three, below ground.

Now, good as our torches were, the light they threw was lost in the chasm's depths : all we could vouch for was that after ten or twelve feet the soil which made up its walls had been changed into stone—I suppose by the action of the water which had made the chasm its bed. Still, this was comforting, for soil can give way and fall, but the petrification we could see suggested, rightly or wrongly, that nothing short of an earthquake would bring it down.

I helped Mansel adjust the timber. Then he bound a second cord to one of the joists and let its coil fall. He then took off his coat, and John Bagot and I, between us, threaded a much finer line up one of the sleeves of his shirt, across his back and down the other sleeve. When it emerged, I tied its end to the cord which was already fastened about my waist. This finer line was to be my signal cord: it could not slip, yet was free to go down with me; and, while Mansel could not now miss any signal I gave, his hands would be free to handle the other cords.

Then the three of us put on our gloves, Mansel and Bagot laid hold of the cord about me, and I let myself into the gulf. While the two of them took the strain, I left the oak and took hold of the second cord. A moment later I had begun to go down.

At first I secured some foothold, but once I had reached the stone, I had to depend entirely upon the cords. In vain I sought for some excrescence or crack, but, as though they resented my intrusion, the walls would give me no help. Indeed, after twenty-five feet they seemed to withdraw; so I gave up trying to reach them and handled my torch, instead. This showed me at once that the chasm had bellied out and gave me some hope that the bottom was near at hand: but when I threw the beam down, its report was valueless, for it lost itself in the shadows almost at once. But one thing I thought I saw, and that was the wink of water, such as a man may see when he looks down a well.

Here I may say that, something to my surprise, the sturdy song of the torrent which I had heard above was hardly any louder than it had been before: this proved, if nothing else, that the water which lay below me had nothing to do with this sound. I, therefore, hoped for some opening into the cavern which I was sure must exist and I strained my eyes and my ears for any sign of one.

I was very near the water, and, as I afterwards found, some ninety feet down, when the song of the torrent swelled into a musical roar. At that moment I saw that the chasm had lost its shape, because the stream that had worn it from West to East had suddenly found an outlet towards the North : and through this outlet was rising the vigorous note of the more important water flowing beyond.

Here then was the opening to my cavern, though whether or no I could take it remained to be seen.

I had to let go my torch, because, approaching the water, I had to have a hand free, not only to bear myself up, but to pull, if I had to, upon my signal cord ; for, once I was down, I had first to discover how deep the water might be, then to find foothold of some sort and then to make up my mind whether or no I could pass where the water went. And what with the roaring and the darkness and the uncertainty, it was more, I confess, by luck than by anything else that I found myself standing in water up to my knees, with a hand upon a small boss, of which I was afraid to let go. However, I had the sense to pull once on my signal cord, which meant that I wished to stay still and be lowered no more. At once the strain was taken by Mansel and Bagot above. Even so, I had much ado to avoid being swept off my feet ; but at last I was standing square, with my back to the wall.

So stablished, I used my torch, to see that I was standing in the midst of a water-slide—I borrow that name from John Ridd, because it exactly describes this remarkable fall which, swift and strong, yet slid on its way in silence, or at least with a sound so slight as to be lost in that of its mightier brother beyond. Its outlet was, in fact, a tunnel or shaft not quite twenty feet long, and eighteen inches higher than the water in which I stood. And beyond the shaft was lying the cavern I sought.

Had the tunnel been six feet high or had I been a dwarf, I could have made my way down it simply enough : but three feet six is a very awkward height—when two feet of that is water and the gradient is one in two. Still, it was passable ; and, after a long look, I thrust my torch into my shirt and pulled twice on the signal cord.

I had a bad moment or two on that treacherous slide, for, before I was halfway down, I put a foot wrong, and, once the water had me, it was not disposed to give up possession again. When I got to my knees, it thrust me off my balance and on to my side : when I drew myself up to my feet, it carried these from beneath me, so that I fell on my face : and when I sat up, to draw breath, before I had drawn it I found myself on my back. At last I realized that I must be clear of the shaft and I had the sense to endeavour to leave the stream ; so I flung out an arm for handhold of any kind. At once I encountered a column, slender, stable and solid, that might have been made and placed for the sake of such as the water was seeking to drown ; and, laying hold of this, I drew myself out of the slide and on to a shelf of rock.

When I had got my breath, I took my torch—in some anxiety : but the water had done it no harm, and when I illumined the column to which I owed so much, I saw, what I might have guessed, that it was a stalagmite.

I find it hard to describe what else I saw, for the beam of my torch was quite lost in the majestic dimensions it did its best to reveal. The place might have been the nave of some cathedral church, with galleries, chapels and natural monuments ; and a long line of stalactites, hanging high up on the wall, rendered the pipes of an organ with great fidelity. That the cavern was full of sound, I need hardly say, for the torrent which had betrayed it the day before was flowing down all its length : I could not see the water, because it was sunk in a channel which it had worn, but, as I had guessed, its steady recitative was echoed and magnified.

Having gone so far, I was, I knew, due to return or else to summon Mansel, to share my discovery. But, since it was perfectly clear that I must return—for I was soaked to the skin and the place was too chill and too damp to allow me to dry—I decided to see something more before I went back. I, therefore, got to my feet and moved carefully down to the stream, proposing to mark whence it came and whither it went. My compass showed me at once that the water was flowing roughly from South to North, but the way up and down was barred. The barriers could be surmounted, but only with time and care : they were natural ridges and walls, all wet as you please, and a man who fell would slide straight into the channel in which the water ran, because he would find no handhold, to stay his course. But two men, roped together, could do very well. Before I turned to go back, I turned my torch on to the water—I know not why. It lighted a little pool, where the torrent fretted a moment before going on. And there, in the pool, was something that was not natural.

Somehow I gained the water and made my catch—and no one was ever more pleased with more worthless things. Tea-leaves, potato-peelings and half an envelope. This bore the name ' de Parol ' and, best of all, was post-marked. . . . The letter had been posted in Paris three days before.

*　　*　　*　　*　　*

I now had some news worth telling, to carry back : in other words I could prove that the water came out of Arx. Whether its exit would make an entrance for us had yet to be seen ; but it looked very much as though this particular cavern belonged to a group, one of which served the château, as Bagot had said.

It was not until I pulled off a gauntlet, the better to stow away the tell-tale document, that I realized with a shock that the chill and the wet together had stolen a march on my vitality. My fingers were already so numb that I could hardly deal with the buttons upon my coat ; and though I did what I could to chafe them back into life, I knew that what they needed was warmer air. So did all my system ; the blood was running sluggishly in my veins. In a word, it was very clear that I must get back.

At once I turned to survey the way I had come.

Till then I had had no idea that I was so far from the shaft. I was full thirty paces away and forty feet lower down, and, though that sounds little enough, the going was very hard and I could no longer move freely as I had done coming in.

I marked as well as I could the way I must go : then I put up my torch, and gave the signal to hoist. This I did clumsily, because my hands were so cold, and I shall always remember how much relieved I was when I felt the cord about me grow steadily taut. At once, as best I could, I laid hold of the second cord, for I am a heavy man, and to put all my weight on one cord was undesirable. So, very slowly, partly dragging myself, but mostly being dragged, I began to go back up the slope to the shaft and the chasm beyond.

Had the cavern been lighted, movement, though never easy, could have been usefully made : but I could not direct my torch, because, of course, I was climbing hand over hand, and so I could make no use of such little aids as there were for the sole of the foot. Indeed quite half the distance I covered, if not on my stomach, upon my knees, for I slipped continually and could not regain my feet.

Arrived at the water-slide, I gave the signal to stop, for, though I knew it was vital that I should get on, I felt I must rest for a moment before going up the shaft. Indeed, it was then that it first came into my mind that, unless we could find some truly waterproof suits, the atmosphere of the place might rule out any attempt to enter Arx by this way. I could endure cold and wet with any man : I had often been soaked to the skin and had stayed so for hours on end, and never had such a condition touched me at all : but now, after half an hour only, I was distressed ; for the cold that had entered my system was stealing away my strength. My progress had been exhausting ; but the rest, which should have refreshed me, had done me no good, and the effort still to be made if I was to reach the chasm, took on a monstrous, not to say desperate air. And here was danger, indeed ; not content with reducing my body, the cold was besetting my soul.

I pulled myself together and gave the signal to hoist
. . .

To this day I do not know how I passed up the water-slide without being drowned. I lost my cord very soon, because my hands could not grasp it, and that is the truth. Mansel and Bagot, between them, hauled me up, but I had to keep my head above water—and this, as I have reported, was two feet deep. I remember gaining the chasm and trying in vain to recapture the cord I had lost : and after that, to be honest, I knew no more, till I found myself lying stripped in the open air, and Mansel and Bagot working to bring me round.

(For this unusual collapse, I cannot account. I must have hit my head when I went up the water-slide, for when they landed me, my forehead was gashed : but that alone would never have laid me out. I think perhaps the truth is that the air within the cavern was short of oxygen and that when my system sought to fight off the cold, my lungs could lend no support to the effort it made.)

" Better, William ? " said Mansel.

I took a deep breath and sat up.

" Yes," I said, " I'm better. If I could get into the sun . . ."

Mansel put off his shirt and slacks and helped me to put them on : then he got into mine, which were wringing wet.

" There's a little meadow," he said, " not very far from here. The sun will be on it by now. D'you think we three can make it ? "

" And Gedge ? ", said I.

" Gedge be damned," said Mansel. " Besides, he's still abed."

" The devil's driving," said I, and got to my knees . . .

With my arms about their necks, Mansel, John Bagot and I passed slowly out of the forest, into the blessed sunshine, over the road to Arx and on to a little green-sward, where the precious scent of the verdure and the lively cheer of the birds were giving the lie direct to the waters under the earth.

And there I was glad to sink down and to take my ease.

" Listen, William," said Mansel. " You've had a very bad go. We'll hear all about it later. I'm going to get Carson and Bell and one of the cars : and John will stay here on guard."

" What time is it ? " I said.

" A quarter to eight."

" Not too good," said I.

" I know. That can't be helped. You've got to get back to the farm."

" I'll be all right," I said, " as soon as I've had some sleep."

" Then sleep your fill," said Mansel : " I shan't be long."

I think he said something more, but the kindness of my

surroundings and the grateful warmth of the sun ushered me into the slumber my state required.

Had I not been awakened, I should, I dare say, have slept for five or six hours : but, after only one hour, as I afterwards found, a sudden pain in my side made me open my eyes.

Then—

"That'll do, Tarquin," said Brevet.   "'*He*, much amazed, doth ope *his* lock'd up eyes.'   You know, I always maintain that *Lucrece* is incomparable."

I propped myself on an arm.

Lousy was standing beside me, apparently itching to kick me again in the ribs.   Brevet was seated as when I had seen him first, that is to say, cross-legged, as tailors sit.   And John Bagot was lying, face downward, some four or five paces away.

As I made to rise—

"As you were," snapped Brevet.

I shrugged my shoulders and passed to where Bagot lay.   I kneeled down and turned him over.   As I did so, he whispered 'Fake.'   I loosened his collar and set my hand over his heart.   Then I opened one of his eyes and made a grimace.

"He needs attention," I said.   "I don't know which of you hit him, but——"

"I'm much afraid," said Brevet, "he'll have to wait. And now sit down where you were."   In view of the pistol he held, it seemed best to comply.   "That's better. And now get this.   I don't want to kill you here, but, if you cross me, I shall.   I don't want to kill you here, because I would prefer that you proceeded to a convenient burial-ground under your own power.   I don't know whether you've ever subscribed to the portage of a carcase, but it is a most exacting exercise.   And now a question or two.   I'd simply love to know how you came by that cut on your head."

"I slipped and fell."

"I see," said Brevet. His eyes came to rest on my shoes, which lay in the sun. "Where did this, er, *contretemps* take place?"

"In the torrent," said I, boldly, "the one that runs through the village—not very far from here. Bagot got over all right, but, just as I was landing, I put a foot wrong."

"Dear, dear," said Brevet. "Ah, well. Boys will be boys. Your trousers seem to be dry."

"I usually roll them up when I'm crossing a stream."

"Of course. How stupid of me. And after you had fallen . . ."

I put a hand to my head.

"You'll have to ask Bagot," I said. "When I came round, I felt cold, and I know I asked him to help me into the sun."

"I observe," said Brevet, "that Bagot's shoes are dry."

"He crossed the stream barefoot," said I.

"Quite. And may I ask what you were proposing to do?"

"Take a look at Arx," said I.

"And Captain Mansel?"

"If it helps you at all," said I, "Mansel's the other side."

"I see. And the rendezvous?"

"Nothing doing," said I.

There was a little silence.

"Trespass," said Brevet. "A very odious offence. Not a crime at law, as no doubt you know. But, to my mind, a deadly sin. The invasion of privacy. And Horace agrees with me—you know whom I mean. I think you met yesterday."

"That's right," said I. "How's his face?"

"Sordid," said Brevet. "Suggestive of the Mile End Road. The result of a marital difference at closing time."

" The penalty of trespass," said I. " A very odious offence."

" Quite," said Brevet. " Quite. There are, of course, other penalties. ' Further and better,' I think is the elegant phrase. ' Further ' . . ."

" Quite," said I.

Lousy laughed aloud, and a tinge of colour came into Brevet's cheeks.

I had, of course, no idea when Mansel would come ; but I knew that I must, if I could, keep Brevet and Lousy in play until he arrived. If I could not do that, then somehow or other John Bagot must make his escape— for both our sakes. Myself, I could take no action, if only because I was still too weary to put up a fight. I was no longer exhausted, as I had been : but I was heavy-laden, and that was about as bad.

" To return to Horace," I said.

" Yes."

" We were unaware that we had any quarrel with him."

Brevet expanded at once.

" Your quarrel with Horace," he said, " is indirect. Horace is tired of Gedge—that's not altogether surprising, for Gedge's interpretation of the laws of hospitality is extremely liberal. He's been tired of him for some time, and when Gedge declared last week his intention of remaining at Arx until you and Mansel were dead, Horace in desperation decided to try his hand. It might have come off, you know."

" It might," said I.

" Though I must confess," said Brevet, " that I was not sanguine. Horace is not cut out for exploit. And his two, er, confederates were rather out of their depth."

" Yes, I noticed that," I said.

" Not that I blame them," said Brevet. " My own respect for the explosive is very high. But Punter, I understand, went so far as to criticize Horace . . ."

" He certainly hit him," said I. " But if ever a wallah bought it, Horace did."

" He would. He's a purchaser. He buys quite a lot from Gedge. So Punter reviled him, did he ? "

" Reviled him ? " said I. " He socked him. Hit him full on the mouth. And Horace was much annoyed."

" So we gathered," said Brevet. " But such was his incoherence, we gathered but little else. Punter actually hit him, did he ? Oh dear, oh dear. You know, I have always felt that Punter's outlook was selfish—that the team-spirit had been omitted from his make-up. Is that your estimate ? I mean, from what he says, this isn't the first occasion on which you have clashed."

" So far as I know," said I, " Punter always did his job. As for yesterday, Horace's leadership was hardly inspiring."

" From the way you speak, you appear to have been in the stalls."

" In the wings," said I. " There was some scenery to shift."

" I stand corrected. Scene Two had to be set. I'm told this was most impressive—' The Last of the Limousine.' Greaser insists that the car is a total loss."

" The ground was against her," I said.

" Poor Horace," sighed Brevet. " Still, your presence at Arx will revive him. What ever will Mansel say ? "

" I've no idea," said I.

" Or do ? "

I shook my head.

" Oh, try again," said Brevet.

" I imagine he'll take some action to get us out."

" I imagine so, too. What action do you think he will take ? "

" To be perfectly honest," said I, " I haven't the faintest idea."

" He hadn't allowed for this ? "

"Not that I know of," said I.

"Ah, well. 'Time's glory is To turn the giddy round of Fortune's wheel.' *Lucrece*, again. And talking of time, what is the hour, Lousy?"

Lousy said that it was ten minutes past nine.

"Then I think we should be moving," said Brevet. "I'm afraid you'll have to carry your little friend."

"What, carry Bagot?" said I.

"Yes. He certainly let you down, but it wasn't altogether his fault. You see, we were very cunning. I wandered into his orbit, head in air, singing a stave from *Patience*, to round the ruse: and Bagot held me up in the time-honoured way. And while he was digesting his capture, Lousy, who was standing behind him, laid him out."

"I must congratulate you."

"Spare me, I pray. Chandos the Great would never have fallen so."

"I might have—easily. John Bagot's a very good man."

"No doubt. A shade Boeotian, perhaps, but undoubtedly sound. Sound. I do hope nobody ever describes me as 'sound.'"

"I shouldn't think you need worry," I said, and Lousy laughed again.

Brevet's eyes narrowed.

"Shall we proceed?" he said.

I got to my feet and passed to where Bagot lay. After feeling his heart again, I made a genuine effort to get him on to my back. In this I failed—I simply had not the strength.

"I'm sorry," I said. "I can't do it. Lousy will have to help."

"Try again," said Brevet, rising.

"Look here," said I. "You find me asleep in a meadow quite close to Arx. D'you think you'd have found me asleep there, if I had had the strength to be gone ? ''

Brevet shrugged his shoulders.

'' That's answer enough,'' I said. '' I'm at your mercy, of course. But it's no good asking of me the impossible thing. I can walk now—without assistance : but I cannot do very much more. As for lifting eleven stone —well, it's simply beyond my power.''

Brevet addressed Lousy.

'' I'm inclined to believe him,'' he said. '' Any way, you'll have to assist. It's not very far.''

Lousy crossed to John Bagot and kicked his ribs. To the latter's eternal credit, he never flinched.

'' It's no good,'' said Brevet. '' You shouldn't have hit him so hard.''

I stood to Bagot's head, set my hands under his arms, lifted up his shoulders and waited for help. With a filthy oath, Lousy moved to his feet and bent down to lay hold. As he did so, John Bagot kicked . . . the kick of a vicious horse, and, yelling ' Run ! ' I launched myself at Brevet who was standing some eight feet off.

Had I only been fit, I might have taken the trick : but, though I spoiled his aim—for the fellow fired upon John . . . an instant too late—I could not follow up my advantage, because my arms were like lead. Brevet went down, to be sure, but before I could seize his wrist, I felt the mouth of his pistol against my throat.

'' One movement,'' said Brevet, speaking between his teeth. '' Only one. A shudder will do.''

I lay very still. I dared not do anything else. Still, Bagot was out of the wood and Lousy was lying dead of a broken neck.

*   *   *   *   *

Looking back upon those moments, I count them among the worst that I ever passed. This was because I feared that Bagot would return to the charge. To take to your heels and leave to his fate your companion is, on the face of the thing, against all decency : yet, had Bagot yielded to his instinct to come to my help, Brevet would have killed me at once and then turned upon him. But John Bagot had the great courage to play a coward's part— the hardest part, I think, for which Fortune can cast a man : and, though, as I afterwards learned, he stayed at hand, in the hope of being able to intervene, he never showed himself, much less made some fatal attempt to set me free. He was, of course, unarmed, for Brevet had taken his pistol as well as mine. In the hope that Lousy was armed, he had waited until we moved and then had searched the body to no effect. He had followed us up to the road to which I led the way, with my hands behind my head and Brevet's pistol thrust into the small of my back. He had seen us wait under cover close to a gate, until, at half-past nine, a car with Gedge and Greaser had stolen up. Clearly it had been arranged that the car should come to that spot to pick up Brevet and Lousy about that time : why they had gone on ahead did not appear, but Gedge's surprise when he saw me showed that they had not expected a meeting with us.

" By ——, I'm happy," he said. " How did you land the swine ? "

" But for Lousy's folly," said Brevet, " I should have had them both."

" —— ! " screeched Gedge. " *Not Mansel ?* "

" Not quite," said Brevet. " Bagot."

" Bagot be ——," said Gedge.

" Quite. But he scuppered Lousy before he left."

" 'E never ! " cried Greaser.

" Wrong again," said Brevet. " For nearly thirty-five minutes Lousy has been in hell. ' And all the *hooters* sounded for him on the other side.' "

" Where's the body ? " snapped Gedge.

" Full in the open," said Brevet, " six minutes' walk from here."

Gedge swore at some length, condemning his late accomplice in shocking terms, because he had elected to die so far from a road.

Then he turned upon Greaser.

" Get the car round," he blared. " This —— goes into the bag, an' then we come back."

At this my heart leaped up, for Mansel might well return before Lousy's remains were gone, in which case such as were charged with the duty of bringing them in—and Brevet would sureiy be one, for he alone knew where they lay—would either become his captives or meet their death.

The car was put about and I was thrust in, always with Brevet's pistol against my ribs. Then Gedge blindfolded me and Greaser let in his clutch.

I knew when we entered the quarry, for I felt the tires take to the timber which we had seen, and the walls gave back the sound which the engine made. Then Gedge got out of the car and after a moment I heard the curtain rise. At once the car went forward. It did not wait for Gedge, but went on slowly enough for, possibly, forty yards. The air smelled cool and damp, as that of a tunnel may. The curtain behind us was lowered, as we were moving along. When the car had come to rest, I heard Gedge pass it on foot, to raise a second curtain directly ahead. Then he whipped into the car and Greaser drove on. A very few seconds later we stopped again, and I was then hustled out, across a strip of gravel and through a door. They need not have bandaged my eyes. I knew where I was.

I was then thrust into a store-room upon the ground-floor, where Gedge and Greaser, between them, bound my ankles and wrists with galvanized wire. Then my bandage was taken off, and Brevet put up his pistol and wiped his face.

"Find Punter," said Gedge, and followed Greaser out of the room.

Brevet looked after him. Then he returned to me.

"A trying fellow," he said. "I make him the sort of present that only the gods dispense, and his response is to use regrettable language because a corpse must be carried four hundred yards."

"I seem to remember," said I, "that it was to avoid such a task that you spared my life."

"True," said Brevet. "True. Still, I feel something should have been said. A graceful word of inquiry as to how I had done the trick. A flicker of commendation. It is the gesture that counts. But there you are. What is poison to us is Gedge's staple food. After all, Napoleon was a most howling cad."

We both heard Gedge let fly.

"Where the devil's that ——, Brevet ?"

"Forgive me," said Brevet. "My services seem to be desired. Make yourself at home, won't you ? I shan't be long."

He shut the door behind him, and I was left alone.

Though I was still very tired, I was too much excited to sleep. Two hours had gone by since Mansel had left the meadow ; and, once he had the Rolls, I knew that he could be back in forty minutes of time. I tried my best to reckon how long he would have taken to reach the farm. He would have made for Sarrat, the nearest town, there to procure a car to carry him on. Such a car would take forty minutes to reach the farm. Everything, therefore, was hanging on the time it had taken him to get from the meadow to Sarrat—some twenty miles. If he had found some vehicle going his way . . . and found it early on . . .

I gave Gedge half an hour in which to collect Lousy's body and bring it back. If he was not back by then, it would mean that Mansel had got him—and Brevet, too.

As the time went slowly by, I could hardly lie still.

Some twenty minutes had passed when the door of the store-room was opened and Mona Lelong came in with a key in her hand. For a moment she did not see me, because the shutters were closed and the light in the room was dim : then her eyes fell on my feet and travelled up to my face.

" God Almighty," she breathed. Then she raised her voice. " Horace," she cried, using French, " come and see what I've found."

The Baron entered the room.

" What is it now ? " he said.

" Behold thine enemy."

The fellow peered for a minute. Then very slowly his battered countenance lighted, as though some lamp within him were being turned up. His eyes, which had been dull, became burning bright, an evil grin stole into his haggard face, and a look of the purest joy supplanted the hunted expression which he had been wearing when he came into the room.

" So," he whispered. " So."

Then he began to laugh, and The Stoat with him.

As on the day before, the tears ran down his cheeks ; but this time tears of mirth and ecstasy. He stamped about the floor in a paroxysm of glee, clapping The Stoat upon the shoulder and indicating my bonds. And the lady threw back her head and laughed full-throatedly.

But my mind was upon a meadow a mile away. If Gedge was not back in five minutes . . .

" Alive," crowed de Parol, " alive. Had they told me that he was dead, I should have been overwhelmed : but to bring him to me alive . . ."

" What ever," said Miss Lelong, " would dear Mrs. Chandos say ? "

" And Mansel," cried the Baron. " How will that *canaille* react ? "

"Try to storm Arx," said The Stoat.

"God is good," said the other, piously.

The Stoat took out cigarettes and looked at me.

"How did it happen, Samson?"

I shrugged my shoulders.

"I was asleep," I said, "and Brevet blew in."

"No Delilah, I trust?"

I shook my head.

"Just —— carelessness?"

"You've said it," said I.

The Stoat approached me and kicked me upon the hip.

"Don't lie to me," she said. "How did you hit your head?"

"Brevet will tell you," I said.

She kicked me again—fiercely.

"I'm asking you."

I told her what I had told Brevet. When I had done—

"A likely tale," she said. "And how did you reach the field?"

"Bagot helped me," I said.

"And Bagot?"

"Escaped," said I.

"From Brevet and Lousy?"

"Yes."

The Stoat bent over me.

"You —— liar," she said, and slapped my face.

"How does that feel?" said the Baron. "To be struck when your hands are tied? Be thankful I do not burn you."

The Stoat lit a cigarette and handed her lighter to him.

"Let him feel the flame," she said.

"Later," said the other. "Believe me, I know how you feel."

"You don't," said The Stoat. "You haven't the dimmest idea. When I was at this man's mercy, he treated me like a leper: he was very polite, as men are—

to a prostitute : he may have knocked you about, but he insulted me as only a ' gentleman ' can."

"He will soon be dead," said de Parol. "Let the swine be."

With that, he urged her out of the room, and again I was left alone—to listen for Gedge's return.

It was natural, I think, that though my ears were pricked for the sound of the car, I should give some grateful thought to Mona Lelong's display. That she hoped to be able to help me was very clear : she had just been paving the way—by making her uncle believe that her hatred was greater than his. And if Gedge and Brevet failed to return, that she would be able to help me I had no doubt. But they would take no chances. They were no fools.

Now I am cautious enough, but when twenty minutes more had dragged by, yet the rogues had not returned, I could have shouted and sung. Thirty minutes should have been ample, and I was ready to swear that they had been gone forty-five. Such delay could mean but one thing—that Mansel had been ready and waiting when they returned to the field.

I saw the *dénouement*, as though I had been ' in the wings.' Gedge and Brevet shot dead, and the others with their hands in the air . . . the bodies conveyed to the car, and this driven into the quarry, bearing its dreadful load . . . Punter raising the curtain, while Mansel stood by . . . Carson and Bell—

And there I heard the car coming . . .

It swept to the door of the house.

Then—

"Get going," snapped Gedge. "And six feet deep, mind you. We don't want to be stunk out."

CHAPTER VI

FORLORN HOPE

A QUARTER of an hour had gone by and an interesting discussion was taking place.

"We may be able," said Brevet, "to use him alive."

"You mean, to string Mansel along?"

"That was in my mind," said Brevet.

"How?" said Gedge, biting his lip.

"I don't know: but Mansel may take some action which gives us a line. Whereas, if we put him down . . ."

Gedge addressed me.

"What'll Mansel do?" he said.

"I've no idea."

"Does he know of the quarry?"

"If Bagot is pulling his weight, he very soon will."

"You knew before."

"Of course we knew the quarry: we didn't know it made away in."

"How d'you know now?"

"I heard the curtain go up."

"Where and when were you to meet Mansel?"

"On the other side of the water, at half-past ten."

"That's no good," said Brevet. "Bagot——"

"—— Bagot," said Gedge.

"I'm not so sure," said Brevet. "He will a tale unfold."

"And then what?"

"Mansel may rush his fences—he'll know he's up against time."

"By ——, he is," said Gedge.

"We stray from the point," said Brevet. "Do I pass him into Paradise now, or must the angels wait?"

I

Gedge stooped to examine my bonds.   As he stood up—

"How long will Lousy keep?"

Brevet shrugged his shoulders.

"Two days," he said.

His eyes fast upon mine, Gedge fingered his chin. Then—

"I'll think it over," he said.

He turned on his heel and went out.

As his footfalls faded—

"The reprieve," said Brevet.   "Your heart must have been in your mouth."

"There's not much in it," I said.

"To be frank, I'm afraid there isn't.   You are as good as pork, as Ben Gunn would say.   Don't you love *Treasure Island*?"

"It's a damned good tale," said I.

"Bagot could play Jim Hawkins, the cabin-boy."

"What makes you say that?" said I.

"He possesses the requisite blend of initiative and mischief."

"Lousy would probably agree."

"True," said Brevet, "most true.   But Bagot didn't stop there.   He actually removed the remains, while we were away—the act of an *enfant terrible*, which, I need hardly say, caused great unpleasantness."

"I gather that you found them again."

"Eventually," said Brevet.   "But it might have been awkward, you know.   Gathering dead at noon is hardly a healthy pursuit."   He sighed.   "Gedge was most out-spoken, as you will believe."

"I can't say I'm sorry," said I.

"That," said Brevet, "would be too much to expect." He took his seat on a table and dangled a leg.   "Entirely between you and me, does Mansel deserve the reputation he has?"

"Yes."

" Achates commends Aeneas."

" No," said I. " I've worked with him more than once, and he's terribly good."

" Do you believe Gedge will get him ? "

" No. He's the better man."

" But the rape of his *fidus Achates* will shake him up."

" He's used to hard knocks," said I.

" Hero-worship," said Brevet.

" Seeing's believing," said I. " The day Gedge sent his challenge, he wrote himself off."

" Our Gedge has his points," said Brevet.

" I know. But he's weighted out. Gedge may be cast iron : but Mansel is high-speed steel."

There was a little silence.

" Well, we shall see," said Brevet. " At least, I shall. Possibly you will, too—from Heaven's battlements. D'you remember this day last week ? "

" Yes."

" How we, er, forgathered at Stère ? "

" Yes."

" You were very downright, Mr. Chandos."

" I tried to be."

" You spoke," drawled Brevet, " of deaths and punishments."

" I did more. I foretold them, Brevet, and so I do again. For the part you played that day, you will die in this world and pray for death in the next. There was some excuse for Gedge, but for you there was none. You're far better read than I am, but I can remember the words ' Better for him that a mill-stone were hanged about his neck and he were cast into the sea.' "

Brevet was on his feet, trembling.

" You damned clod," he mouthed. " Who are you to condemn me ? I could have moved mountains, if I had had your chance. You—you cumber the earth ; but I could have been a proconsul. Instead, I'm a criminal—

and you are a country squire. D'you wonder that I hate you, Chandos? D'you wonder that I look forward to spilling what brains you have?"

"No," said I, "I don't. And I could have been sorry for you if you hadn't laid hands on my wife."

Brevet's face was working. So were his hands. I watched his fingers curling into his palms.

After a little, he left me without a word.

*   *   *   *   *

I was glad to be alone, for I felt more weary than ever, because, I suppose, my hopes which had risen so high had been so suddenly dashed: and I knew that if some effort should presently have to be made, I should not be able to make it, unless I had slept. The store-room was pleasantly warm, for the sun was striking the corner to which it belonged and, luckily, its floor was of wood, so that I was not cold. My hands being tied behind me, I could do nothing at all to unfasten my bonds, but, seeing a pile of sacks a few feet away, I made my way up to them and, dragging some into position by using my teeth, I furnished myself with a pillow of which I was very glad.

Here perhaps I should say that I could hear, though but faintly, the definite rush of water not very far off. This water was not without, but within the house, and it seemed to me likely enough that this was the very stream upon which I had turned my torch a few hours before.

But I was too tired to consider what that might mean and, with its rustle to lull me, I fell asleep.

When at length I awoke, the store-room was dark. This meant that I must have slept for at least ten hours. Be that as it may, although I was very hungry, I was myself again.

The first thing I did was to see if in any way I could manage to free my hands. But this I could not do, for they had been bound too well. Then my thoughts turned to the water which I could hear. If indeed it belonged to the stream which entered the cavern I knew and if the rope I had used was still hanging down, that way lay a chance of escape. It was a very slight chance. First, I had nothing to tell me that this was in fact my stream : if it was, could I gain the cavern, or should I be jammed and drowned before I could get so far ? And if I could reach the cavern and find my rope, could I possibly climb it unaided before that unearthly chill had taken away my strength ? It was a very slight chance. There might be another way out which a captive could take : but I felt that this was unlikely—Arx was too strong. Still, anything was better than being butchered by Brevet the following day.

It must not be thought that I was blind to the fact that, unless my hands were freed, I could make no attempt to escape, but was, as Brevet had said, ' as good as pork.' But, in my desperation, I forced myself to assume that The Stoat would see me over this dreadful stile. That she would do what she could, I had no doubt : and she knew as well as did I that nothing at all could help me, so long as my hands were bound.

I afterwards found it was nearly ten o'clock before the door was opened and Brevet switched on the light.

I saw at once that the man had recovered his poise.

" Had a nice rest, Mr. Chandos ? "

" Yes."

" Good. ' Weariness can snore upon the flint,' can't it ? I believe that's *Cymbeline,* but I can't be sure. Never mind. D'you think you could toy with a *chaud-froid* ? "

" I should be glad," said I, " of something to eat."

" That's what I thought," said Brevet. " I proposed that Greaser should serve you with some sort of cheer. But Miss Lelong had a very much better notion, and so

I am here to bid you to sup with us. In fact, we have had our meal, but we are still at table, to which, as often as not, we sit very late. And some broken meats remain. D'you think you can rise?"

"Not with my feet tied," I said.

Brevet picked up a pair of pliers and, standing well to one side of me, cut the wire.

I managed to get to my knees and so to my feet.

"Can I have a wash?" I said.

"Of course. And may I say how very moving it is to meet someone who thinks of washing before he eats. Even Horace regards ablution as waste of time: while, compared with Gedge and Punter, the average private-schoolboy is, believe it or not, 'the mould of form.'"

He led the way into a kitchen which stood beside the store-room in which I had lain. The farther wall of the kitchen was natural rock. At once I heard the water most loud and clear.

Now running water speaks many different tongues. There is the speech of a fall, the speech of a troubled torrent and that of a steady stream. And this was the third of those—the swift, smooth rush of a vigorous head of water, meeting no let or hindrance and sliding, rather than running, down some steep place.

Brevet saw me look round.

"Every convenience," he said, and pointed to an opening which had been cut in the rock. That gives to an underground stream: all refuse goes out of that hatch and is seen no more. Myself, I believe that the stream would accept a corpse; but lower down there may be a bottle-neck, and if that was suddenly corked, conceive the inundation that would result. So, in spite of all temptations, we bury our dead."

There was a sink by the opening, which was some three feet square. To this I made my way, to put my head under the tap.

" May I ask you to turn it on ? "

Brevet obliged.

The water was very cold, and it did me a world of good to feel it running over my head and face.

I turned about and held my hands under the flow.

At length—

" That's better," I said.

Brevet turned off the tap and led the way out of the kitchen, along a passage and into a dining-room. The windows of this were wide, and the lights were on.

About the table were seated the four I had expected to see.

De Parol was facing Punter, asprawl in his chair : on his right, The Stoat was sitting, smoking, with her elbows upon the board and her chin in her hands : between her and Punter sat Gedge, who was picking his teeth : a cigar glowed in his ashtray and a bottle of champagne was standing within his reach.

The Baron rose at once.

" Ah, welcome, dear Mr. Chandos." He bowed from the waist. " This is a privilege indeed. Yesterday you entertained me : to-day I have the great pleasure of returning the compliment. Sit here on my left—where we can see you. Brevet, some soup for milord. A spoon would be out of place. He shall lap like a dog."

It seemed best to take my seat.

Brevet busied himself at the sideboard, while the others regarded me in silence, as though I were some strange fish.

Brevet placed before me a plate of cold soup.

" I can recommend this," he said.

For a moment I hesitated. Then I bent my head and began to drink. It was not a pleasant operation, but I knew that I needed food.

In one of my pauses for breath, a hand came down on my head and pressed my face into the soup.

" ' Drink, puppy, drink,' " said The Stoat.

Punter sniggered ashamedly.

That was the first of many indignities.

By the time I had made my meal, my face was a mask of grease : but for that I declined to care—I was making my enemies sport ; but they were giving me back the strength I required.

Disgustedly The Stoat surveyed me.

" The landed gentry," she sneered. " How galling it must be for him to keep such company."

" Juvenal says," purred Brevet, " that——"

" Blast what Juvenal says. When does he die ? "

" Depends on Mansel," said Gedge.

" You're not going to sell him ? "

" No."

" Then——"

" I know my stuff," snapped Gedge.

" Why so uncommunicative ? " said Brevet. " The gentleman stands condemned. He is already a shade. Except, therefore, to some sympathetic seraph, he is debarred from reporting the circumstances of his decease."

Gedge vouchsafed no reply.

" ' And some fell on stony ground,' " sighed Brevet. He turned to me. " We don't usually run to tombstones, but if there is any short epitaph on which you have set your heart . . ."

" Let's choose him one," said The Stoat.

" ' Is this the face ? ' " said Brevet.

" Too topical," said The Stoat. " What about ' The Blight that Failed ' ? "

" Oh, very good," cried Brevet, and even Gedge gave a half-laugh. " Greaser shall draw it out on a number-plate. And you shall photograph God's acre and send the relict a print."

" Goody, goody," cried The Stoat, and jumped in her chair. " But will Nature's darling get it ? "

"Every time," said Brevet. "She's not as naïve as she looks."

"I regret," said the Baron, "I very deeply regret that I had not the pleasure of entertaining her here."

"Don't despair," said Brevet. "When Mansel and Bagot have ceased to strut and fret, the invitation may very well be renewed."

"When," said Punter, sagely.

The word might have been a goad.

Gedge turned upon the fellow, with blazing eyes.

"You palsied ——," he cried. "You creeping ——. 'Cause Mansel burst ' Rose ' Noble, he won't burst Daniel Gedge. I've only got to see him. He's kept away for a week, because he's afraid. But now I've forced his hand. Where Chandos is, he'll come."

"' Rose ' 'ad Chandos," said Punter. "An' Mansel came."

For a moment I thought Gedge would strike him.

Then——

"Let him come," he said, and sucked in his breath. "Let him come, as he will, by the quarry. Let him force the outer curtain—to say he's there. Let him come to the second curtain—an' then force that . . ."

There was a little silence.

Then——

"I do not like this," said the Baron. "I do not like this at all."

"Then go an' stop him," sneered Gedge. "You know where he lives."

"Curse and damn," screamed de Parol. "You brought him here."

"You want him fixed, don't you ?"

"It is essential, of course : but I do not want battles here. For years I have——"

"—— what you want," spat Gedge. "You've had a —— good run."

" —— ! " screamed the other. " I will not bear your brunt. This is my property, and if those entries are forced——"

" They will be," said Gedge, " to-night. Bagot knows : and Mansel will come that way. But that's the last move he'll make. —— it, the thing's too easy. He lifts the first an' warns us : to lift the second'll take him all of an hour. An' then . . ."

Again he sucked in his breath.

De Parol covered his face and rocked himself to and fro.

" Don't worry, Horace," said Brevet. " The curtains can be repaired : but to reconstruct Captain Mansel will be a magician's job. The simplest way will be for him to be born again."

The Baron waved him away.

" You are wolves in sheepskin," he said.

The Stoat was glaring at me.

" Take Samson away," she said. " He makes me sick."

Brevet glanced at Gedge.

" Take him back," said the other. " I'll be along."

As we passed down the passage—

" Can I wash again ? " I said.

Brevet shook his head.

" Gedge would misconstrue the indulgence ; and as I think it likely that we shall be roused to-night, I don't want to have a scene just before I retire. Besides, if Gedge is right, and Mansel does force the curtains, you, too, will put on incorruption within the hour."

Feeling desperately uneasy—

" How many volts," said I, " is he going to meet ? "

" None," said Brevet, opening the store-room's door. " He'll just be flood-lit. That's all. He will be blinded, but we shall be able to see. Lie down where you were before. He'll like to bind you himself."

I moved to the pile of sacks and wiped my face upon them as best I could. Then I sat down by the pillow which I had made.

Brevet took his seat on the table and picked up the pliers.

"'The Blight that Failed,'" he said. "There are times, you know, when Mona is very quick. She's a girl of parts, The Stoat : and terribly good at her job."

"What is her job ?" said I.

"She carries the excellent notes which Horace turns out. All over the world. And never puts a foot wrong. They're a wonderful combination. But they never flood a market—that's where the coiner falls down. But she doesn't seem to like you. What did you do to annoy her on Tuesday last ?"

"I may have been rather blunt."

Brevet nodded.

"Diplomacy is not among your failings. People dislike being shown that for you to touch them with a barge-pole would go against the grain. And Mona has her sensitive moments. She was a lady once . . . Is there any last office I can do you ?"

"None, thank you," I said.

"Quite. I only asked, because though I fully expect to be the instrument of your translation, our Daniel is sometimes wayward in matters like this. I remember— Ah, here he comes."

A moment later Gedge was followed by Punter into the room.

Gedge turned me over and looked at my wrists. Then once again, while Punter held my feet, he bound my ankles with wire.

He stood up and looked at me. Then he laughed a high-pitched laugh.

"'Rose' Noble had you, had he ? Well, you'll be seeing him soon and you can tell him from me that when

I have a man, I have him for keeps. And if he doesn't believe you—why, Mansel'll back you up."

Then the three withdrew and again I was left alone.

It was now past eleven o'clock and I hoped very hard indeed that they meant to retire. I had never had any doubt that Mansel would strike that night and would come by way of the quarry, as Gedge had said. And now if he came that way, he was almost certainly doomed. He would know, of course, that he was playing into their hands: but he would take any chance in the hope of saving my life. So now I had not only to save myself, but somehow to reach the quarry in time to stay him and the others from throwing their lives away.

Everything was depending on Mona Lelong. As I have already said, I simply declined to believe that she would not manage to reach me and free my hands. The trouble was—how soon could she come? Time was terribly precious, for Mansel might start his assault at any time now. Yet Mona Lelong could not come till the others had gone to bed. And would they all retire? Or would someone sit up to watch? I decided that no one would watch, for, from what Gedge had said, it was clear that the raising of the first curtain would sound some alarm. And when I was free—what then? Without a pistol I dared not engage the enemy. And even if I were armed, the odds against my survival were very high. And I had to survive somehow—five lives might well be hanging upon my own. . . . There was simply nothing for it— unless The Stoat could get me out of the château, I should have to take to the water and hope against hope.

Of such were my reflections in that most desperate hour: but as the time went by, but Mona Lelong did not come, the hopes I was holding so fast seemed more and more forlorn and an agony of fear beset me that she would come too late.

And then at last, at midnight, the door of the store-room was opened, and Mona Lelong slid in.

Two things I must make clear. The passage without was lighted all night long ; and the rush of the sliding water swallowed all lesser noise. With the store-room's door ajar, one could, therefore, see to move ; while, if one moved with care, the movement could never be heard.

She glided up to my side and fell on her knees : and then, before I could speak, she had lighted a little torch and was sponging my face.

" Say you understood," she breathed.

" I knew you'd come."

I heard her catch her breath : then she stooped and brushed my face with her lips.

" Listen, Mona. I'm terribly up against time. The pliers are on the table. I want you to cut the wire about my wrists."

In a little less than a minute, my hands were free.

I took the pliers from her and freed my feet.

As we stood up together—

" D'you know a way out ? " I whispered.

She clapped her hands to her face.

" I don't, Richard. I've racked my brains all day. You'll have to come back to my room. You see, by night the château——"

" Hopeless," I said. " Mansel will strike any minute, and if I can't stay his hand he'll lose his life. And so will Bagot and the servants. They haven't a chance."

" But you *can't* get out, Richard. By night——"

" Can you find me some rope ? " said I. " Never mind what for."

" Yes," said the girl, looking round. " The rope's over here."

I followed her to a corner, and there, by the light of her torch, she showed me four or five coils of good, strong cord. As I picked one up—

" And now an iron bar," I said.

A hand went up to her mouth.

" I don't know where there's a bar."

" Dogs," said I. " Fire-dogs. Is there a fireplace here ? "

" Behind those cases. Be careful. There may or may not be dogs."

There were—and across them, as I had expected, was lying a bar. I extracted it carefully—again by the light of her torch.

" Into the kitchen," I said.

She opened her eyes at that, but she led me out of the store-room without a word. As I closed the door behind us—

" And now you must go," I breathed. " God bless and keep you always for what you've done. The pliers will lie for themselves—they shouldn't have left them there."

" I don't do things by halves," said Mona Lelong.

Not daring to argue in the passage, I followed her into the kitchen and closed the door.

" Mona, for God's sake go. You can't do any more."

" I'm the best judge of that. If you don't want to waste your time, I should put me wise."

I hesitated. Then—

" So be it," said I. I pointed to the hatch or opening which gave to the sounding stream. " I'm going to go down that drain."

I heard her gasp. And then she had caught my arm.

" You can't, you can't," she cried. " It's a subterranean stream and you'd die a terrible death."

" Listen, Mona," I said. " Unless I'm jammed, I know that will let me out. Know. And now please give me your torch. I haven't an instant to lose."

Torch in hand, I surveyed the water. This was running in a channel that looked about three feet wide. I gave her the torch again and fastened the rope to the bar.

I had counted on the length of that bar. I had hoped that it would be longer than the opening was broad, so that, once it was in position and I had taken the strain, I could depend upon it as though it were fixed. But when I applied it to the opening, I found that the bar spanned this with less than an inch to spare.

I drew in my breath.

I dared not trust myself to a bar so placed ; for if it moved half an inch—well, bar and rope would follow me down the stream.

I decided to prove the water—to see if the bar could be jammed between the sides of the channel in which the water ran. This would be more satisfactory, for so the rope would fall straight.

"I'm not going yet," I said. "Please hold the bar and give it to me when I ask."

She took it without a word.

And then I was through the opening, standing in water and holding on to the sill.

The stream was four feet deep, but it slid straight into a tunnel against the roof of which I could brace my back.

So I took my stand : then I put out my hand for the bar. Mona was ready and put it into my hand. I drew it through the aperture, still with the rope attached, and set about trying to jam it in the channel or bed of the stream.

This was no easy task.

I dared not bend down squarely, for had I done that and slipped, I must have been swept away : so I had to keep one hand on the edge of the tunnel's roof and do my best with the other to jam the bar. And the water was opposing my efforts with all its might, as though it resented the trespass which I was seeking to do.

At first my heart sank down, for the channel was wider than the bar was long : then I found that, well under water, the channel's sides drew closer, and after a frantic struggle, I lodged the bar.

I say ' lodged ' because I mean ' lodged.' Without two hands I could not jam it. Yet, if I ventured to take my hand from the rock . . . All the time, the moments were flying.

I let go the rock and put both hands to the bar. With all my might I thrust this squarely downward. I sank it perhaps two inches. Then I took hold of the rope, set my back to the roof of the tunnel and took the strain. . . . But the bar never moved.

I took a turn of the rope about my wrist. Then I stood to the opening and spoke to Mona Lelong.

" The rest of the rope," I said. " Quick."

She swung the coil on to the sill. As I made to sweep it into the water, she caught my hand.

" Richard, you'll never do it. Even if you get down you'll never get out alive. Think of——"

" I give you my word," I said, " that I've more than an even chance. And it isn't only my life : it's Mansel's and Bagot's and——"

" And if you're jammed."

" I'm sure I shan't be. The water's flowing too fast. And now I must go, Mona dear, and you must get back. Could you possibly spare me your torch ? "

And as I spoke the words, above the rush of the water, I heard the Baron's voice.

No one could have failed to hear it. So, perhaps, maniacs cry.

" Mona ! " he screeched. " Traitress ! " The man was in the passage beyond the kitchen door. Then I think he must have entered the store-room, for he let out a scream that must have torn his throat.

With both her arms on the sill, the girl was standing so still she might have been turned to stone. The torch being between us, I saw her face. One look at this was enough. She knew that her hour was come.

There was only one thing to be done.

"Hold fast to the torch," I said.

I swept the rope into the water, took her under the arms and lifted her out of the kitchen and into the stream.

With my left arm about her waist—

"Wrap the torch in your skirt," I said, "and put an arm round my neck."

As she did these things, the light in the kitchen went up.

With the rope in my right hand, I gave myself to the water, and in an instant of time we were out of sight.

The tunnel was not very long—about twenty-five feet. Although I could not see, I knew from the sound of the water that we were out—and, what was more, in a cavern of some considerable size.

I took a turn on the rope and managed to find my feet. Then I spoke in Mona's ear.

"Lift the torch clear of the water, and then lay hold of the rope with your other hand." I felt her move. "All right?"

"Yes."

"Now let me take the torch, and put both hands on the rope."

She did as I said.

The torch, which was still alight, showed me the end of a cavern which might have been mine: but, once again, its light was lost in the place. I could not see the cavern's dimensions or how it ran, though such features as I could make out were not unlike those I had noted the morning before. But one thing was very clear —that we must stick to the water and not attempt to move by its side, for to traverse such ridges and shelves would have taken us far too long.

Now Mona could not proceed without assistance from me. The water was far too deep and the current too strong. Yet I could go no farther with only one hand on the rope.

How I got the girl on to my back, I shall never know : but somehow, between us, we did it : and then I began to go down, with both my hands on the rope and her arms about my neck.

It was a nightmare progress.

I had, of course, to move backwards, chancing what might be coming, although she tried to help me, by looking over her shoulder, torch in hand. Staggering, stumbling, sliding, I plunged down that sounding water, round sudden bends, beneath overhanging rocks and over miniature falls. All the time I was praying that this was indeed my stream : all the time I was cursing my folly, because I had taken only one coil of rope : all the time I was calling for light and looking wildly about me for any feature I knew.

I have fought with Death and I have fought against Time : but never as then have the two withstood me together with such malevolence. And my body alone could do battle : my mind had to take what punishment they chose to inflict. This was severe, indeed.

Any moment now, the rope which I was holding must come to an end ; and then, though the cavern was mine, with nothing to hold to, how could I reach my pool ? And if I did reach my pool, would my cord be there ? Mansel might very well have withdrawn it, before leaving the head of the chasm and seeking the upper air. And if my cord was still there, should I have the strength to climb it . . . up the slide into the chasm . . . and then up ninety feet—ninety feet without foothold, fit work for an ape ? And if I could do these things, should I be in time ?

Such a burden was sore enough, but Irony made matters worse.

In the hope of saving my life, the others were bent upon

forcing the jaws of Death, when, if only they turned to the cavern, they would risk nothing at all and Mona and I should be saved.

I could have cried aloud for the pain of the iron in my soul.

At last I felt that I must have a moment's rest. So I turned my side to the stream and lay back against the rock.

"Lift me a little," said Mona, "and I can sit on the edge."

"Only for a moment," said I. "We've got to get on."

And then her weight was gone, and I could straighten my back.

"Throw the beam round," I said.

It was as she swept the beam up that I saw my cord . . . lying just as I had left it . . . with its end running into my pool, three paces away.

*   *   *   *   *

So far I have said nothing about the cold : but I make no shame to confess that, while I was still in the store-room, I had been heartily frightened of courting again that evil which had nearly cost me my life the morning before. Whilst we had been in the kitchen, when I was placing the bar, all the way down the water, I strove to fight off all thought of this deadly foe, for if that stepped into the arena, then Mona and I were doomed. But now, when I left the water and had my own rope in my hand I realized with a shock that the awful chill of the place was already at work.

My rest had done little for me : my members were cold and clumsy : all effort seemed hard to make. *And we had the water-slide coming and the chasm—ninety feet deep.*

I sometimes wonder why I did not despair : but God, they say, tempers the wind to the shorn lamb. Be that as it may, I made up my mind to this—that it was the air of the cavern that was stealing away my strength and that if I could gain the chasm, before I was too far gone, the air from above would revive me and all my strength would come back.

If this were so, there was not a moment to lose.

I put my arm about Mona, sitting on the slope beside me, with the cord—my cord—in her hand and the lighted torch in her lap.

"Come, my lady," I said. "We're half-way home."

She looked up at me and nodded : but when she endeavoured to rise, her legs gave way.

"Sorry," she said, "I'm done. And I can't hold the torch, Richard. My fingers won't work."

There was no time for explanation.

I stuffed the torch into my pocket and fastened the rope about her under her arms.

"Listen, Mona," I said. "You must try and fight off this weakness as best you can. I'm going to pull you up, for it's all straight sailing now and I know the way."

"I think . . . you'd better leave me. Better that one should get out than that——"

I laid my cheek against hers and held her close.

"We've much in common," I said. "I don't do things by halves."

Then I laid hold of my cord, surveyed my way for a moment, put away the torch and began to climb.

Although my strength was failing, I reached the water-slide with something to spare and, aware how futile it was to take any rest, I started to draw up Mona without delay.

I fear that she had a rough passage, but at least there was no obstruction upon that slope ; and it cost me less to drag her those thirty paces than it had cost me to cover the ground myself.

I lodged her against a stalagmite, standing on the brink

of the slide : then I lighted the torch and took her hand in mine.

" One more ordeal, great heart, and then you can take your rest. We've got to go up some water, instead of down. Only a little way, and I'll be as quick as I can." I threw the beam on the slide. " That's the water beside you. When you feel me take the strain, you must take a very deep breath and let yourself go. You may go under water, but have no fear. Try and float on your back : but if you can't, don't worry, because we're going to be saved."

" Oh, Richard, I can't believe it."

" Try to believe it," I said. " It's perfectly true."

Then I left her lodged on its brink and went up the water-slide.

How long this passage took me, I cannot tell. Perhaps it took me three minutes. But it was the only period of that exacting time when I forgot Mona and Mansel and Gedge and all his works ; when I forgot Arx and the cavern—and Jenny, asleep at Maintenance, all the sweet of the fairy-tales snared in her lovely face : when I forgot past and future, because I was ruled by the instinct to try and save my life.

And then I was out . . . in the chasm . . . scarce able to hold myself up . . .

I took a turn on the rope and leaned back against the wall. Rest I must now, whether or no. If this air was not to revive me, then Mona and I were done. If my strength was not to return, then she must die in the cavern and I where I was. I had reached the end of my tether. Unless I could be restored, I could not go on.

But the vain thing which I had imagined proved to be true. Drawing deep breaths of air, I felt refreshed. After a little, I knew that in two or three minutes I should have strength enough to haul my companion up.

Whilst I was waiting, I drew my torch and looked

round. At once I saw a ledge, some three or four paces away. This would accept Mona. Here she could lie, while I climbed—for both our lives. And something else I saw—that I had not noticed when I was there before. Just beyond the shelf, the chasm shrank to a cleft. In other words, the chasm was roughly wedge-shaped. My cord was hanging over the base of the wedge : but the thin end was much more narrow—say, three feet wide : and the sides were rough and broken—hand-hold and foot-hold were there. At this my heart leaped up, for to climb a ninety-foot rope is a fearful thing. (Of course I could never have done it. My weight was too great. Perhaps some gymnast could have : though, had he been spent as I was, it would have cost him dear.) But if I could climb up the chasm, using my rope to help me . . .

This discovery helped to revive me—of that there can be no doubt : for I forgot my condition, to remember—almost with a shock—that I was up against time . . . that I had to get to the quarry, before the second curtain was raised.

It cost me little enough to draw the girl up the slide and get her on to the ledge : but that she was greatly exhausted was very clear. Mercifully, she was not sense-less, as I had been ; but the atmosphere of the cavern had stolen into her system and robbed it of all but life.

Something had to be done if she was to live.

I pulled her house-coat open and tore it away : then I ripped her slip from her chest ; for her to be naked was better than for her to be swaddled in clothes which were full of the coldest water that ever I knew.

" Draw in this good air," I cried : " and chafe your body and limbs as soon as ever you can. You must make the effort, Mona : we're very near out of the wood."

She obeyed at once, beginning to draw deep breaths.

" I'm going on," I continued. " It's not very far. I'll take the strain as before, and by then you must be

ready to—to bear a hand." She looked at me wanly
enough and I patted her cheek. " You must, Mona, you
must. You see, when we get up this chasm, we'll still
be ten feet down and unless you can stand on my
shoulders, we shan't get out."

As I spoke, my words shocked me. In my search for
a saying to spur her, I had stumbled upon the truth.

Here she lifted an arm, and the beam of the torch
illumined the dial of the watch on her wrist.

Fourteen minutes past twelve. Less than a quarter
of an hour since she had entered the store-room, to set
me free. The thing was absurd, of course. The watch
had stopped—fallen foul of the water, as we were coming
down. But, in fact, it had not stopped. As I was
staring upon it, its minute hand was approaching a
quarter-past twelve.

(And there was the reason why I had not succumbed
to the chill which had cost me so dear the morning before.
Though, upon this occasion, my efforts had been much
greater, I had spent in the cavern no more than eight or
ten minutes, instead of near half an hour.)

It took me twenty-five minutes to climb that cleft.
Had I not been desperate, I do not believe I could have
done it and I doubt very much if I could do it again.
I realized at once that my cord would give me no help.
This was natural enough, for the cord, of course, wished
to hang plumb, and, when I put weight upon it, it did
its best to draw me out of the cleft, into the breadth of
the chasm beneath where our timber lay. Indeed, so far
from helping, it hindered me. That I should keep it was
vital, because, to reach the grotto, the time would come
when I had to leave the cleft : and when once I had
nearly lost it, I managed to pull up some slack and loop
it about my neck.

But it was the darkness that slowed me down.

Each time, before I moved, I had to draw my torch and

survey the cleft, observing and carefully marking holds for my hands and feet. And then I would put up my torch and grope for the projection or crevice which I had seen. And three times I was so placed that I could not draw my torch, but had to go on blindly and hope and pray for hand-hold of any kind.

Still, in the end, I reached the top of the cleft. And, when I put up my hand, I found it had a ceiling of soil.

So far as I could judge, this meant I was twelve feet down; for it will be remembered that at the head of the chasm, its sides were of earth. Indeed, it was clear that I must be beneath the 'chamber,' in which Mansel and Bagot and I had stood the morning before. But the opening through which I had been lowered lay several feet to my right.

To gain this, I had my cord. But when I saw how I must use it, I felt very sick.

A gymnast would have made nothing of it. But I was not a gymnast. More. I was heavy and tired, my hands were torn and bleeding and I must move in the dark.

I think it will be clear that I had to hold fast to my cord and swing out over the depths; and then, when the cord hung plumb, to climb it up to the timber some twelve feet above.

I suddenly realized that I was streaming with sweat . . .

Now I have found that when you are bound to take some desperate step, it is best to take it as quickly as ever you can. The longer you contemplate it, the more sinister it appears, until the requisite effort seems wholly beyond your power.

I, therefore, rubbed the palms of my hands on the earth above my head, laid hold of my cord and cautiously let myself go.

I had had the sense to put out my feet before me, to take the shock when I met the opposing wall: this was as well, for they met it heavily, but I was not much shaken, because I bent my knees, as a man coming down from some jump.

I was something encouraged to find that the wall was of earth : for this meant that I was, indeed, but a few feet down : but, before the cord had stopped swinging, I started to climb, for this was already beginning to cut my broken hands.

Looking back, I know very well that, had I now to choose between once again climbing the cleft and covering those few feet of cord in mid-air, I would sooner climb the cleft, be it twice as high.

I was very nearly spent : I had to depend entirely upon my hands : an agony of mind as of body prejudiced every hoist. How far I could go, I knew not ; but I knew that I could not go far. There is a limit of endurance which no man born of woman can ever pass.

And then my hand touched the timber . . .

For an instant I fumbled frantically. Then I had a hand on a joist. One desperate heave, and the joist was in my armpit. And there I hung for a moment, not knowing how to go on. Then I found the other joist with my other hand, and, after a fearful struggle, I was lying on my face in the grotto, ten feet from the open air.

*　　*　　*　　*　　*

I rested for perhaps three minutes. Then I put on a pair of the gloves which I knew would be there and without any more ado I pulled Mona up. This was child's play to what I had done before ; but all the time I was hauling, I was praying that she would be fit to play her part : for without her help I could not reach the hole which gave to the mountain-side. But if she was fit, I could put her upon my shoulders, and if she could make the effort, she could get out. And then she could make fast the rope, and I could follow her up. But if she was not able to do these things . . .

To my immense relief, she had her senses about her and was just able to stand.

I put my arm about her and pointed up.

" See, Mona, there is the moonlight. We're back in the world."

Tears began to course down her face.

" Out of the valley of shadow. Oh, Richard, I can't believe it. Death's been so terribly close."

" I know, my dear, I know. But we've spoiled his game. And now I must save the others. Listen to me."

By my direction, she mounted upon my shoulders and put her hands on the rim of the hole above. Then I seized her ankles and thrust her up. And then she was on her knees and clear of the hole.

As I bade her do, she took the cord from her body and made it fast at once to the nearest tree. And then I followed her up and into the open air.

After a hasty discussion, with her consent I put her back into the grotto, there to await my return, because I was so much afraid that the night air might do her ill; for there was not so much as a sack to wrap her in. But the grotto was warm. And then I set off down the mountain as fast as ever I could.

I did not make directly for the quarry, because, for all the moonlight, I feared I might miss the place. I headed, instead for the road, which I could not miss. This at break-neck speed, for, now I was ' in the straight,' I had nothing to lose. And at last I saw the meadows below me and, between them and me, a black sash.

I gained the road and started to run . . .

After what seemed an age, I rounded a bend, to see the mouth of the quarry some fifty paces ahead.

My legs were giving out, but I shambled up to its jaws.

And then I heard the rasp of a curtain—the sound a steel curtain makes when it is moved up or down.

"*Mansel!*" I roared. "*Mansel! For God's sake stop!*"

"By God, it's him," shouted Mansel.

And a figure leapt out of the shadows to set a hand under my arm.

"Oh, thank God, sir. Thank God."

Bell.

The honest fellow was trembling.

Then came a heavy explosion, and right on its heels a thunderous, rumbling crash.

* * * * *

Two hours had gone by.

Mona Lelong was asleep in John Bagot's bed, and I was at ease in my own, with a quart of champagne inside me and brandy within my reach. Bell was standing by the window, Mansel was sitting beside me, and Bagot was leaning upon the end of my bed.

I had made my report, and Mansel was now to tell me the little I did not know.

"In the first place," he said, "you must wonder why I left you alone with John Bagot and went for the car. That was because you were wearing the colour of death. I've known you a good many years, but never before have I seen you look so ill. I was going for a doctor, William. I meant to bring a doctor from Sarrat, as quickly as ever I could.

"Well, my luck was dead out. I had to cover three miles before I fell in with a lorry, and I never got to Sarrat till a quarter to nine. There are only two doctors there, and both were out. I tried in vain to run one or other to earth : but at last I threw in my hand and sought for a car. I meant to drive straight to the meadow and pick you up. If you will believe me, there wasn't a car to be had ; for every one had been taken by so many idle fools as had an urge to visit the scene of the accident. Observe the unkindness of Fate. Every one of those cars had been driven to a spot ten minutes from where I wanted to go. But all were gone. The last had left two minutes before I arrived. . . . I got a lift in the end —from another idle fool who had come from farther afield, but I never got to the farm till ten minutes to ten.

"It didn't take me long to get back, with Carson and Bell. But I was just too late. When John Bagot ran into the road, and I saw his face . . ." He stopped there and covered his eyes. "I've had some bad moments, William, but I cannot remember when I've been hit so hard. Of course I knew they'd got you, before he opened his mouth. And I knew that you would receive no mercy at all. The only question was how soon they would put you to death.

"Well, something had to be done. But, for once in my life, I didn't know what to do. One thing was most painfully clear—that we could do nothing by day.

"I naturally thought of the sink-hole, but that I dismissed at once. You see, I knew nothing at all of what you had found, and in view of the shocking condition in which you emerged, it seemed the height of folly to try to get in that way.

"I decided to survey the dingle—from where you saw it on Thursday. I did, before mid-day—to no purpose, of course. There's no approach from the mountains. There must have been once, of course : my theory is that the landslide closed the gate.

"I then considered the château—to no avail. There was nothing for it but the quarry, as you and Gedge had perceived.

"Now there could, I knew, be no doubt that when we raised the first curtain, we should also raise the alarm : so that, when we raised the second, our friends would be ready and waiting to pick us off. I mean, that was elementary. Yet both curtains had to be raised, if we were to strike. And so I fell back on the Baron's infernal machine.

"I never mentioned the fact, but, after you had retired, on Thursday night, Carson and I went out and retrieved the bomb. This, for two reasons. First, to leave it under the culvert was a most monstrous act. Some innocent being or beings might very well stumble upon it : and if and when they did, they would almost certainly stumble into another world. Secondly, it might come in useful—one never knows.

"And so I determined to use the infernal machine. It would certainly raise the second curtain much quicker than could our hands. What was more to the point, its effect would be disconcerting. Gedge and Brevet and Punter would hardly be at their best. And that would give us a chance.

"Well, there you are. After a fearful day, we left full strength for the quarry, complete with bomb.

"The first of the curtains took us an hour to raise. Then we entered the tunnel, and I placed the infernal machine. I wired it up and then withdrew with the leads. You heard us pull down the first curtain, to stop any flying stuff. And then you heard the explosion . . .

"I think that's all."

"Tell me again," I said, "what Carson found."

"He and Rowley could only raise the curtain a foot— the first curtain, of course, the one we had just pulled down. Then Carson crawled underneath—to find the tunnel gone, for its roof had collapsed. He says you would never have known there had been a tunnel there. That being so at our end, what is it like at theirs ? Of course, quarries will be quarries : they're chosen because their stone is easy to win.

"Had you not already escaped, I should have ruined

our chances of getting you out. Of that there is no question. All I can say for myself is that it never entered my head that de Parol possessed an explosive so savage as that. But since you have saved yourself, William, it's really turned out very well. The enemy's transport is frozen; and only by way of the château can they themselves emerge. One or more may have been bent when the cracker went off. The strong probability is that Horace is out of his mind, and I'm sure that Gedge and Brevet are having their beastly being like men possessed. But that is more your fault than mine, for your escape, William, will bruise their cold, black hearts. My God, I give you best for getting out of that jam. I don't believe I could have done it, and that's the truth."

"But for Mona Lelong," said I, "I should still be there."

"Perhaps. But, but for your spirit, you'd both be entombed alive."

"We were very lucky," I said. "I don't have to tell you that. Next time I go down——"

"Next time?" cried Bagot, but Mansel only smiled. I nodded.

"I've some scores to settle, John. And unless they've discovered my bar, within the week I shall see that kitchen again."

CHAPTER VII

TWO IS COMPANY

AT six o'clock that evening the three of us sat in a meadow and talked with Mona Lelong. The spot was that above and behind the farm, from which I had watched the Baron's attempt on our flat. Carson and

Bell were on guard, and Rowley was keeping the farm, a furlong away.

The Stoat and I had rested the whole of that day, and neither of us was the worse for what we had undergone. But my hands were still very sore. She was wearing clothes that Mansel had bought for her—a dark-blue shirt and slacks, which suited her very well.

"The thing," said Mansel, "is this. You have broken with Arx and you cannot go back. That is the price you have paid for saving Chandos' life. Now we can make no return, for no one can make return for valour like that. For his sake you staked your life—and you very nearly lost it, Miss Mona Lelong. But though you didn't lose it, you have lost everything else. Well, of course we are at your service from this time on. Any help you wish, you shall have. That is understood. But there is another point. Chandos took you with him, to save your life— not at all with the idea that you should come in with us. If you like to come in with us, that is to say, to help us to bring Gedge and Brevet down, we shall be very glad. But that would mean giving us the lay-out— telling us all we ask about the Château of Arx. And if you don't want to do that—well, there's an end of the matter. We shall put no pressure upon you : we shall not question your decision in any way. Perhaps I ought to add this—that we know your uncle's profession : and when we have dealt with Gedge, we shall destroy his plant. We shall not inform the police : we shall not hurt your uncle, except in self-defence : but we shall draw his teeth. That's all I want to say, except to insist upon this—that there is no reason at all why you should come in with us. You have done enough, Miss Lelong. You have done far more than we had any right to ask : and, as a result, you have turned your life upside down."

Mona Lelong raised her eyebrows.

"As a matter of fact," she said, "I've put it the right

side up. You've pulled me out of the slough. I've got
a little money—ill-gotten gains, of course ; and if I can
get to England . . . Not yet, you know. I'm going to
see this through. I told Richard yesterday that I didn't
do things by halves. Without me, my uncle's finished :
but, as I daresay you'll believe, I owe him nothing at all.
He made me what I am ; and, though I've always played
square, again and again I've had to stand up for myself.
I've taken ten per cent. of what he has made—and he's
never forgiven me. Yet he couldn't get on without me,
and mine was the dangerous job. So, you see, I've no
compunction. As for Gedge and Brevet . . ." She
drew in her breath. "And now let's get down to
things. Tell me in so many words what you want to
know."

"Can we enter Arx," said Mansel, "except by the way
you came out ? "

Miss Lelong considered.

Then—

"No," she said. "You might have done it by the
quarry, but now you say the tunnel is blocked. The
château itself is impregnable."

"When you say 'impregnable' . . ."

Miss Lelong frowned.

"It isn't by day," she said. "But——"

"We can't try by day," said Mansel.

"Well, at dusk, throughout the château the inside
shutters are closed. These are of steel, and every one is
wired to give the alarm. So, of course, are the gates.
If you managed to force the wicket—well, they'd be
waiting for you inside the *porte-cochère*."

Mansel bit his lip.

"Electricity," he said. "Any chance of cutting that
off ? "

The girl shook her head.

"We make our own. Turbines. They're underground. The place is a natural fortress. Between the house and the château there's a cavern as big as a church."

" Servants ? "

" All crooks. Most of them badly wanted—that's why they stay. And they never squeak—why kill the golden goose ? "

There was a little silence.

" Tell me," said Bagot. " Have they got a car in the château ? "

" No," said Mona Lelong. " We kept the limousine there, but you did that in. Until they can clear the tunnel, they'll have to hire."

" Then they'll hire for some time," said Mansel. " To clear that tunnel would take a gang six weeks."

" And now," said I, " for the question that really counts. Will they guess which way we went—eighteen hours ago ? "

" I don't think they will. The rope would not be missed ; nor would the bar. You say they were both out of sight. We didn't light the kitchen, and so there was nothing to show that we had been there. They would assume that I'd taken you back to the château : and when they drew blank there, they'd start on the cavern's depths. While they were searching those, Captain Mansel made his—demonstration. So they'd have to let the search go, and, when the tumult had died, begin all over again. And they'd do it half-heartedly this time and presently give it up. But, if they did think of the drain, they'd make sure we were dead. To be frank, I don't know that I blame them."

Mansel nodded.

" Such an assumption," he said, " would be entirely warrantable. And now may we have the lay-out ? "

" Give me pencil and paper," said Mona. " I'll draw a plan of the house."

Long before we went to our dinner, we knew all there was to be known about Arx and Petit Arx. For reasons which will appear, I shall not set it all down, but they made the sort of retreat of which a malefactor must dream. In the neighbourhood the Baron was accepted as a rich, eccentric recluse: and until he had had the misfortune to be discovered by Gedge, the cloak which he wore was a cloak of darkness indeed. It seemed, even now, most unlikely that anyone dreamed that he was devoted to crime: but the comings and goings of Gedge and his confederates must have impaired the legend of the recluse. For this reason alone, the Baron was mad to be free of his beastly guests; while the thought that they might be followed to his abode—I mean, of course, by the police—was a continual torment. As I have already shown, Mansel's arrival had set him beside himself; and I quite agreed with Mansel that Mona's and my disappearance and then the tunnel's collapse must have reduced him to that condition of mind which marches with Insanity.

Be that as it may, we decided that three full days must pass before we attacked. (This was simply because of the state of my hands. For one thing only, until these were healed, I could not have fired a pistol and hit my man.) We should then attack in force, entering Arx by the way by which Mona and I had escaped.

"And unless," said Mansel, " they have a guard in the kitchen—well, that should be the end of Brevet and Gedge. But, before we change the subject, I think I should just say this. This three days' delay is trying— we all know that. But let us be sure that it will be just as trying for Daniel Gedge."

"That's right," said Mona Lelong. "I know he wants to be gone. He's got some job in the offing—I don't know where or what. But he had a wire about it the other day—and the way he spoke about you for ' holding him up ' ! Brevet improved the occasion. ' The priest abuses the goat which is late for the sacrifice.' "

Mansel made no reply, but I saw his brows contract.

*   *   *   *   *

We knew no peace the next day.

No doubt because it was Sunday, scores of strangers came to inspect the dell : and, because they had plenty of time, a great many brought their lunch. Cars were continually moving along our little-used lane, and families broke their fast in the curtilage of the farm. Since we wished to attract no attention, the doors of the barn were kept shut and we did not leave our rooms till seven o'clock that night : but the day was immensely hot, and the flat was like a furnace that afternoon.

I think this made Mansel insist that Mona and I should drive into the hills on Monday and pass the whole of the day in that majestic peace which only high places know.

" Take Bell and the Lowland," he said. " Make for Cluny and eat your lunch above Jules. Then go to sleep in a beech-wood. You won't be worried up there."

" And you ? "

" John Bagot and Carson and I shall go to Toulouse. We must get some proper gear for the fun and games which will open on Wednesday next. I know just what we need, and it shouldn't be hard to find. But I will not attack without it. Twice the bowels of the earth have nearly taken your life, and we've quite enough risks to run without treading on Nature's toes."

So it came about that at nine the following morning Mona and Bell and I drove into the topless hills.

Once we had passed Cluny, we met no traffic at all ; and a mile and a half beyond Jules, we might have had the world to ourselves. And then at last the mountain road we had chosen came to an end.

I knew the spot though I had seen it but twice. Shepherds and fishermen know it; and I suppose that surveyors have passed that way. But if others know it, it does not reflect their acquaintance, but seems to have lain untrodden since Time was young.

That we had been seen and followed, I could not believe. Still, I felt it was prudent that Bell should stay with the car: so Mona and I took our lunch and made our way South.

A mile from the end of the road, you come to a hidden valley, of which the *Pic de Merlin* makes one stupendous side. At its foot a blue and white water tumbles and darts and flashes and sings its eternal song. From this rise up three lawns—three velvet, emerald lawns, the one above the other, in natural terraces. And this magic of lawns and water is sunk in hanging beech-woods, jealously guarded by forest, as Sleeping Beauty's castle was kept in the fairy-tales. The eye of the great sun sees it: birds and beasts are at ease there; and sheep, I think, must tend the terraces. But it is very private—a little powder-closet of Nature's own.

As we gained the middle terrace—

"And how do you like this?" I said.

After a long look round, Mona sat down on the turf.

"I have no words," she said, "but those of the Queen of Sheba. Yes, I have. I think the gods must love it. I feel we're trespassers."

"It reduces Gedge and his works to their true proportion," I said.

"Gedge is a myth," said Mona. "This place **denies** his existence. But doesn't it conjure up Jenny?"

I threw myself down beside her.

"To tell you the truth, it does. I don't know how you know, but this is the kind of place to which my wife belongs."

"I know from what Brevet said. He was—immensely impressed. He quoted Milton, comparing Jenny to Eve."

"Brevet has eyes to see—as Satan had. Jenny is unusually natural. She wouldn't marvel at this: she'd love it, of course—but her love would be familiar; she'd feel at home."

"Tell me about her, please."

I did my best. When I had done—

"And isn't she worried about you?"

"I'm afraid she probably is. But she has a natural faith. It's very hard to describe. But it was natural to her that, when Jonathan Mansel was menaced, I should stand fast by his side. What is natural, to her is right. And that God will defend the right, she has no doubt at all."

"Her faith is impregnable?"

"I truly believe it is. And such a faith is powerful. I think it disconcerts the hounds of Death."

We lunched and dozed and we talked of many things: and then we went down to the water, which seemed to be flowing for us.

As we strolled the lawn beside it—

"We've stolen a day," said Mona. "At least, I have." She threw out an arm. "This doesn't belong to my portion. But no one shall take it from me. I'm not too bad at sticking to stolen goods."

"You have robbed no one," said I.

"Nor did Prometheus. The gods still had their fire. But all the same—he stole."

"Mankind was the fence. I hardly think you will be punished."

"I don't care if I am. I've got it—and no one can take it away."

"It's only the first of many. You're out of the slough."

She shook her beautiful head.

"They won't be like this. This will stand by itself—always. Will you do something for me?"

"Of course."

" Go on strolling, then : as if you were all alone. Just
for a minute or two. I'm going to leave the stage and sit
in the stalls."

She moved to the middle terrace and stood there, watching me, whilst I, feeling something foolish, pretended she
was not there. And then she came running back, to set
her arm within mine.

" I just wanted the picture," she said. " Adam strolling in Eden—and thinking of Eve."

" I decline to believe that Brevet compared me to
Adam."

" No. He was less complimentary. He doesn't like
you very much. He's jealous of you, Richard. Gedge
just hates you like poison : but Brevet is jealous, too."

" I'm sorry for that."

" It's not your fault. It's Brevet's. Gedge may be a
mad dog. But Brevet's way is that of a cat with a mouse.
But don't let's talk about him. He—hardly belongs."

" You do, though," said I. " Many a girl would be
bored with five minutes of this."

" I don't agree," said Mona. " I know quite a lot of
women who'd want to scratch my eyes out, if they could
see me now."

" I won't argue the point," said I, " for I don't know
much about women, and that's the truth."

" That's a very nice failing, Richard. Why do you
say I belong ? "

" Because you're happy here, Mona. There's nothing
to do but sit in the lap of Nature, study her lovely lines
and hear her speech. But that is enough for you, as it is
for me."

Mona nodded gravely.

" I am happy here. Very happy. But you contribute,
you know. You've shown me how to read this beautiful
book. You've held my hand. You've made it . . . live,
Richard."

"I'm used to high places," I said.

"But not to giving lessons to good-looking girls."

"You're a damned good pupil, Mona."

"Better than you think, Richard. I've learned much more than you've taught me—such lovely stuff. And I shall never forget it, as long as I live."

"I'm out of my depth," I said, "when you talk like that."

Mona put up a hand and touched my hair.

"The squire of Nature," she said. "I hope the dame won't be jealous, because I am here with you."

*　　*　　*　　*　　*

I find it hard to believe that a stranger operation was ever deliberately planned than that for which we made ready the following day. That men have entered strongholds by conduits, I have no doubt : and it is common knowledge that others explore, as a pastime, the caverns under the earth. But features of both such adventures distinguished our enterprise ; for, while we must wrestle with Nature, to have our way, all we did had to be done in secret from first to last.

Mansel had returned from Toulouse with ropes and timber and two stout, waterproof packs : but, best of all, he had brought a small, powerful windlass, for which he had paid a great deal. This was geared ; and so, although it could raise a weight of six hundred pounds, a child could have turned its handle, without any fuss. I need not insist on the difference which such a machine would make : but its greatest virtue in our eyes was that it made for speed. And, as I have shown, speed was truly vital, if we were to enter Arx and to 'live to tell the tale.'

John Bagot begged very hard to be allowed to lead us not only into the cavern, but up the stream, "for I have done nothing," he said, "but let Chandos be taken alive."

This was a monstrous saying, and Mansel and I denied

it with all our might. But when we had done, we told him in so many words that, if only for Audrey's sake, he must stay at the head of the shaft.

"Please look at it this way," said Mansel. "The quarrel is ours. That being so, if you come to any harm, what can we say to Audrey, with whom at this very time you should be on your honeymoon? Of course you have pulled your weight—it's made a world of difference— having another man. But when two can do the trick, I refuse to make it three. I won't let the servants go down —I haven't the right.

"You and Bell will control the windlass—with Mona Lelong standing by. If we should find ourselves failing, then we shall signal for help and you will come down. If we are gone more than an hour—then you will come down. But not otherwise. And now you must give me your word to do as I say."

Poor John looked mutinous: but, after some hesitation, he gave his word.

"That's right, John," said Mansel. "You see we're older than you."

"And Carson and Rowley?"

"They will keep the Rolls moving upon the road. They'll touch the quarry for a moment twice in the hour. But I dare not leave one man alone on the road to Arx."

"And the Lowland?"

"Will be berthed in a wood by Sarrat. As long as we have the Rolls, she can always be reached."

"And I watch and pray?" said Mona.

Mansel laughed.

"I don't think you would consent to stay at the farm: yet I decline to believe that you wish to re-enter Arx."

"Not by way of the cavern. I'll give you that."

"And all you want is your passport?"

"Yes. You know where it is. And there's twenty thousand francs in the drawer. If I am to pay my debts,

I'd better have that. But for God's sake don't risk your lives to get that trash. Passports have been lost before now, and new ones issued instead. But they don't do that with lives."

"We won't—I promise. But I'd like to have a look at the château, when once we have opened the road."

At half-past one the next morning, all was in train.

To get our gear to the sink-hole had entailed the kind of labour which men, who once have made it, prefer to forget : but, because they were not to go down, Bagot and Bell and Rowley had borne the heaviest stuff. (This was not, of course, division of labour : had Mansel and I been tired before we went down, the atmosphere of the cavern would have been harder to fight.) Then Rowley had returned to the quarry to meet the Rolls.

I threw a glance round the grotto.

Mona was looking at me, with a hand to her mouth : Bell was adjusting the straps of Mansel's waterproof pack : and Bagot, with a hand on the windlass, was trying to light with a torch the chasm's depths.

All this I could see by the glare of a powerful lamp—one of two which Mansel had brought from Toulouse. The other was wrapped in oil-skin and was hanging about my neck.

Mansel and I were wearing bathing-shorts—and nothing else except heavy, climbing boots. From throat to ankle, our bodies were covered with oil.

I glanced at my waterproof watch.

"Half-past one," I said. I looked at Mona and smiled. "What'll you bet we're not back by a quarter-past two ?"

"Give me a chance," said Bagot. "I'd like to have a look round."

I laughed and took hold of the rope.

Carson had made a 'swing-seat'—that is to say such a seat as children employ with a swing : and sailors use them when they are 'painting ship.' Upon this I settled myself. A moment later I was sinking into the chasm's depths.

I need not describe my journey. Enough to say that it was most easily made. So can that become child's play, which, for lack of a helping hand, has been a most desperate matter of life and death.

When I had passed down the slide, I unwrapped and lighted my lamp. This I set down in the cavern, to flood the way to my pool. It made an enormous difference, as did my climbing boots : for now I could see where to tread and, because of the nails in my soles, I did not fall.

I reached my pool, to find my faithful rope waiting to lead me up : and though I did not enjoy the last twenty-five feet of the race—I was, indeed, most thankful to reach my bar—I was not at all fatigued and did not feel very cold.

When I had got my breath, I found my feet and stood up and set my back, as before, against the tunnel's roof. That the kitchen was all in darkness, I saw at once. I undid my signal cord and made it fast to my bar : and then I pulled it four times, to report that all was well.

I climbed through the hatch and stood listening. Except for the rush of the water, I heard no sound.

I pulled off my gloves. Then I undid my pack and took out my pistol and torch. The latter, I ventured to light and lay down in the hatch. Then I put off my boots and my shorts and put on a pair of trousers and rubber-soled shoes. Before they were fairly on, I saw Mansel's arm in the hatch . . .

As I helped him into the kitchen—

" My word, William," he said, " I'm devilish glad to be here. Your itineraries are exacting—to say the least. I didn't like the slide very much, but those last twenty-five feet would make a porpoise think."

Two minutes later he was changed.

I put out the torch, and he opened the kitchen's door.

The passage without was lighted, as we had thought it would be.

We left the kitchen and closed its door behind us, because we wished to diminish the sound which the water made. At once we heard someone singing.

A tremulous falsetto was singing the line of a song.

Nous avons fait un bon voyage . . .

This was, I believe, the first line of a pretty duet, which had been the rage of Paris some years before. But now that one line was rendered over and over again. And the man who was singing the line was short of a voice.

" De Parol," breathed Mansel. " He must have gone over the edge. And I'm much afraid this means that our birds are flown."

With his words, my heart sank down. They had to be proved, of course : and he might be wrong. But I knew how unlikely it was that Gedge would allow an idiot to trouble his ears.

The pitiful wail went on.

Nous avons fait un bon voyage . . .

The sound was coming from the dining-room, the door of which was shut. We passed it by and made for the stair beyond. We knew our way, of course, for Mona had shown us exactly what to expect.

No light was burning on the landing : but the first door we came to was open—and that had been Gedge's room. And when, after waiting a little, I lighted my torch, we saw that the bed was unmade and his things were gone.

And Brevet's and Punter's rooms were empty, too.

I will not describe our disappointment, for I think that it may be imagined without any words of mine. But I think that we felt, perhaps, as a robber may feel—who has taken infinite pains and has run exceptional risks to reach and open some safe, only to find it empty and, so, all his labour and cunning but waste of time.

Mansel sighed.

"I was always afraid of this. From the moment that Mona said that Gedge was waiting to get to some other job." He shrugged his shoulders. "Oh, well . . . As we're here, we'd better have a look at de Parol. He may have lost his reason ; but people who've lost their reason sometimes talk."

The singing had ceased now, and when we stopped by the door of the dining-room, we heard no sound but that of a muffled rattling and then the irregular smack of some objects let fall.

"He's throwing dice," breathed Mansel, and opened the door.

The Baron was sitting at the table, and all the lights were on. Two places only were laid. On the floor, by the second, lay Greaser, plainly as drunk as a lord.

The Baron peered at us, dice-box in hand.

His face was foul and unshaven : his hair was wild : and his eyes were wide and staring—you only had to meet them to know that the man was mad.

He rose to his feet and bowed.

"Enchanted," he said. "Sit down and drink, I pray you. To-morrow we die." He resumed his seat and pointed to Greaser's body. "He's dead, you know. Entirely between you and me, I think they poisoned his wine. But I promised to stay with him ; and once I have passed my word . . ." He threw his dice again. "Dear me. An ace and a two. I'm losing to-night. But I shall win it all back. And then I shall denounce Mona." He slammed the table. "I'll have her boxes searched. No, no, don't argue with me. Greaser tried to argue, and look at him now. It's very degrading, of course : but what can I do ? The money was on my table. Three hundred and fifty francs. And Greaser wouldn't take it. Besides, he's dead."

Mansel took his seat at the table.

"What of Gedge and Brevet?" he said.

The other's finger flew to his lip.

"Hush," he whispered. "They're sleeping. They want all the rest they can get. There's going to be a battle, but don't say I told you so. And all the dead will be laid in rows on the green." He threw his dice again. "There's another nine for Lousy. He was the first, you know. I saw him lying there with his head on one side. A most unnatural posture. But that's the worst of the dead."

"Gedge and Brevet have gone."

The Baron appeared to consider. Then he burst out laughing and slapped his thigh.

"You're perfectly right," he crowed. "They took the 'bus and they've gone to—let me see . . . I gave them a letter to our Ambassador there. My grandfather was his butler—or, rather, his butler's father. That's years ago. If he could see me now, how proud he would be. But he's dead, too. But I shall never die. You see, I've drunk the water of everlasting life."

"But they're coming back?" said Mansel. "Gedge and Brevet, I mean."

"They must," cried the Baron. "They must. Who's to bury Greaser? I really can't ask the servants to dig a grave."

"Did they have a wire?" said Mansel.

The other nodded his head.

"A lovely wire. And very happily worded. 'Love,' it said. I think it was Brevet's birthday. D'you know he's twenty-two? And I shall be thirty-five when Lousy's dead. But the 'bus couldn't manage the tunnel. Somebody's filled it up." He laughed and laughed, till the tears ran down his face. "I oughtn't to laugh, you know. Besides, I'm going to complain. That curtain was most expensive. And what about Mona's taking two hundred francs?" Mansel rose to his feet. "Now don't say you're going. You promised to stay with Greaser, and you must keep your word."

"You must excuse us," said Mansel.

The Baron rose and bowed.

Then he sat down and once again lifted his voice.

Nous avons fait un bon voyage . . .

As the door closed behind us—

"Well, that's that," said Mansel. "And now for Mona's passport. It isn't worth wrecking his plant—he'll never use it again."

For myself, I was thankful to leave the dining-room. Never before or since have I stood and witnessed the way of a man who has lost his mind. Absurd as had been his chatter, I never felt less like laughter in all my life : for, though I dare say I am wrong, I had the clear impression that some malevolent spirit had come to possess his soul . . . had found it untenanted, and so had entered in, to make a mock of his betters, who, with all their faults, had been made in the image of God.

A door, quite close to the kitchen, admitted us to a passage, hewn through the rock. This led us into a cavern—much longer, but not so spacious as that we knew. An easy path had been made through all its length, and, in this, lines had been laid, to take a trolley we found at the other end.

A second door admitted us to the château, the front of which we had studied so many times.

The house was all in darkness, and, if the servants were there, they must have been fast asleep. In Mona's bedroom we found her passport and money, as she had said we should. Then we made our way back to the hall, through which we had come.

And on a table there was lying a telegram.

D' Aniel Château d' Arx Pres Sarrat.

Mansel ripped it open, and the two of us read it together by the light of my torch.

For August eighth read August eleventh but advise immediate attendance.

RUST.

The wire had been sent on Tuesday from Châteaudun.

"I'm much obliged," said Mansel. "That makes me feel very much better. In fact, it was well worth coming to learn this news. And now let's be getting back."

In less than a quarter of an hour, we were once again in the grotto, and Bell was wiping the oil from my back and legs.

Mona was speaking.

"And all for a scrap of paper. Don't say you'll do it again."

"I hope we shan't have to," said Mansel. "And I have travelled first-class. How you two survived is more than I understand."

"I was in the guard's van," said Mona. "And he looked after me."

With that, she produced some hot soup : and whilst we were drinking this, we told in detail the tale I have just set down.

When we had made an end—

"I'm not surprised," said Mona, "that my uncle has lost his wits. And I can't pretend that I am greatly concerned. He had only one use for me, as I've told you before. And Greaser will care for him. He may get tight, but he'll never let him down. He's immensely rich, you know : and they'll hardly take action now, whatever they find."

We left our gear in the grotto, for, while we might need it again, we could not believe that it would ever be found. Then we made our way down to the quarry, where after some twenty minutes Carson and Rowley arrived.

And so we came back to the farm, just as the sky was paling, before the cocks had made up their minds to crow.

CHAPTER VIII

WE ATTEND A CONFERENCE

AT half-past ten that morning—Wednesday, August the fifth—we held a council of war. We had rested and bathed and eaten, and now we were listening to Mansel, who was speaking very quietly, as though he were thinking aloud.

" This wire "—he pointed to the form—" is clearly the second wire, correcting the first. The first said that something was fixed for August the eighth. I don't know when it arrived, but it made Gedge leave at once—no doubt for Châteaudun or its vicinity. When he meets Rust, he will learn that he need not have been so precipitate—and will be very much vexed. What is more to the point, he will learn that Rust has wired him again. And that will infuriate him, for he will immediately fear that, if we break into Arx, that wire will fall into our hands.

" Though I'm using the future tense, all this has happened by now, for to-day is August the fifth.

" Now I think we may take it for granted that Gedge won't come back. Once he is there, he will stay till the job is done. But he'll be on the tips of his toes, in case we appear on the scene, to queer his pitch. And when we do appear on the scene, as we most certainly shall, the vials of wrath will be poured out.

" Very well. I'd rather have killed him in Arx, but that can't be helped. What we must aim for is to strike when he's actually doing the job. Then, though we may be observed, we shall be excused. So the first thing we've got to find out is where the job's going to be done : that will probably show us the nature of the job. It's almost certainly a jewel robbery—jewels are Gedge's field. And it is going to be committed not far from Châteaudun. Châteaudun is a little town not quite thirty miles from Chartres. And for Chartres I propose that we leave—this evening at seven o'clock. We'll eat our dinner at Pau and drive through the night. We shall be at Chartres for breakfast, and then we can get down to things. If we can't get wise in five days, we deserve to be shot."

Be sure we agreed with him.

And so it came about that by six o'clock that day the cars were packed and that, after a dinner at Pau, at ten o'clock that night we took to the open road.

We had four hundred miles to go and plenty of time. Mansel and I shared the driving, and Mona Lelong and Bagot chattered or slept. The servants, using the Lowland, followed behind. It was as we rose out of Tours that the dawn came up. I never saw such a heaven as I saw then. The whole of the sky was fretted with tiny clouds, and every cloud was ablaze with a crimson glow. Above and beyond was the blue ; but this was overlaid by a crimson coverlet. And the magic of this brocade came down to touch the earth. Highway, meadows and trees rendered it helplessly. For three or four minutes the whole of the world was red. Then the great alchemist rose and, using his ancient prerogative, turned the firmament into the purest gold. But the saying stuck in my mind, *Red in the morning, Shepherd's warning*. Foul weather was ahead.

Arrived at Chartres, we drove to a small hotel where Mansel was known. Here we fared much better than we should have fared anywhere else ; for, because we were with Mansel, we were no ordinary guests, and nothing was too much trouble, so long as we had what we wished. So we bathed and broke our fast and rested till lunch. And at three o'clock that day Bagot and Bell and I set out to prove the country which lies about Châteaudun. But Mansel, with Carson and Rowley, drove into the town itself.

Before we left—

"What we want is a château," said Mansel; "a country-house—with a rich, persevering owner who loves to get big people beneath his roof. We all know the type. He doesn't care for his guests: as like as not he hates the sight of them: but he wants to be able to say, 'When so-and-so was staying with me this summer . . .'. That is for him the freedom of heaven itself. Now when I say 'big people,' I don't mean people who count: I mean people who are 'news.' He'd rather have an itinerant divorcée who was notorious than an ex-Viceroy of India in failing health.

"Mark you, I may be quite wrong. It may not be a house-party that Gedge desires to attend. It may be a sale or a wedding: it may be a business deal. But I think it is a house-party. And when I reach Châteaudun, I'm going to try the tradesmen that serve the neighbourhood. Your action will be more direct, for you will locate a château and then have a drink at a hamlet a mile or two off. But for God's sake watch your step. Gedge caught me bending once—at a village inn."

I will not set down our progress because for fifty hours it did not deserve that name. Though no one could have worked harder, our luck was out. On Friday and Saturday morning Mona did more than her share, visiting Châteaudun's market and shop after shop, while Mansel searched the country I had not had time to reach. But pick up the scent, we could not: Gedge had passed off our map.

To save the face of my proverb, a thunder-storm had broken on Thursday night : but the sky had cleared very soon and the following day had been excessively hot. Since Saturday had promised to be even hotter still, we arranged to ' call it a day ' at half-past four and to rally at five o'clock at our own hotel.   And so we did.

It was, I confess, a sober gathering.

For two days' very hard labour, we had precisely nothing to show. And time was running short. To-morrow would be the ninth : and whatever was due to take place would take place in two days' time.

" Any suggestions ? " said Mansel.

" Not from me," I said.   " Except that Châteaudun should be counted out."

" I agree.   In fact I've been forced to the conclusion that Châteaudun was a blind. I mean that Rust wired from there because Châteaudun was *not* the nearest town. That was, of course, always on the cards : but once you leave Châteaudun, which way do you go ? Vendôme ? Orleans ? Chartres ? "

I made no answer, because I had none to make.

" Vendôme's the smallest," said Mona.   " And it's only twenty-five miles."

" Vendôme be it," said Mansel.   " Will you do the market to-morrow ? The shops will be shut."

" I will, indeed.   I'd like to be there at nine."

" So you shall," said Mansel.   " We'll pick you up at mid-day. And now let's forget the matter for two or three hours. We can work out our routes after dinner : it won't take long."

For half an hour or so we talked about other things, and then I went out to send a wire to my wife. And when this was done, I strolled to the great cathedral, to look at its lovely glass—for, as all the world knows, the panes of Chartres cathedral are finer than precious stones.

I could not, I think, have gone at a fairer hour, for the evening sun was pouring into the shrine, printing the glorious colours upon the cold, gray stone and making majestic magic on every side. Indeed, they remembered the rainbow that paints its own reflection for two or three minutes of time : for there was the real wheel-window, ablaze with light ; and there, on pillar and flags, was its delicate counterpart.

For a quarter of an hour I stood or moved in the church, quite forgetting that I had been tired, gazing upon the beauty which Nature was drawing from Art and wishing very much that Jenny was there by my side, to see the miracle. And finally I sat down on one of the high-backed chairs at the side of the nave, proposing to rest for five minutes before I took my leave.

It was, I think, as I sat down that I heard Brevet's voice.

" My dear lady, you must hold me excused. Many a better man than I has endeavoured to describe the windows of Chartres. And every one has failed—for the very good reason that they are indescribable. As well attempt to describe a rainbow snared in a fountain or the miniature of a maid in her lover's eye."

The man was pacing the aisle. At the moment a pillar was rising between him and me. But in two or three seconds he would have passed the pillar, and I should be clear to be seen, three paces away.

Standing against the pillar was a confessional.

In a flash I was inside this, and the faded curtain was drawn.

It was as well I moved.

My chair had been the last of its row : and its row was the first of its batch. Brevet turned directly beside it, leaving the aisle for the nave. And his companions with him.

One was an elderly woman, very highly made up, very

expensively dressed, whose shoes were too tight. Her pearls, if real, must have been most valuable. The other was a girl who might have been twenty-three. An enormous solitaire diamond winked on her ill-shaped hand. Her expression was disagreeable and she was patently bored.

But, though I observed these things, I was not thinking of them. A car was waiting outside—the car that had brought the three and, when they emerged from the shrine, would take them away. It would take them whence they had come . . . to the château for which we were seeking . . . where the house-party was assembling . . . the house-party of which Brevet made one.

The thing was so clear—so obvious. All things were possible—with Brevet within the gates and Gedge without.

Somehow I had to get out and to follow that car.

Brevet and the two women were standing in the midst of the nave. He was, of course, discoursing and pointing to this and to that. As they turned to go on, a body obscured my view. The next moment a priest had entered the confessional. He had, no doubt, seen me go in and now was come to hear what sins I had to report . . .

As Brevet passed out of sight, I thrust a note through the grating and fled for the Southern door.

I was descending the steps, when a hired car disgorged two ladies of middle age.

" I'll wait here, m'm," said the driver. " You'll see all you want to see in a quarter 'v an hour. An' then I'll take you back to *The Grand Monarque*."

I looked to the right, and there was the car I sought. There was no mistaking it. It went with the gorgeous pearls and the very expensive dress. Its footman was talking to its chauffeur with a lackadaisical air.

For a moment my brain zig-zagged . . .

And then I saw what I must do.

I could not approach the servants and I could not follow the car. But the hired driver was English, and he should serve my turn.

I took out a thousand-franc note and whipped to his side.

" Can you speak French ? "

" I can, sir."

" You see that turn-out ? " I said.

" Can't 'ardly miss it, sir, can you ? "

" I want to know whose it is and where it belongs." I slipped the note into his hand. " Find those things out from the servants before the owner comes back. And then report to me at *The Grand Monarque*. There'll be another thousand if you make good."

Without waiting to hear his reply, I whipped to a little lane on the other side of the square.

When I could turn, I saw he was hard at work. Both servants were listening to him, and the chauffeur was nodding his head. Presently he took out a map, which the footman and he explored. And then he produced a pencil . . .

It was as he was taking his leave that Brevet and the women came out.

I watched them enter the car. Then I turned on my heel and strolled to *Le Grand Monarque*.

Five minutes after I had reached it, I saw the hired car enter the *Place des Epars*.

When its occupants had left, I stepped to the driver's side.

" Seein's believin', sir. The footman was that obligin', he wrote it all down."

I stared at the margin of the map.

Mrs. Dieselbaum, Château Robinet, Morle.

" Well done, indeed," said I, and gave him his thousand francs.

" You're very generous, sir."

" It's my day out," said I, and meant what I said.

*   *   *   *   *

We drank champagne that evening—and two hours later we all of us left for Vendôme. Chartres was too close to Morle—a short thirteen miles, and, though it had served us well, my one encounter with Brevet was more than enough.

*   *   *   *   *

Soon after dawn the next morning, Mansel and I were standing within a wood, east of the Château Robinet, half a mile off. Bagot and Bell were at hand, and Carson was in charge of the Rolls, a mile and a half away.

The body of the house was plainly extremely old, but this had been bedizened time and again. Harmony and proportion had gone by the board, and though the work done was good work and must have cost a great deal, the result was an architect's nightmare, and that is the truth. But it did look very expensive : and that, I suppose, was enough for Mrs. Dieselbaum.

It stood in a pretty big park and was approached by two drives : a private golf-course marched with the woods to the west : finally, the buildings were moated and the drawbridge was up.

" There must be a foot-bridge," mused Mansel ; " the other side. With the village ten minutes' walk, the servants would never consent to being locked up all night."

" Garage ? " said I.

" It must be within the moat at the back of the house. If it is, what a place to crack ! The drawbridge goes up at dusk : throw a spanner into its works, and it can't come down. And so you can't be pursued. And now let's make our way round to the mouth of the northern drive. The other's too close to the village, so that is the one they'll use."

Forty minutes later we came to the mouth of the drive. There stood the façade of a gate-house, but nothing more. There were no gates.

" The Bonneval road," said Mansel. " Turn to the right for Orleans and turn to the left for Chartres. And with a start of a minute, who knows which way you've gone ? And now we'll take to those woods and view the house from the West."

That we moved with the greatest caution, I need not say ; for that Gedge was somewhere at hand, there could be no doubt. After a short consultation, the four of us entered the woods.

These proved to be very thick, and it soon became very clear that, unless we came down to their edge, we could not observe the house. Still it was early enough—it was not yet seven o'clock, so when we had gone some way, we turned towards the golf-course, which I have said we had seen from the opposite side.

Some twenty yards from the meadows we came to a decent path. This seemed to run through the woods, by the side of the course, and we afterwards found that it led from the house to a spot quite close to the mouth of the drive. Since it curled to and fro, like a stream, it was easy enough to watch, so Bagot and Bell took cover to right and left, while Mansel and I passed straight on to the meadows' edge.

The first thing we saw was the foot-bridge which Mansel had said would be there ; the next, an obvious garage within the moat. (I think I should make it clear that the château did not rise from the moat, but stood a good twenty feet back from the water's edge. So a car which crossed the drawbridge and turned to the right would leave the front door on its left and then pass round

the château, between the house and the moat. It follows
that, as Mansel had said, so long as the drawbridge was
up, a car could leave the garage, but not the island on
which the garage stood.)

As we looked, we saw shutters opened, and smoke
began to rise from one of the many stacks. Then a clock
which we could not see declared it was seven o'clock.

"Time to withdraw," said Mansel, "and think over
what we've seen. We'll come again to-morrow, before
it's light. I want to have a look at the mouth of the
southern drive. Just to be sure, you know."

And with his words, a figure approached the foot-
bridge, golf-clubs in hand.

"Brevet," breathed Mansel. "It's Brevet."

And Brevet it was.

We watched him cross the foot-bridge and make his
way to a tee . . .

"By God, I've got it," said Mansel. "He's going to
meet Gedge. This is the way they do it. Brevet goes
round in the morning at this unearthly hour . . . and
pulls a ball into these woods . . . and while he's trying
to find it, Gedge comes along this path."

Mansel could rise to an occasion as no one I ever knew.
The more urgent the crisis, the keener his wits became.
He knew that if the rogues saw us, we should have lost
our match ; for Gedge would never touch Robinet, did
he but guess we were there. More, it would come to a
battle—the very last thing we wanted at such a time and
place. Yet, if we could attend this interview . . .

"Watch Brevet," he breathed, and was gone.

Two minutes later he was back—and Brevet was holing
out, with a shocking five.

"Bell moves by the path," he said, "with Bagot behind.
The moment Bell sees Gedge coming, he gives a signal to
Bagot and fades away. Bagot runs back down the path,
whips across to the meadows and pitches a piece of dead

wood on to the nearest green. Meanwhile we stick to Brevet and watch the greens."

We moved abreast of the fellow, just out of his sight. We watched him play three holes. As he strolled to the fourth tee, I glanced behind. Something thin and brown lay full on the second green.

I touched Mansel's shoulder twice.

" That's right," he breathed. " He's just had a look at his watch. And now he'll drive into the woods."

And so Brevet did. More. To round the picture, he raised his arms and shook his fists at the heaven, all clear and blue. Then he pushed back his soft, brown hat and turned to the woods.

He left the meadows ten paces from where we stood, but, perhaps because he was a townsman, he made enough noise for three. Since we knew how to move, it was easy to follow the man and even to draw very close, without being seen or heard.

Then he stepped on to the path and at once we heard Gedge's voice.

" You lazy ——," he said. " It's a quarter past."

" I know," said Brevet, coolly. " I saw no reason for waiting a quarter of an hour. Only a fool or a knave would look for his ball in these woods ; and a fool would look for five minutes—no more than that. If I know that, others do—so shall we come to the point ? "

I heard Gedge suck in his breath.

Then—

" All O.K. ? " he snapped.

" The traditional bed of roses. Far the easiest thing that we've ever done."

" What about the bridge ? "

" My affair," said Brevet. " Just count it out."

" Go on. Spill it," said Gedge.

Brevet cleared his throat.

" The gear is controlled from a cellar, which has one

door. That door has a Yale lock, of which my host has the key. By day, the door stands open : but at dusk, when the drawbridge is raised, that door is shut. When my host is called in the morning, he gives his servant the key : the man then opens the door and brings the key back."

" What then ? "

" Before I leave," said Brevet, " a very small piece of metal will enter that good Yale lock. The key-hole, I mean. It follows that, when night falls and the door is shut, no one will be able to open it, key or no key."

" How long to break it down ? "

" Half an hour, perhaps. It's three-inch oak."

" And you leave here at six ? "

" You may lay to that," said Brevet. " Time and tide and alibis will not wait. I shall sit down to dinner at Tours precisely at half-past eight. It'll be an agreeable change—the food here is too elaborate. And I like *The Univers*. They've a very good pastry chef."

" Meanwhile we're lifting the stuff."

" Taking it up," said Brevet. " I'm handing it to you on a plate. Punter and Rust could do it without any help from you."

" I see," said Gedge. " Well, get this and get it good. I don't fancy Tours."

" What the devil d'you mean ? " said Brevet.

" This," said Gedge, shortly. " Tours is too far. Ninety miles from here. That means an hour and a half —and going like hell."

" You're cutting the line in the village—the line to Chartres."

" I know all that, but an hour and a half's too long. And Tours is a —— to pass. The pastry chef may suit you, but that long, narrow High Street don't suit me. If you're on the run, it doesn't give you a chance. So I'll pick you up this side. You can dine at Vendôme."

" At *The Beau Sejour* ? " said Brevet. " I'm much obliged."

" Why not ? " spat Gedge. " I don't own the —— place. And I shall have left that morning. Besides, it's a house of call. A party blew in last night at eleven o'clock."

" Vendôme's too close," said Brevet.

" Be your age," said Gedge. " It's fifty miles. You're in the hotel at eight and you leave at a quarter to ten. We strike at a quarter past nine—an' pick you up on the road at ten-fifteen."

" Where ? "

" There's a sign-board twelve miles on which says CHÂTEAU-RENAULT 6. The first on the right after that. Fifty yards down you come to a ruined barn."

" And then ? "

" We buzz off," said Gedge, " and you toddle along to Tours. Stay the night there an' follow along the next day."

" Suppose the long, narrow High Street doesn't suit me."

" One man in a different car ? An' the stuff in Abraham's bosom ? You're getting loose."

There was a little silence.

At length—

" You're a wilful blackguard," said Brevet.

Gedge laughed his high-pitched laugh.

" Maybe," he said. " But you know my sums come out."

" Yes," said Brevet, slowly. " I'll give you that. Your, er, mental arithmetic is usually very good."

" Then that's that," said the other. " When and where do I pick you up ? "

Brevet repeated his orders.

" Snags to come ? " said Gedge.

" In that unlikely event, you'll see a towel in my casement—as once before."

" Right. An' I see you here on Tuesday at seven sharp."

" And there you're wrong," said Brevet. " I'll jog Coincidence's arm, but I'm damned if I'll pull her leg. Three times I've pulled into these woods between seven and seven-fifteen. I'm not going to make it four."

" If I say——"

" I don't care what you say. If a towel's in my window to-morrow, then I shall be here on Tuesday at seven o'clock. Otherwise, you will wait in vain. The thing's absurd, and you know it. We've basted the joint enough."

Gedge appeared to reflect.

Then—

" Perhaps you're right," he said. " We don't want to slip up now."

There was another silence.

Then—

" What's Mansel doing ? " said Gedge.

" That's very easy," said Brevet. " If Chandos has not re-appeared, he's pulling down Arx. If Chandos has re-appeared, he's hanging round Châteaudun."

As though Brevet had not spoken—

" Mansel's fly," said Gedge. " I'll get the —— down, but he's half a crook."

" Wishful thinking," said Brevet. " Mansel means to see you, and he is a dangerous man. If you'd fade out, as I say——"

" You white-livered ——," said Gedge.

" Sorry," said Brevet. " But I am above abuse. If you mean to return to Arx, I shall have to conform. But I shall ring up from Sarrat, before going on ; and I very strongly advise you to do the same."

There was another silence.

Then—

"I'd give a monkey," said Gedge, "to know where he is."

Brevet laughed.

"Why worry," he said, "if he's only half a crook?"

Before the other could answer, he had re-entered the wood.

For a little Gedge stood where he was. Then he turned on his heel and retraced his steps.

As his footfalls faded—

"To Gedge on a plate," breathed Mansel. "To us in a lordly dish. But I'm sorry to think that we're sharing the same hotel." He moved, to glance down the path. "Go back and watch Brevet, will you? I'm going to see Gedge out. Tell Bagot and Bell to play connecting-file."

As a man in a dream, I carried out his instructions; for all my thoughts were fast on *The Beau Sejour*. It was a small hotel, and if Gedge got back before us—well, Mona and Rowley were there *and had not been warned*. And the Lowland was in the garage, for all to see.

It is sometimes the whim of Fortune to give with the right hand and take away with the left. At a stroke she had made us free of the enemy's plan of action. More, of his *revised* plan of action, for only that morning the rendezvous had been changed. Time and place and method—all had been detailed to us by Gedge himself. Such a gift was fantastic—unique. And all the time, entirely unknown to us, the dame had put in peril the whole of our enterprise.

I tried to think what we must do.

We could not move till Gedge was out of the way. It would take us at least an hour to reach the Rolls. Because it was Sunday, we could not telephone except from a town. We could—from a private house: but where was the private house?

For one desperate moment I thought of crossing the foot-bridge and asking to be allowed to speak from

Robinet. But trunk-calls take time to make, and Brevet
was up and about. Besides . . .

And there I saw the man turn and make for the seventh
tee. He was coming back. Eight holes were enough
for him.

Five minutes later, perhaps, Bell gave me a message
from Mansel.

"Please get back to the car as fast as ever you can."

* * * * *

The Rolls stole out of the thicket and on to the Vendôme road.

As he settled himself in his seat—

"We must assume," said Mansel, "that Gedge has
gone straight back. I saw him into his car, and he went
this way. But we shall turn off in a minute, in case of
accidents. So he'll go in from the North, but we shall
come up from the East. I say 'come up,' for we must
not drive into the town. So Bagot and Bell and Carson
will take the Rolls and drive to *The Fountain* at Blois,
while you and I will go in and get Mona and Rowley out.
Gedge doesn't know Rowley by sight : but Rowley
doesn't look French, and so the moment Gedge sees him,
he'll go to the porter's lodge and ask who he is. And so
we can only hope that Rowley keeps out of his sight.
Mona will breakfast upstairs, and I think we ought to be
there before she's down. As for the Lowland—well, Gedge
has missed her once, and with luck he'll miss her again.

"Now if Rowley should recognize Gedge—and I'm
sure, if he sees him, he will—his instant idea will be to
put us wise. So he'll be in the streets somewhere, waiting
to stop the Rolls. For that reason, I think, we'd better
stroll in from the North, for that's the direction from which
we should normally come. And we must look out for
Punter. It's most unlikely that he's at *The Beau Sejour* ;
but I have no doubt at all that he's in Vendôme."

He raised his eyebrows and sighed.

" It's all very trying, of course : but it might have been worse—for Gedge might not have mentioned that he was our fellow guest.   And then we should have bought it."

" The Lowland's the danger," said I.   " We can lie up all day : but we can't lock up the garage.   And once she catches his eye, the fat will be burnt."

" I won't be beaten," said Mansel.   " We'll get her out while he's at church."

But though I was glad to laugh, I knew in my heart that, if Gedge had returned to Vendôme, yet did not retire to his room, our chance of a happy issue was painfully slight. The felon was ' on the job ' : and so his eyes were wide and his ears were pricked.   More.   He was most uneasy —lest Jonathan Mansel should find him before ' the job ' had been done.   And we had to watch this man—who was watching for us . . . wait till his back was turned . . . move in a flash and be gone, before he looked round.

" What's his car like ? " I said.

" A good-looking Whistler," said Mansel.   " Very fast, no doubt.   Astonishing how these big fellows are never short of a car.   Of course they're special clients, specially served."

" I'd rather have a Lowland," I said.

" So, I expect, would he.   But his Lowland's at Petit Arx, and the door is shut.   He must be sore with us, William."

" Very sore," I said.   " In fact, for our peace of mind, it's just about time he went out."

" I entirely agree," said Mansel, and left it there.

*   *   *   *   *

And here, if I may, I will describe our hotel.   Since I had hardly seen it, I could not then have described it, as I shall describe it now : but I came to know it better before that day was out.

The Beau Sejour stood in a street. By its side, a decent archway gave to a cobbled yard and a garage beyond. These were capacious and might very well have belonged to a bigger house. In the left-hand wall of the archway was the entrance to the hotel. A revolving door hung in the entrance and admitted to a pretty big lounge, at the opposite end of which were the lift and stairs. On the left of the door was, as usual, the porter's lodge : on the right of the door was a window, serving the lounge. The back entrance to the hotel led out of the cobbled yard. It follows that no one could enter or leave the house, that no car could enter or leave the cobbled yard without being able to be seen from the porter's lodge. *Or from the window of the lounge on the opposite side of the door.*

* * * * *

I saw the faithful Rowley before he saw me.

He was standing beside an alley, less than a hundred yards from *The Beau Sejour*. His eyes were upon the road along which the Rolls would have come.

As I approached, he saw me . . .

And then we were both in the alley, and Mansel was lounging on the opposite side of the street.

"Drove into the yard, sir," said Rowley, "just fifty minutes ago. I knew it was him the moment I saw his face. But he never saw me or the Lowland—our luck was in. She was out in the yard—I'd just washed her : but, just before he drove in, the hotel 'bus comes back from meeting the early train. She's a clumsy brute, that 'bus, an' 'er driver was backing her round. An' he got between me an' Gedge. If Gedge had let him go on, he couldn't have helped but see me, but, though there was plenty of room, he shouts to the fellow to stop until he's got in. And so we were saved.

"I watched him out of the yard. Then I slipped in the back way, to go an' warn Miss Lelong. But there

N

ain't no back stairs, sir, and Gedge was fast in the lounge, with his eyes all over the place. I didn't dare go by him —there weren't enough people about. So I prayed she'd stay in her room and ran back to the yard. I had to get out to warn you, but I thought, if I could, I must get the Lowland away. So I started her engine up. Then I left her ticking over and walked to the end of the archway, just in case . . ." He wiped the sweat from his brow. "Upon my soul, sir, you'd think he knew we was here. There he was in the window, beside the door. For ten solid minutes I watched him—of course he couldn't see me. Then a waiter arrives with a drink and a pile of sandwiches ; an' down he sits in a chair and begins to eat, always with his eyes on the archway . . .

"Well, I put the Lowland away. Then I wrote a note in pencil to Miss Lelong an' told a servant to take it up to her room. 'Don't leave your room, miss,' I said. 'There's somebody here.' An' then, by the grace of heaven, a van comes into the yard. Delivering ice. The fellow was all alone, so I gave him a hand ; and when he was through, he lifted me out of the yard and into the street.

"And there we are, sir. It's only the Lowland now : but if he looks round that garage—well, there she is."

I was just going to make him some answer, when Mansel put a hand in his pocket and turned to his right.

"Fade," I breathed, and whipped to the nearest doorway, six feet away.

With my eyes on the street I waited. Rowley was adjusting a shoe-lace, quite six paces off.

Punter passed the mouth of the alley, strolling along the pavement towards *The Beau Sejour*.

It occurred to me that Gedge was waiting for Punter. Not that the two would meet, but at certain times, no doubt, the subordinate had to report. This he did by passing the archway, for Gedge, from where he was, could just see into the street.

As Mansel strolled back into view—

"That was Punter," I said.

"I know, sir," said Rowley, grimly. "We ought to have put him away ten years ago."

"I'm afraid you're right," said I. "And now you go over and take Captain Mansel's place. One moment. Except by the archway, there's no way into that yard?"

"No way at all, sir."

Two minutes later Mansel strolled into the alley and took my arm.

"Tell me the worst," he said.

"I will," said I, and told him Rowley's tale.

As I made an end—

"The trouble is," I said, "that no one can watch the swine. We can't even watch that window, except from the yard. For all we know, he may have gone to his room, and it may be perfectly safe to take the Lowland away. But until we can enter that yard, we can't be sure."

"And we've got to be sure," said Mansel. "The fellow's instinct is working. That's why he sticks to that window. He has been warned."

Now, had the day been a week-day, there would have been plenty of traffic between the street and the yard— delivery-vans and lorries and stuff like that : but, because it was Sunday, a full half-hour went by and only one car turned in.

At a quarter to twelve—

"I assume," said I, "I assume that he'll go to lunch."

"He may or may not," said Mansel. "He may have more sandwiches there. I don't think that very likely : but I doubt if he'll go to lunch before half-past twelve."

Both hands were in Rowley's pockets and he had turned to the left . . .

From half-way down a basement, I watched the alley's

mouth—and saw Gedge saunter by, with his hat tipped over his eyes.

In a flash I was at the corner which the alley made with the street. Then I took a deep breath and looked round.

Gedge was walking straight on, with cross roads ahead. Rowley was twenty yards on, on the opposite side of the way.

I let Gedge reach the cross roads. Then I turned out of the alley and walked to *The Beau Sejour*.

Not daring to glance behind me, I darted under the archway and into the cobbled yard.

A moment later, the engine of the Lowland was running, for Mansel and I had always a key of each of the cars.

And then I was out in the yard . . .

Another car entered the archway. There was but room for one, and I had to wait until it had entered the yard. And then my way was clear. But I had to turn to the right before I could turn to the left, for here a very long ' refuge ' divided the street into two. And, as I turned to the right, I saw Gedge coming towards me, some twenty-five paces away.

I saw the man start and slow down. Then he turned to look into some window, as though he hoped not to be seen.

And the gesture gave me my cue.

With her tail just clear of the archway, I stopped the car and got out. Then I walked into the hotel.

I laid a hundred francs on the porter's desk.

" Send for the luggage," I said, " from Rooms No. 71 and 72."

" Monsieur is leaving ? "

" Yes," I said. " I've got to get on to Dieppe. My bill in five minutes, please. I'll pay you as I go out."

" Certainly, sir."

I made for the stairs and walked up to Mona's room. Mercifully, she was dressed.

" Listen," I said. " Gedge is below. He's staying in this hotel. He has seen me and the Lowland, but no one else. In a minute or two he is going to see you and me . . . to watch us get into the Lowland and leave Vendôme for Dieppe. And I think he will follow us . . . to make quite sure that Dieppe *is* our destination. He'll probably be in the lounge, as we go by. But don't you see him, Mona. It's got to be his day out. And now you've one minute to pack. A boy's coming up for our things."

I entered my room and thrust my stuff into my case. As I pressed the hasps into place, a knock fell on the door.

Thirty seconds later, Mona Lelong and I were descending the stairs.

Gedge was stooping in the shadows—I saw him with the tail of my eye.

I paid our bill and tipped the porter again.

" Monsieur is crossing to-night ? "

" Madame is," said I. " I've got to get back to Pau."

With that, I followed Mona out to the car.

I dared not glance at the alley, as we went by, but I lifted a finger to Mansel, to tell him to stay where he was.

Three minutes later, the Lowland was clear of Vendôme and was heading for Chartres.

CHAPTER IX

GEDGE CALLS THE TUNE

" AND now, please," said Mona.

" First, move the mirror," I said, " so that you can watch the road." She did as I said. " Now keep your eyes on that, while I tell you my tale. He'll be using a dark-blue Whistler, but please report any car that seems to be hanging on."

I told all there was to tell: but just before I had finished, she interrupted me.

"There's a dark-blue car behind. I can't see the make."

"Is it coming up?"

"Not very fast."

"Light a cigarette," I said.

After a minute or two—

"It's still coming up," said Mona.

"When it's less than a hundred yards, put out your arm and shake the ash from your cigarette."

This she did.

A quarter of a minute later—

"He's falling back," she said.

"It's Gedge all right," said I. "He had to be sure it was us, and your good-looking scarlet sleeve has said that it is."

"Go on with your tale. I'll watch."

"There isn't much more to tell. For some extraordinary reason it had never entered my head that, if we appeared to Gedge, he would try to avoid being seen. I had thought that he'd lose control—that he might even shoot. But the moment I saw that he'd seen me *and turned away*, I knew that we had a chance of saving the game. That I should ship you to England is a perfectly natural thing: that being so, it is also perfectly natural that we should stay at Vendôme—and take it easy to-day, for Dieppe is not very far and you won't go aboard before ten. So I threw the fly . . .

"How far he will follow us, I neither know nor care: but by the time he gets back, Mansel will have talked to the porter and wiped his memory clean. If, on his return, Gedge asks questions, he will be told that no one but you and I arrived very late last night at *The Beau Sejour*."

With her eyes on the driving-mirror—

"It's him all right," said Mona. "He's always there."

"Good," said I. "We'll lunch at *The Grand Monarque* and take our time ; and he can wait outside in the *Place des Epars*."

"I should think you're the only man who has ever bluffed Daniel Gedge."

"Rot," said I. "Besides, he was badly placed. He is on the edge of committing a highly profitable crime. If we are upon his track, he's got to abandon that crime. When he saw me, he feared that we were upon his track. *But he hoped so much that we weren't that he wasn't sure.* He *should* have been sure, of course. He *would* have been sure—if he hadn't cared about losing some ten or twelve thousand pounds. Wishful thinking has warped his judgment. And when I threw my fly, I encouraged the wishful thought."

"It was damned quick of you, any way. When I got Rowley's note, I felt weak at the knees."

"I'd had my shock," said I. "When he said where he was staying, it took a year from my life."

"Why did he leave the hotel and then come back ? "

I shrugged my shoulders.

"Instinct, perhaps. Mansel says his is working, and Mansel is usually right."

"How far will he come ? " said Mona.

"God knows," I said. "Say Rouen."

"Supposing," said Mona, " he follows us into Dieppe ? "

"If he does," said I, " you'll have to take the boat. I'm sorry, my dear, but you see it's the only way."

"I shall come straight back," said Mona. "I will be in at the death."

"All right," I said. "But it hardly seems worth while —unless, of course, you want to revisit Arx."

"I'm through with Arx. I don't want to see it again."

"Then, if you have to sail, why don't you stay ? I mean, it might help us, Mona. We'll have to fade out, you know, when we've put Gedge and Brevet down."

"I know how to fade out," said Mona. "And I may have my uses—you never know."

We ran into Chartres at exactly a quarter-past one, and there we lunched in style at *The Grand Monarque*. The Whistler waited for us—on the other side of the *place*.

I hope Gedge enjoyed his vigil, which lasted for nearly two hours—we had plenty of time. Then we visited the cathedral—as much to twist his tail as anything else. We took the road to Rouen at four o'clock.

I had hoped he would leave us at Rouen: but as we gained the country which lies beyond—

"He means to see us," said Mona. "He's coming on."

Now I must most frankly confess that, had I been placed as was Gedge, I should have done the same. His plans were made and he had nothing to do. Why not, therefore, make certain that he was not being misled? For all that, his persistence annoyed me, for I was tired of the game. I did not mind dining at Dieppe: but I did not want all the fuss of seeing Mona on board, of hanging about on the dirty, ill-lit quays . . .

And there for the first time I saw why Gedge was intending to follow us into Dieppe. He meant, when Mona was gone, to take my life.

Once seen, the thing stood out.

Night, the deserted quays and the empty sheds. . . . A shot in the darkness, a spurt up a narrow street, and a stroll up the front. . . . A couple of drinks at the bar of some hotel, and then the Whistler again and the open road.

Had I not known he was there, it would have been too easy. Even though I knew he was there, it might not be very hard.

"What do you know?" said Mona.

"I wish," said I, "you'd keep your eyes on that glass."

*   *   *   *   *

I cannot pretend I enjoyed the excellent dinner we ate : for I wanted to be alone, to lay my plans. So far from being alone, I had to play up to Mona with all my might, for, had she perceived what I had, she would not have gone aboard.

I had started the game, and I had to play it out. By the rules of that game, Gedge must observe me, but I must not observe Gedge. Now, if I broke those rules, I should lose the game : but if I kept those rules, I might very well lose my life.

Gedge would watch me take Mona on to the ship : and then he would watch me come off, to walk back to the car : and I should not know where he was—I knew the place very well, and the darkness and shadows could hide a hundred men.

I could not think what to do ; and I presently gave up trying, for Mona was looking at me, as though she suspected that something was on my mind.

After dinner we sat in the bar, until it was nearly ten : and then we strolled out to the Lowland, to drive to the quay.

The weather was very fine, and Dieppe was gay. Quite a hundred cars were in waiting, on the road that was running between the hotels and the sea.

As we came to the Lowland, Mona spoke very low.

" The Whistler is twelve cars off."

Gedge must have been in the Whistler, waiting for us to appear ; for, as we swept up the road, Mona saw him coming and told me so.

" He's taking no risks," I said grimly. " He means to see you aboard."

At last we turned to the right and took a side street to the quays.

The front had been well lighted, but, as I had expected, a man who was roaming the quays could have done with a torch. Very few lights were burning, and these were far between.

I had asked where the boat would be berthed, and I very soon saw where she was.

" Is he coming ? " I said.

" I'm not sure. Yes, there he is. He's using his parking lights."

The street, the sheds and the quay made three long parallel lines. I could have passed on to the quay between two sheds. Instead, I ran the length of the street, rounded the last of the sheds and then passed on to the quay. So the Lowland was facing the way we had come. There were only two lamps burning in more than a hundred yards. I stopped midway between them. At least the darkness should serve me—as well as Gedge It was the best I could do.

I switched off the engine and lights. Then I took the key from the switch and we left the car.

I took Mona's ticket at the office, which was right at the end of the sheds. Then I picked up her suit-case and led the way to the boat.

" He's stopped in the street," breathed Mona : " and turned the Whistler round."

" Where exactly ? " I asked.

" A long way down. Not very far from the street that leads to the front."

I nodded.

That would do. Once Gedge had gained the Whistler, he could be clear of Dieppe in less than three minutes of time.

The gangway to the steamer was lighted—I have no doubt that the fellow watched us take it, to gain the deck.

To secure a cabin was simple . . .

Mona sat down on the bed and looked at me.

" We do get about, don't we ? Yesterday Chartres : to-day Dieppe ; and to-morrow *The Fountain* at Blois."

"Cut out *The Fountain* at Blois and make it the
Berkeley Grill, say, this day week."

Mona shook her head.

"Tomorrow night," she said, "I shall sleep at *The
Fountain* at Blois."

"As you will," I sighed. "I can't keep you away."

"I've been very—dutiful, Richard."

"Yes, you have," I said warmly. "You've watched
that swine behind us for nearly two hundred miles and
you're suffering great inconvenience to save our game.
I'll never forget it, Mona. I don't know another girl
who wouldn't have kicked."

"What about Jenny?"

"I . . . except Jenny," I said.

"Well, I don't," said Mona. "Jenny would never
have left you—*with Gedge on the quay.*"

I sat very still, and presently Mona went on.

"Did you think that I would leave you . . . and sit
here and wait for the shot?"

I put a hand to my head.

"Mona, I beg you——"

"I've done my bit," said the girl. "I've saved your
game. He's seen me on to the ship—but I'm damned if
I'll sail."

"We'll settle that later," said I. "And now let me
think."

It was an immense relief to be able to concentrate.

I had so berthed the Lowland that Gedge would be
unable to watch both her and the ship. He would have
to choose between them: and, once he had seen us
aboard, I had no doubt at all that he would choose the
car. He would find the car and then he would pick his
position: and then he would wait for the sheep to come
and be killed.

He certainly held a good hand—a very much better
hand than he had held by a light-house three weeks ago:

but I had one valuable card, for I knew that he was there, yet he did not know that I knew.

And then I saw very clearly the first of the steps I must take.

Before I did anything else, I must locate Gedge.

Now if my judgment was good and Gedge was watching the car, I should be able to leave the ship unobserved. Then I must take to the shadows and make my way—not, indeed, to the car, but to her vicinity. And there I must wait and watch, till Gedge, by some sound or movement, declared where he was.

(Here, perhaps, I should say that I had plenty of time, for the ship would not sail till twelve, when the train had come in. And, for all Gedge knew, I might stay aboard until then.)

Now though I tried very hard to see what next I must do, my efforts were vain ; and I had to make up my mind that once I had taken the first step, I should be able to see what my second must be.

I turned to Mona and told her what I proposed.

" But I think you must see," I said, " that you cannot be on in this scene. For one thing only, my shoes are soled with rubber, and I shall make no sound. If you decline to sail, you must leave the ship : but you must not approach the Lowland, because, if you do, you may tear the whole thing up."

Mona took my hand and led it down to her foot.

She was wearing rubber-soled shoes.

" And don't be afraid," she said, " that I shall tear anything up. We won't leave the steamer together, for that would be—well, unwise. I shall give you three minutes' law, and then I shall start. So tell me which way you're going."

I knew that to argue was hopeless, and time was going by.

" There's a crane," I said, " on rails about twenty paces

ahead of the bows of the ship. Then comes a row of trucks rather nearer the sheds. And then there's another crane. The second crane is just this side of the Lowland.

" I shall make for the second crane. I don't think Gedge will be there. I think he will be by the sheds, for the sheds make very good cover between the two cars."

Mona Lelong nodded.

" All right. Don't fear I shall cramp your style. But I've got to be there, Richard ; for this is down Gedge's street, and I may be of use."

I stood up and took her hand and put it up to my lips.

" You're a damned brave girl," I said.

Then I left the cabin and made for the upper deck.

*   *   *   *   *

I have said that the gangway was lighted : but the light did not spread very far. As I approached the ramp, I saw two men at its foot and another one half-way up. The two were pressing the third to turn and ' come back ' with them. As he decided to do so, I followed him down to the quay and, moving behind the three, passed out of what light there was. Then I turned to my right and stepped to the crane.

If Gedge had been watching, he would have seen me beneath the gangway light : but, because of the figures before me, he must have lost me again, as soon as I reached the quay. But I hoped that he had not been watching : for, if he had, when two or three minutes had passed, but I failed to return to the car, his ever-ready suspicions would be aroused.

For a minute or two I stayed beside the crane, for I wished to accustom my eyes to the darkness in which I must move. Then I passed from the crane to the line of motionless trucks.

I now had excellent cover—if Gedge was close to the

sheds. But I moved very carefully, stooping low when I passed the couplings and continually straining my ears.

Now the last of the line of trucks was rather nearer the Lowland than I had thought. Crouching close to its end, I could see her familiar shape some twenty paces away.

I had left her, it may be remembered, roughly mid-way between two electric lamps. These lamps were held by brackets, fixed to the wall of a shed. I had passed the first some way back, but, though it was not powerful, it did diminish the darkness between the last truck and the car.

Surveying these twenty paces, I sought for any cover which Gedge could use. There was the shed's big door-way; but this was shut. I was sure that he was not standing against a jamb. There was a bin for refuse, but that was too slight. Search as I would, I could see no cover at all. He might, of course, be waiting beyond the car: but that I thought unlikely, and I could remember nothing which might have helped him there. He might be crouching beside the car itself: but I felt that he was this side—that he meant to let me go by and then fall in behind me, before he fired.

And there I heard the man move.

He was waiting two paces away, standing between the buffers of the last of the trucks.

I have no excuse to offer, for Gedge had simply chosen the obvious place. Indeed, I think that a child would have picked it out. But I had overlooked it, because I had made up my mind that he would stick to the sheds.

I could not see the fellow, for the corner of the truck was between us; but, had I moved clear, I doubt if I could have seen him, for the truck was casting a shadow, if you can give it that name.

Now I was sorely tempted to strike there and then. Our positions were now reversed, and I was very well placed. Though I did not use my pistol, I could, I was sure, have killed him, because I should have seized him before he knew I was there. But I was afraid that, though I seized his wrist, the fellow might fire; and then I could not kill him, because of the instant attention the shot would draw.

And there I remembered Mona.

God only knew where she was. She might by now have come to the second crane. This was ten paces on, not far from the edge of the quay. But she might not have got so far. Somehow I had to find her and 'put her wise.'

I began to steal back, past the trucks. But though I passed right down the line, she was not there.

Cursing under my breath, I peered at the second crane.

Now had I not known that Gedge would be waiting for me, I should have returned to the car by one of two routes. Either I should have taken the way by the sheds, that is to say, the way by which Mona and I had gone, or I should have struck obliquely across the quay and have crossed the railway line between the row of trucks and the waiting car. To deal with either movement, Gedge was very well placed. It follows that he was well placed to deal with any movement at the base of the second crane. Not so well placed, of course; for the crane was off the line which I should have taken between the ship and the car. But the crane was full in his view, and its base was not in such darkness as that in which he stood.

Still, there was nothing for it—Mona had to be warned: and since she was not by the trucks, she must be making her way towards the crane.

I left the line of trucks and passed directly across to the edge of the quay. There I turned to my left, proposing to keep by the water, until I was opposite the crane.

I had nearly covered this distance, when I perceived

some object, say, ten feet above the ground. Drawing a little nearer, I saw that it was a gangway, with one of its ends in the air. (It was a see-saw gangway—that is to say, a ramp that was mounted on wheels: and the wheels were in the middle, instead of at either end.) Since this was slanting directly towards the crane, I turned to move beside it ; for though its cover was slight, it was better than none at all. And as I reached the end of the gangway, I saw a slight figure ahead.

I was much too near Gedge to speak, so I closed to within a yard and then touched her wrist.

At once she stood still as death.

I put my lips to her ear.

" Turn and follow," I breathed. " I'm going to the edge of the quay."

And by the time we were there, I had made my plan.

A moment or two before I had seen the gangway, I had marked on the edge of the quay a flight of steps. For this I made, and when I had found the place, I took the girl's hand in mine and led her down.

" Sit down and listen," I said. " We're all right here."

" You've found him ? "

" He moved and I heard him. He's by the last of the trucks."

" How far is that from the Lowland ? "

" Just about twenty paces. And now, Mona, listen to me. In a minute we're both going to move and to follow the edge of the quay. When I am two hundred yards up, I shall walk across to the sheds and back to the car. The danger is very slight, for he is expecting me to approach from the opposite side. I shall open the near-side door, for he can't see that : and though he will hear the car start, he cannot possibly reach me before I move.

" And now for you.

" You will keep to the edge of the quay until you have passed the sheds. Then you will turn to your left and

walk across to the street that leads to the front. You
will go up that street until you come to the front ; and
there you will wait, at the corner, until I come. And
there I'll pick you up—and then we'll run for Blois as
quick as we can."

" Let me stay with you," said Mona. " Two can slip
into that car as quickly as one."

" My dear, he must not see you."

" You said that he couldn't see the near-side door."

" I don't think he can : but when it opens, he might.
And if he should—well, if there are two to get in, it just
doubles the risk."

There was a little silence.

Then—

" D'you think he'll follow ? " said Mona.

" He won't if he's wise. He didn't come here to kill
me : he came to assure himself that we had stayed at
Vendôme *en route* for Dieppe. Two birds with one stone
is attractive : but one with one is as much as man has
a right to expect. But let him follow, my dear. He's
quite a long way to run, to reach his car, and as the
Lowland can cut any Whistler down . . ."

" And what will he think . . . when he sees the Lowland move off . . . but you haven't gone by ? "

" I've no idea," I said, " but I can tell you this. If he
sets eyes upon you, then we might as well have stayed at
Vendôme—and have booked a table for Brevet on Tuesday
night. And now will you do as I say ? "

" All right," said Mona, at last.

" That's a good girl." I shot a glance at my wrist.
" It's now eleven-fifteen. I shall give you five minutes'
start, for you've farther to go."

She got to her feet.

" You will be careful, Richard, and wait your chance ? "

" I promise," I said. " But I don't think I can go
wrong."

We climbed to the head of the stair, and there she pressed my fingers and glided away.

I gave her full five minutes. Then I stole the way she had gone and counted my steps. At two hundred paces I turned and crossed to the sheds. And then I turned left again, towards where the Lowland stood.

Since I knew where Gedge was waiting, the risk of approach was slight, for, once I had picked up the car and the trucks beyond, I had only to keep the car in line with the last of the trucks. So the man could not see me, because, of course, the car would be blocking his view. For all that, I was very careful—Gedge might have moved.

I had the switch-key all ready, for, if he saw the door move, I should have to be quick. And, in case of accidents, I felt my pistol and put off the safety-catch.

But everything went very well.

In the wake of a shambling porter, I passed the danger-point—which one of the lamps was making some seventy yards from Gedge, and after waiting for the footfalls to die away, I stole, like any shadow, straight to the car.

Bent double, I moved beside her, until I was abreast of the door. Then I put an arm in at the window and, after a little fumbling, slid the key into her switch.

I passed the door and turned round. Then I set my hand on the handle and pressed it down.

And, as I made that movement, a light behind and above me came suddenly on.

I suppose it was half-past eleven : that on Sundays, at half-past eleven, the lamps that were out were lit, because of the train that was coming in half an hour. Be that as it may, as I slid on to the seat, the mirror showed me Gedge, with the light beating down on his face. He seemed to be—interested . . .

As I had hoped she would, the Lowland's engine

started upon the switch. And then I was in gear and was moving . . .

As I switched on my lights, a bullet shattered the window behind my head and, passing beside the mirror, drilled its way out of the car.

I put down my foot. That Gedge was blind with rage was perfectly clear. . . .

My headlights picked up Mona—half-way down the street that led to the front. I hung on my heel for an instant and, crying " Look out for glass," took her into the car. Then I whipped into third . . . into top . . . and let the Lowland go.

The girl was shaking all over.

" I'm s-sorry I broke my word : b-but I had to come back."

" That's all right, my lady. I thought you would."

Few cars were now to be seen, and those that were there were still. As though she were a gust of the wind, the Lowland swept the length of the front. Then I swung to the left and we took the Rouen road.

" He damned near got you, Richard."

" Damned near," I admitted. " If the Lowland hadn't been moving . . ."

" You said that he wouldn't see you."

I told her what had occurred.

" All's well that ends well," I added. " But if I'd been three seconds later, it mightn't have been so good."

Her eyes were fast on the mirror.

" He'll follow now."

I took a hand from the wheel and patted her knee.

" Don't waste your time," I said. " You won't see him again to-night."

" I know. All the same . . . I wish you'd turn off at Rouen."

" I will, if you like," I said. " As a matter of fact, I

think it's a good idea. We don't want to average sixty all the way."

We were up and over the hill that neighbours the port, and there was the rolling country, a limitless stage of shadows, on which the splash of our lights was playing Will-o'-the-Wisp.

So we whipped through the night at eighty, using the road as a track ; for we had the world to ourselves and I knew those thirty-five miles as I knew the palm of my hand.

And then, twelve miles from Dieppe, the Lowland coughed.

My eyes flew to the gauge ; but the tank was three-quarters full.

The Lowland coughed again, and the needle was falling back.

" My God, Richard, what is it ? "

" I think," I said, " it's a speck of dirt in the jet. She may clear it out herself."

" And if she doesn't ? "

" I shall have to take the jet down."

And with my words, the Lowland's engine stopped.

I brought her to the side of the road.

Once I tried to start her, but once was enough. In a flash her lights were out, and I was down in the road.

As I opened the near-side door—

" Out you get, my lady. And up and over that bank."

" Richard, I——"

" Do as I say."

I watched her do as I said.

On the farther side of the bank, she turned and looked at me.

" Lie down and stay down," I said. " On your obedience both our lives may hang."

Then I took up a spanner, opened the bonnet and lit

my inspection-lamp. All the time I was straining my ears for the sound of a car.

The job was simple enough, and I had just cleared the jet and was putting it back, when I heard, most sharp and clear, the snarl of the Whistler's engine, ripping the lovely silence as though it were tearing cloth.

Now, because I knew the road, I knew where the Whistler was. Little more than a mile away. I had not heard it before, because it was climbing a hill. And now it had come to the switchback—the two-mile switchback on which we had come to rest. But we were down in a dip. It follows that Gedge would not see us, until he was a hundred yards off.

I let my spanner fall and ran down the road towards Rouen as hard as ever I could . . .

As I heard the Whistler breasting the rise behind, I threw myself down on the turf by the side of the way.

I knew Gedge would see the Lowland, and I knew he would overrun her, because he was going so fast. He *did* overrun her by nearly three hundred yards : but I never thought he would be such a fool as to back.

But back he did—with his head hanging out of the car. And, as he passed me, I rose and ran beside him, just clear of his head-lights' beam.

As he slowed to a standstill, I dropped.

I watched him whip out of the car and turn his back.

For a moment he stood, crouching . . . poking his head at the Lowland, pistol in hand.

Then my left hand fell upon his right wrist.

And, as he leaped at my touch, I seized his throat.

So we stood for a moment, face to face.

And then he fought for his life, writhing and kicking and flinging himself to and fro.

It was all I could do to hold him, strong as I am : and I had the strange idea that I was gripping a serpent in human guise. His movements were those of a serpent that has been scotched. And as a serpent, so held, will lash its tail, so he attacked with his left hand—not striking, but clawing and scratching, as wild cats will.

He was trying to reach my eyes, so I snapped the arm that I held and captured his other wrist.

And then I saw fear in his eyes.

"Yes," I said. "You're dying. I've always been pretty strong : but you gave me a strength one evening, against which nothing could stand. That evening, at Stère, I told you that I should put you to death. And now I'm doing it, Gedge—I'm keeping my word. First, Lousy : now you : and then Brevet. You see, I'm going to meet Brevet . . . four miles from Château-Renault . . . on Tuesday night."

The man's eyes were starting, his swollen face was working : his teeth were bared.

And then his whole body went slack.

But I was taking no chances.

I lowered him to the ground, still holding fast to his throat. And so I stayed for five minutes, for serpents take long to die.

At last I knew he was dead.

I let him go and stood up. Then I stepped to the ditch at the foot of the bank. This was some two feet deep and was overgrown. And there I laid Gedge to such rest as a bloody murderer has. Then, using my handkerchief, I picked his pistol up and laid it beside his hand. If the gendarmes knew their business, they would find that one round had been fired. At last I straightened my back—to see Mona standing, silent, three paces away.

"Finish Gedge," I said, and wiped my hands on the grass.

"I know," she said quietly. "I saw it. I'm not so obedient to-night. But I didn't come to help you. When you told me to take that bank, I knew that he hadn't a chance. I don't suppose you know it, but there was death in your voice."

I nodded.

" I knew I was going to kill him, the moment I heard the car. I've had the feeling before. It's a very great help. It gives you confidence."

Mona regarded me.

" Your face needs bathing," she said.

" There's a stream a mile on," said I. " We'll stop for a minute there. And now you can help me, Mona. I want you to drive the Lowland, for I must return his car."

" Return it ? " cried Mona.

" Of course. To *The Beau Sejour.*"

" Supposing you're seen."

" I shan't be," said I. " At four o'clock this morning, the whole of Vendôme was dead. But we mustn't throw time about, for it's nearly twelve. And now I must fix that jet. It's clear enough now."

I turned and walked to the Lowland. Two minutes later her engine was idling sweetly, as though it had never stopped.

From one of the Lowland's pockets I took some wash-leather gloves. As I drew them on—

" Take your seat," I said, " and follow me on to the stream. I shan't be a moment there, and——"

" I'm going to bathe your face."

" You spoil me," I said. " Any way, after that, you will lead me back to Vendôme. You will stop just short of the town and wait by the side of the road. And then, when I come back, I'll drive you to Blois. One moment. Do you feel sleepy ? "

" Sleepy ? " she cried. " Is the play as dull as all that ? " I began to laugh. " God in heaven, Richard, you're out of the Middle Ages. That's what's the matter with you."

We stopped by the drowsy water, where more than once I had lunched, and Mona bathed my face as though I was four years old. And when she had done this, she slid an arm round my neck.

"Hold me a moment, Richard."

I put my arm about her and held her close.

The world about us was breathless : the poplar boughs above us might have been done in stone ; and all the sound we could hear was the lisp of the little stream.

"Calm after storm," said Mona. "Havoc's gone west with Gedge. You sat down to play with Death three weeks ago : and you kept on raising him : and now the game is over, and you have won."

"But for you," I said, " I should be lying in the dingle . . . with two feet of earth above me and more than a scratch on my face."

She nodded. Then—

"Do you know why my uncle came down—on that awful night ? "

"I assumed that he was uneasy."

"He was—because he knew me. He feared, the moment he saw you, that I might have fallen for you. That's why at dinner that night I laid it on with a trowel. But my uncle wasn't convinced—and that's why he went to see if I'd left my room."

"You're the bravest girl, Mona."

She shook her head.

"No," she said. "You're brave. You sat down to play with Death."

"So did you that night. And to-night you've done it again."

"I know. But not out of . . . bravery."

Before I could make any answer, she had put up her face and kissed me—and slipped away.

Then we re-entered the cars and set out for Vendôme.

During the run I endeavoured to look ahead.

So far as I could see, I had done no evil, but good. Château Robinet would not be entered on Tuesday night : but Brevet would not know this and so would make his way to the rendezvous. And when we had dealt with him, we could withdraw to England quietly enough. Unless I was much mistaken, Gedge's body would not be found for at least three days : and another three days would go by before it was found to be that of the man who had stayed at Vendôme. Still, there was one loose end—which must be tied up. Punter. When Punter missed Gedge, he would at first count himself lucky and would take no action at all ; for initiative found no favour in Gedge's eyes. But when Tuesday morning came, but Gedge was still not to be seen, Punter would feel that something ought to be done. And if he wired to Brevet, then Brevet would fail to appear at the rendezvous. And what of Rust ?

I decided to discuss with Mansel the action which we must take, for I was determined that Brevet should pay his debt. In a way he was worse than Gedge : for Gedge's vice was inherent—he was a criminal born : but Brevet was not. And Brevet had spoken with Jenny, had seen for himself how rare was the grace that she had—and then had sought to carry her into a den of thieves.

*   *   *   *   *

It was not quite half-past three, when the Lowland came to a standstill a lady's mile from Vendôme.

As I ran alongside—

" Is this all right ? " said Mona.

" Splendid," said I, " and thank you very much for coming so well. I'll be as quick as I can, but I doubt if I shall be back under half an hour."

" Time for a nap," said Mona. " I'm sleepy now."

Five minutes later perhaps, with lowered lights, the

Whistler stole under the archway and into the cobbled yard of *The Beau Sejour*.

To my relief, a place had been left in the garage, no doubt against her return ; and when I had driven her in, I took the key from her switch and put it into a locker beneath the dash. And then I left the car and, when I had shut the door, I took off my wash-leather gloves.

As on the morning before, all the hotel was in darkness, both back and front : and a very few moments later I stepped out into the street.

I had walked for two or three minutes and had seen no one at all, when Bell fell in beside me and touched his hat.

" Ah, Bell," I said.

" I'm thankful to see you, sir. When you took the Whistler in, of course I thought it was Gedge. An' then you came walking out. I take it, sir, he won't need a car any more."

" He's had his last run," I said. " He put a foot wrong —and I put him where he belongs."

" I'm glad to hear it, sir. If ever I saw one, there was a dangerous man."

" Where's Captain Mansel, Bell ? "

" At Blois, sir. And not so easy. He was here himself till two. But he's staying at Blois till six, so we've plenty of time."

As we made our way to the Lowland, I told him what had occurred.

" And the moment we're in," I said, " you and Carson must plug that hole in the car. I don't think it's very obvious, but it might make somebody think."

" Very good, sir. A plated bolt would be the easiest way."

" Good for you," said I.

Bell was ever the soul of ingenuity.

As we left the town, some clock chimed a quarter to four, and ten minutes later I saw the Lowland ahead.

"There she is," I said, pointing. "I expect Miss Lelong's asleep. She's stood up devilish well, but she's had an exacting day."

And then I knew she was sleeping; for else she would have seen us and put on her parking lights.

Very gently I opened the door . . .

But she was not asleep. The Lowland's cushions were empty, and Mona Lelong was gone.

*   *   *   *   *

I should have sought for her, but I saw a little note-book beside the driver's seat. It had belonged to her bag—a bag I had bought for her use, when we were in Chartres.

By the light of the ceiling-lamp, I read what she said.

I have served your turn, my dear, and now I have faded away. It's very much better so; for soon you must fade away and you don't want me round your neck. And there are other reasons.

I've so much to thank you for. But most of all for being yourself with me. I don't quite know how you did it. Captain Mansel tried, and John Bagot—and they were sweetness itself. But you were yourself. You gave me forbidden fruit—fruit that I've often gazed at and longed to have: but it was forbidden to me, because I was an outcast—a thief and a confederate of worse than thieves. You knew all that, but it cut no ice with you. That day we spent in the mountains—I touched high-water-mark then. The dog had its paws on the table: but if you noticed the outrage, you gave no sign.

But now the play is over—at least, it will be over on Tuesday night. And then you'll go back to the world to which you belong—to Maintenance . . . and Jenny . . . And, you see, I can't go with you. We both know that. Your birthright will admit you. But I—I sold my birth-

right, as Brevet did. Of course I could pass—as he does. But that would cost me what self-respect I have. And so I have faded out.

Will you give my love to Jenny? Tell her the truth about me and then give her my love. She'll understand quite a lot that I haven't said.

Goodbye, Richard darling.

I am so proud to have been

Your loving friend,

THE STOAT.

PS.—Don't worry. I'm through with crime.

PPS.—The switch-key is under the mat.

For a long time I stared through the wind-screen, although there was nothing to see. Then I put up the little note-book and put out the ceiling-light.

" Miss Lelong has gone," I said. " The switch-key is under the mat. You take the wheel, Bell. I'm—rather tired."

CHAPTER X

BREVET KEEPS AN APPOINTMENT

WHEN I said that I was tired, it was no more than the truth—I had had but three hours' sleep in forty-eight hours. But I am well accustomed to going without my rest and, in fact, I had not felt weary until I saw the note-book that told me that Mona was gone.

The girl's abrupt departure had hit me hard. I knew she was right to go, not only because her presence might soon have embarrassed us, but because, ' when the play was over,' she could not step back, as we could, into the life we led. She had put herself out of court by doing as she had done, and, though we had been willing to help her, she would never have sailed under colours which she had no right to fly. She had said as much in her letter. But though she had done what was best—for herself as for us, her going had shaken me ; for I had grown fond of Mona, and she and I together had been taught terrible things. Besides, she had saved my life . . . And here was, of course, the reason why she was more easy with me than with Bagot or Mansel himself ; for when two together have stared Death out of countenance, they share for ever something which neither the one nor the other can share with anyone else. But what distressed me most was the knowledge of what it had cost her to take her leave. The price had been very high. She that had nothing had given up that which she had. For she had been happy with us. For eight tumultuous days she had lived and moved with men of her father's standing, with men whose hands were clean. And now the interlude was over. She had not returned to dishonour : but she was gone into a world in which she had no place ; for her heart was with her own kind, yet run with them she could not, because of the days before.

My mind was still full of her going, when Bell drew up at the door of *The Fountain Hotel.*

" Room 202, sir. I'll see to the car."

A night-porter took me up to the second floor, and one minute later I entered a pleasant suite.

Mansel, who had been dozing, was up in a flash.

" All well ? " he said.

I nodded.

He sighed with relief.

" And Mona ? "

" Has taken her leave."

" And our gentleman friend ? "

" Is dead."

" Damn you, William," said Mansel. " I wanted to kill him myself."

I laughed, and he poured me some liquor, of which I was very glad.

And then I sat down on a sofa and put up my feet, and Mansel called Bagot in and I told them my tale.

When at last I made an end—

"William," said Mansel, "you've taken Time by the forelock—and pulled it out. But I don't mind admitting I'm glad to see you back. You see, I saw something you didn't. I saw Gedge's eyes, as he followed you out of Vendôme.

"I didn't dare come after, for fear of spoiling your game. I very nearly did. When I'd had a word with the porter, I very near rang up Bagot and told him to bring the Rolls. And then I decided not to. You'd bluffed Gedge, good and proper—a really remarkable feat : and if I looked over your shoulder, I might tear everything up. But the moment I saw him go by, I knew he was out for blood. My only comfort was that he thought he had caught you bending, and I hoped very hard that that would turn the scale. But I did not like the thought of Dieppe on a Sunday night. However, as I say, I felt you must play the hand."

"You think he meant to get me before he drove out of Vendôme ? "

"Of that," said Mansel, "I have not the slightest doubt."

I laughed.

"It never occurred to me till we had left Rouen behind."

"Perhaps," said Mansel. "But you hadn't seen his face."

"And but for a speck of dirt, he'd be alive now."

"That's the way it goes," said Mansel. "An empire falls—because some printer's devil has missed his tram."

There was a little silence. Then—

"I'm sorry," said Bagot, "that Mona Lelong has gone."

" So am I," said Mansel. " But it's very much better so for all concerned. I'd a great regard for that girl, and now I've a great respect. Her right hand offended her—and so she has cut it off. We can all do that, you know : but devilish few of us do."

I could not follow him there ; but I did not pursue the point—in case he asked for the note-book which I had kept to myself.

" And now," said Mansel, " for the future. So far as I can see, you've covered up very well. There's only one thing—but, first of all, tell me this. Was the steamer English or French ? "

" French," said I.

" Good," said Mansel. " And now we needn't worry. You see, there's Mona's suitcase, which will be found on board. But the French will take no action—or if they do, the channels employed will be so tortuous that weeks will go by before the hunt is up. And long before that, the scent will have disappeared. Besides, all her stuff was new ; so it wasn't marked. And now for Punter . . .

" When Punter appears this morning outside *The Beau Sejour*, Gedge will not be in the window, to take his report. What, then, will Punter do ? "

" Nothing," said I : " unless he's very much changed."

" I quite agree," said Mansel. " Gedge was a jealous lord, and I'm sure that he firmly discouraged what he would have called ' butting in.' So Punter will take no action. His orders certainly were to pass, but on no account enter *The Beau Sejour*. That's only common sense ; for the wicked who assemble in public, are apt to assemble in jail. So I think we may safely assume that Punter will do nothing to-day. But when to-morrow comes, but Gedge isn't there, Punter will grow uneasy. After all, to-morrow's ' the day.' And as to-morrow goes on, but Gedge doesn't appear, Punter will feel that something has got to be done. He will, therefore, communi-

cate with Brevet—probably by wire. They must have
arranged some method, in case of accidents: and the
Post Office Telegraph offers the simplest way. And, as
Brevet is as shrewd as they make 'em, Brevet will disappear. So he must not wire to Brevet. And to keep
him from wiring to Brevet, we must pick Punter up.

"If I know Punter, it shouldn't be very hard. He
crumples easily. When he sees the Rolls beside him, he
will go quietly enough, whatever the hour of the day.
And two of the servants can hold him, till Brevet has left
the château, *en route* for Vendôme."

"And Rust?" said John Bagot.

Mansel raised his eyebrows.

"About Rust we can do nothing, because we do not
know him by sight. And it's too late to get to know
him. So if he puts a spoke in our wheel—well, it can't
be helped. But as Punter is reporting to Gedge, I think
it likely that Punter gives orders to Rust.

"And so we can take to-day off." He came to set a
hand on my shoulder. "And now, if I were you, William,
I'd take my rest. You show no signs, but I think that
you must be whacked."

"I am pretty tired," I said slowly. "I'll write out a
wire to Jenny and then I'll go to bed."

But when I entered my room, there was Bell with
peroxide and ointment, with which to dress my face.
And he would not let me be, until he had cleaned and
anointed the two or three scratches I had.

He had bought some sterilized lint, with which to do
the work: and that, I suppose, was more fitting than a
little square of linen, soaked with wayside water and
smelling very faintly of Mona Lelong's perfume.

* * * * *

At nine o'clock the next morning Punter emerged
from the yard of *The Beau Sejour*, Vendôme. I know

this because I was standing some twenty-five paces away.

For a moment he stood by the archway, biting his nails. Then he turned to his right and began to walk down the street.

I nodded to Rowley, and Rowley nodded to Bell—who was sitting at the wheel of the Rolls, perhaps sixty yards off.

As Punter passed the alley, Mansel fell in beside him, and I was three paces behind.

"I want you, Punter," said Mansel.

The man started violently. Then—

"Oh, my Gawd," he said. "You didn't 'alf give me a turn."

As the Rolls slid alongside—

"In you get," said Mansel.

Punter shot a frantic look round. Then he saw me and Rowley: and then he got into the car.

As the car moved off—

"Where's Gedge?" said Mansel, sharply.

"Gawd knows," said Punter, with bolting eyes. "I 'aven't seen 'im since Sunday, an' that's Gawd's truth. 'Is car's in the garridge all right. I think 'e must be sick."

"You're lying, Punter," said Mansel. "You'd better come clean."

"S'elp me Gawd, I'm not, sir. I wish I was."

"Why do you wish you were?"

"'Cause we got a job comin' off—on Thursday night. An' Brevet in Paris, an' all."

"Where's the job?" said Mansel.

"This side of Châteaudun."

"I thought it was at Morle," said Mansel. "The Château Robinet. And I don't think Thursday's right. You should be at Arx on Thursday."

Punter expired.

"There you are," he said. "I always knew Auntie wasn't up to your weight. In course I never said so. But I tole 'im I knew your shape an' 'e'd better leave you alone. But 'e wouldn' listen to me. Talked about amaterze an' wot 'e'd do to your guts."

"What's his car?" said Mansel.

"Dark-blue Whistler," said Punter. "She's in the garridge all right."

"Where were you meeting Brevet?"

"Pickin' 'im up in Chartres at 'alf-past eight."

"Where?"

"In the station yard."

"You're lying, Punter," said Mansel.

"No, sir," said Punter. "You can 'ave Brevet for me. A proper leper, 'e is. Ole school tie be ——. 'A major operation,' 'e calls it, when 'e does a —— in. 'I've lost another patient,' 'e says." He turned to look at me. "Fancy you gettin' out o' that jam, sir. I thought you was for it, then. Auntie was like a madman and Brevet got a crick in 'is neck. The things they said of The Stoat. An' even then we couldn' see 'ow she done it. An' then the bomb goes off an' the tunnel comes down." He wiped the sweat from his face. "I was only ten feet off an' I thought I was dead. An' all the fuses gone, an' nobody's got a torch. Gawd, wot a night! I don' wonder the Baron goes balmy."

I was shaking with laughter, but Mansel steadied his voice.

"That'll do, Punter," he said. "I want to know where Gedge is."

"In course you do," cried Punter. "An' so do I. Well, it doesn' matter now, as you've pulled me in. But I 'ave been wantin' to know for twenty-four hours. Unless he's sick or in bed, I dunno where he is. I tell you, 'is car's in the garridge."

"At *The Beau Sejour*?"

Punter hesitated. Then—

"You saw me come out," he said. "I ain't given nothin' away."

He had, of course, in the beginning : but I think he may be forgiven, for Mansel's sudden appearance had thrown the man off his guard.

We presently stopped by a wood, some thirty miles West of Vendôme. Mansel and Bagot had picked it the day before, for it lay six miles from a village, and that had no telephone.

And, as the Rolls came to rest, Bagot and Carson appeared.

" 'Ere," cried Punter. "You ain't goin' to bump me off?"

"It's all you're fit for," said Mansel.

"Oh, not an ole frien', sir," cried Punter. "I've known you more than ten years."

We all broke down at that, and Punter looked greatly relieved.

"Not this time," said Mansel. "But cross me again, Punter, and I will show you no mercy—I mean what I say. So if ever you see me coming, Gedge or no Gedge, you'd better get out of my road. By rights, I should put you to death. If you'd helped to abduct Mrs. Chandos——"

"I tole 'em not to," shrilled Punter. "I tole 'em that if they pinched 'er, you and Mr. Chandos would foller 'em down into 'ell."

Mansel continued sternly.

"I say, if you'd been in that show, in ten minutes' time you'd be hanging from one of those trees. But, as we don't know that you were, although you're a rotten blackguard, we're going to spare your life. Get out and go with Carson. He and Rowley will see that you don't get into mischief this afternoon."

Punter left the Rolls. And when Carson showed him some handcuffs, he put his wrists together without a word.

" Take him on, Rowley," said Mansel. " Carson, come here."

As Carson stepped to the door, Rowley followed Punter into the wood.

" In view," said Mansel, " in view of the lies he has told us and which he may think we believe, I think you will have to leave him at half-past six. But take all his money and leave the handcuffs on. Until he is rid of them, I don't think he'll give his mind to getting in touch with Brevet or anyone else."

" Very good, sir," said Carson, grimly.

" That means you'll have time to burn. So get some supper somewhere, before coming on."

Then Bagot got into the Rolls, and we took the way we had come.

We did not stop at Vendôme, but turned to the right for Tours, and a short four miles from Château-Renault we turned to the right again.

Almost at once we perceived a ruined barn . . .

The spot was solitary. Gedge had chosen it well.

Forty minutes later, we made our way back to Blois.

* * * * *

The four of us lunched at *The Fountain* and left the hotel with our luggage at three o'clock. We took the Paris road, for all to see : but we left it beyond Orleans, to stop three miles from Morle. Then, leaving Bell with the Rolls, we made our way to the wood from which we had first observed the Château Robinet. And there we lay down and talked, with our eyes on the hideous pile.

" I think," said Mansel, " that everything's cut and dried : but I'll just run through it again, for we shan't have another chance and it is so very important that no mistake should be made. And if either of you sees any snag, he will please interrupt me at once.

" When the curtain comes down to-night, Bagot and

Rowley will leave at once for Boulogne. They will take the Lowland, for the Lowland is Bagot's car. They will drive leisurely and they will go by Paris, instead of going direct. To-morrow afternoon Audrey will reach Boulogne: where John and Rowley will meet her and take her to Amiens. And there they will stay in their villa—the villa in which they have stayed and in which they were going to stay, when once they had left Anise.

"So much for John and Rowley. And now for us.

"As soon as the curtain falls, you and I and the servants will take the Rolls. We shall drive to Pau and there we shall turn for Bayonne. And soon after nine to-morrow, we shall cross the bridge at Hendaye and enter Spain. We shall then drive down to Gibraltar, stopping two nights on the way: and there we shall ship the car and sail for England as soon as ever we can."

"I can't better that," I said. "I'd like to see John in England: but the Lowland's numbers are French and it's better that he should do as he had arranged to do."

"Nothing will happen," said Bagot. "And if it did —well, I spent the crucial hours at *The Fountain* at Blois."

"And the Lowland?" said Mansel.

"Was at Vendôme. If some unauthorized person took her out . . ."

"You'll do," said I, and laughed. "Give Audrey my love."

And then we discussed the last scene, which soon shall speak for itself.

So we passed the time, until, at ten minutes to six, Brevet came out of the château and left in a black Delage.

* * * * *

Little more than four hours later, I saw the Delage again.

As it turned into the lane, I rose and moved behind it,

while Bagot, who had been with me, ran down the road towards Tours. Bagot was gone to tell Mansel that the rat had entered the trap.

There was room to turn by the barn, and I thought that Brevet would use it: but, though he got out and examined the space there was, I suppose he decided to wait for the others to guide him, for, when he returned to his car, it was only to switch off her engine and put out her lights.

Then he shut her door and lighted a cigarette.

In my left hand I had my torch, and, as he threw down his match, I put the light on his face.

"Don't move, Brevet," I said.

The cigarette fell from his lips, but the man did not start. He stayed as the light had caught him, with his right hand a little extended and the match-box fast in his left. And so he still was standing, as though he was bound by some spell, when Bell, who was just behind him, took hold of his wrists.

He made no resistance at all, but only stared straight at the light, with a frozen look on his face.

I put up the torch and bound his arms behind him, using a scarf. Then Bell released his wrists and laid hold of the scarf, instead.

Brevet gave a light laugh.

"I fear," he said, "I was foolish to visit *The Beau Sejour*. I take it you . . ."

"I know the hotel," I said.

"Quite," said Brevet. "The moment I entered the house I felt that you did. Of such is instinct—that lovely messenger. And so, as you know, I withdrew—to dine at a humbler board. But, of course, the damage was done. But I must felicitate you—you follow with great discretion. I had my chin on my shoulder all the way."

I saw no reason for shattering Brevet's belief, but, in fact, I had not seen him since six o'clock.

" I told you I'd get you," I said.

" Quite," said Brevet. " Twice. On the second occasion, I felt you were optimistic. But you were right, Mr. Chandos, and I was wrong." He threw a glance round. " Is this to be the scaffold ? "

" Yes."

" Indeed. A dramatic setting. *Scene 4*: A Ruined Barn. And now let me tell you something. You lighted upon me by chance. I'm sure you've tried very hard and you must be sick of the sight of Châteaudun. But it was the purest fluke that you and I should have clicked at *The Beau Sejour*. Now I'm not going to try and make terms, because I am perfectly sure that you'd turn them down : but I'm going to tell you something which you will be glad to know. We two have little in common, but one emotion we share. And that is a hearty dislike of Daniel Gedge.

" In a very few minutes from now Daniel Gedge will be here. And he will expect to find me, but he won't expect to find you. If, then, with my hat on your head, you walk up to his car . . . You're bigger, of course, but all cats are gray in the dark. And our friend will be unready. And in case I should lift up my voice, I'm quite prepared to be gagged.

" Think it over, Mr. Chandos. And if, when Gedge is no more, in spite of the service I've done you, you still feel that I should die—well, I shall be at your disposal, as I am now."

There was a little silence.

Then—

" Treachery, too," I said. " How low can you sink ? "

Brevet shrugged his shoulders.

" My values," he said, " are dictated by instincts other than yours. Pray take it from me that the portion of Ishmael tends to blur, so to speak, the finer shades of good form."

" Gedge won't be alone," I said.

" No, no," cried Brevet. " Punter and Rust will be there. But they ' are spirits of another sort.' Your man can look after them. Once Gedge is out, they'll give no trouble at all. They're typical jackals, you know. But Daniel Gedge . . . You know, you'll be doing Mansel a very good turn. Gedge means to get him, Mr. Chandos. And, frankly, it's fifty fifty. I know Captain Mansel's brilliant. But so, in his way, is Gedge. And I think that, if I were you, I should accept this chance of assuring the life of your friend. And now, if you're going to gag me . . ."

" I'm not going to gag you," I said.

Brevet bowed.

" It's very pleasant," he said, " to deal with a gentleman." I felt rather sick. " Forgive me, but Time's getting on. And our vulgar friend may be early. And since I must not appear, may I suggest that I should re-enter my car ? I—can't very well emerge, if my hands are tied."

Now whilst we had been talking, more than one car had gone by on the main highway : but as Brevet made his suggestion, I heard the sigh of the Rolls. An instant later she had swept into the lane.

" Here he is," hissed Brevet, and started aside.

But Bell held him fast.

" You fool," cried Brevet, struggling. " I mustn't be seen."

" Not Daniel, but Mansel," I said.

Brevet stood still as death.

The Rolls stole on towards us. Then she came to a standstill, and Mansel got out.

" I see," said Brevet, slowly. " And Gedge ? "

" Is not coming," said I.

" Quite. A—previous engagement ? "

" Yes."

Brevet laughed—rather shakily.

" My, er, premises seem to have been faulty. ' Pleased to the last, he crops the flowery food, And licks the hand just raised to shed his blood.' Pope had a knack, you know. But the heroic couplet is a medium for which I cannot care. If ever Shakespeare employs it, he almost always nods."

He never heard the Lowland approach from the other side.

" No trouble ? " said Mansel, shortly

" None," said I, and, with that, I drew my torch and threw its light on the ground.

Brevet's voice was trembling.

" Before you do this," he cried, " I beg that you will reflect. I have no quarrel with you. From first to last, my hand has been forced by Gedge. It has gone against the grain to——"

" There's nothing doing, Brevet," I said. " We don't like ' losing patients,' but——"

" *What ?* "

I put the light on his face. This was distorted with hatred. The mask was off.

" Is the euphemism familiar ? "

And, as I spoke the words, Mansel flicked him under the chin.

His head went back, but Bell held his body up.

" Quick," said Mansel. " He won't be out very long."

Now we had early decided that, when Brevet's body was found, the police must be led to believe that he had taken his life. To that end, we had laid our plans.

In the Rolls we always carried a length of hose, so that, wherever we were, so long as there was a tap, she could be easily washed. From this hose twelve feet had been cut—and carefully sponged with petrol, because there were finger-prints there. What was left of the hose was now at the foot of a village well.

Wearing gloves, Carson took the tube and a morsel of cotton waste . . .

Two minutes later, the Delage's engine was running and carbon monoxide was stealing into the car.

Mansel put in his head.

"Good enough," he said, and switched on the ceiling light. "Get him inside."

Whilst Bagot held Brevet up, Bell undid the scarf. Then Bagot and I, between us, lifted him into the car.

Then Bagot and I stood back, and Carson shut the door.

"Watch him, Carson," said Mansel. "The other two turn the cars."

Whilst this was being done, we strolled down the lane in silence—Mansel, John Bagot and I, as we had so often strolled about this time.

"End of a reptile," said Mansel. "Upon my soul, I think he was worse than Gedge."

I told them of Brevet's betrayal—of how he had sought my favour by teaching me how to kill Gedge.

"I'm not surprised," said Mansel. "But that is something that Gedge would never have done."

"Gedge was animal," said Bagot.

"Yes," said Mansel, "he was. A ruthless, dangerous beast. But what was Brevet ?"

But to that we could find no answer, and after a little we let the question go.

And then we turned and made our way back to the cars.

"He's never moved, sir," said Carson.

"Good," said Mansel. "Give me the scarf and gloves."

With the gloves on his hands and the scarf about his face, he opened the door of the Delage and put out the ceiling light. Then he shut the door again and put off the scarf and gloves.

We shook hands with John Bagot and Rowley.

"You two get going," said Mansel. "I want to watch your withdrawal. And then we'll go."

"See you in Town," said John Bagot, and Rowley touched his hat.

Three minutes later, perhaps, Bell signalled that all was clear, and the Rolls stole out of the lane and turned to the right for Tours.

*   *   *   *   *

At six on the following evening, we entered Madrid.

We had bathed and changed and were drinking some excellent sherry before we sat down to dine, when a man climbed down from a stool and stepped to our side.

"Well, Jonah," he said.

It was Captain Toby Rage.

"Sit down and drink," said Mansel. "What are you doing here?"

"You do well to ask," said Rage. "It's all your fault. I ought to be at Biarritz—fleetin' the days as they did in the golden world."

"How is it my fault, Toby?"

"You left me holding the infant, last time we met."

Mansel raised his eyebrows.

"I remember the occasion. Murder had just been done. And I told you——"

"Quite so," said Toby. "You told me what action to take and then you—withdrew."

Mansel smiled.

"I begin to see daylight," he said.

"Do you indeed?" said Toby, bitterly. "Well, I wish you'd let me see some on that Arabian night."

"I said that the ways of the police were bad for my heart."

"You didn't say that they would corrode the soul." A waiter appeared. "A double sherry, please. The finest you have. At this grandee's expense. And now, where was I ? Oh, yes. The ways of the police. You didn't say they'd conduce to leprosy. You didn't say that their stench would offend high heaven and poison the very cesspools under the earth."

Both Mansel and I were laughing. Toby regarded us gravely and then drank my sherry up.

" Let's have it, Toby," said Mansel.

Captain Rage took a deep breath.

" You baited the trap," he said, " and I walked slap in. You gave me information which was above all price. You said that the robber-chief—and, no doubt, first murderer—had parked the swag in that half-built house next door. And you showed me the obvious truth that he would return to claim it, before the workmen arrived to pursue their honest toil. Well, I'm not very bright, as you know : but even I could perceive that an ambush or ambuscade would almost certainly bring forth refreshing fruit.

" Now in view of the fact that the robber-chief was impulsive, but I myself was unarmed, discretion suggested that I should seek assistance and not lie in wait alone. My boon-companions, however, inspired no confidence. Now that the coast was quite clear, their valour blinded the eye : but they'd hidden it under a bushel, until I declared the fact that the rogues were gone. And so I thought it was best to wait for the police." He raised his eyes to heaven. " So the congenital idiot awaits the pretty carriage that is going to carry him off to the mental home.

" Well, the police arrived in three cars.

" The first thing those experts did was to surround the villa—not the half-built house, the villa in which the crime had been done. When that stratagem had been accomplished, the guests were herded into two separate rooms : men in one, women in the other—a needless precaution, I felt, for dalliance had been discouraged by what had occurred. What next they did, I don't know, because, of course, I was confined. It wouldn't surprise me to learn that they turned the water off. But I fairly fell upon the *agent* who was standing beside our door.

"I demanded to see the head wallah without delay, as having most vital information about the crime. I might as well have demanded to watch some Mother Superior having a bath. When I became insistent, I was desired to have patience and calm myself. Nerves and tranquillity were mentioned : repose was recommended . . .

"Subduing a thirst for blood, I started all over again.

"'If you'll do as I say,' I said, 'you will not only recover the stolen jewels, but you will take alive the principal thief.'

"The *agent* lifted a hand.

"'All in good time, Monsieur.'

"'And that's where you're wrong,' I said. 'You haven't a moment to lose.'

"'We are losing no time, Monsieur. Be sure of that. The finger-print experts are coming.'

"'The thieves were gloved,' I said.

"'Ah, so you think.'

"'Think?' I cried. 'I saw them.'

"He gave me a professional smile.

"'The photographer also,' he said, 'will soon be here.'

"I felt rather faint.

"And then I had a brain-wave. At least, that was how I saw it. I little knew that it was in fact inspired by the malignant tenant to whom you had let my soul.

"'D'you want to lose your pension?' I said.

"The sinister suggestion shook him. Within two minutes I was speaking to a plain-clothes man.

"I gave him your information, chapter and verse. And he replied—I'll give you his very words.

"'Monsieur is ingenious. But the police will deal with

the crime. It is very right and proper that Monsieur should wish to help. But we have no need of assistance. Where others suspect, we know. You see, unhappily we are familiar with crime. And so we always know what the criminal does—and will do. That is how we bring him to justice—by looking into his mind. Now, in the first place, Monsieur, no robber would ever park such very valuable booty so close to the scene of his crime.'

" ' Go and look,' I said, trembling.

" ' Secondly, these three men made off in a car.'

" ' They didn't,' I yelled. ' They couldn't. Their car was done in.'

" ' Thirdly, you may be sure that they have been stopped by now. All the roads have been closed, and we only await the news that they are under arrest. And then you shall help us, Monsieur; for you shall identify them.'

" ' Don't you know they were masked ? ' I said.

" ' What of that ? We shall mask them again.'

" I began to wonder if I was losing my wits.

" ' Look here,' I said. ' Police or no police, you've got the wrong sow by the ear. Your theories may be superb, but I am dealing with facts. The stuff is lying next door. Take me out and I'll find it and you can take it away. And if you put three men there, when the robber-chief comes back you'll get him, too.'

" The other drew himself up.

" ' This is not,' he said, ' the theft of a bicycle. We are dealing with desperate assassins—whom we shall outwit. Never fear that, Monsieur. But it is by reading their brains that we shall bring them to book.'

" I won't repeat my reply—which I don't think he got. This may have been as well. In any event just then a local photographer arrived—with his wife, to play assistant and help him to change his plates. It seemed they were friends of the other, for they all shook hands once or twice and the policeman asked after their dog.

" Then he returned to me.

" ' Monsieur will excuse me,' he said. ' He may not perhaps comprehend the highly important part which the camera always plays in the detection of crime.'

" I looked at him very hard.

" ' Mind you photograph the piano,' I said.

" ' Why the piano, Monsieur ? '

" ' Because the thieves didn't play it. That ought to send them down.'

" I think he suspected that saying. Any way, a moment later I was back in the morning-room. And there I stayed for four sodden, soul-searing hours, listening to my colleagues explaining how, but for the presence of the ladies, they would have dealt with the thieves.

" At half-past six my name and address were taken and I was allowed to withdraw. And, as I stepped on to the pavement, I saw a workman approaching, suit-case in hand. I need hardly say he had come from the half-built house. He showed it to an *agent* : and after an altercation, the *agent* shrugged his shoulders and carried it into the villa, to show it, I suppose, to his chief.

" I admit I was greatly surprised, for it meant, of course, that the big shot had not been back. Still, at least, it confirmed my story—which warmed my heart. If only I'd known . . .

" From then on, for fourteen days, the police never left me alone. They declared they had found the jewels before I had opened my mouth : but they wanted to know how I knew where the jewels had been parked. I told them a stranger had told me—a passer-by : that I didn't know him from Adam and hadn't seen his features because it was dark. And then I asked what it mattered —because he'd have kept his counsel, if he was a rogue. And then, at last, they said the obvious thing. They said that the passer-by must have seen the robber-chief.

" I must have made twenty statements—and signed the lot. Wherever I went, there was some policeman waiting, to ask me some drivelling question, like the date of my father's birth. Then some wallah comes down from Paris, an' they start all over again. Identification parades of people I'd never seen. Evil-smelling offices. Statements in triplicate. Furtive consultations, to which I was not admitted, although I was three yards off. Hand-shakings *ad nauseam*—I shook hands with a prisoner one day, supposing him to be the detective who had him in charge. Believe me, the mistake was venial. But when I heard what he was charged with, I felt that I'd done enough. So I just packed up and withdrew— and here I am.

" I need hardly say that the robber-chief and his band are still at large. And so long as they stick to France, I should say they're as safe as a wolf in a barn full of sheep. But if they were taken tomorrow, I shouldn't care. You see, I've lost interest in the matter. They say you don't care for the play, when once you've been conducted behind the scenes."

" I apologize, Toby," said Mansel. " I never dreamed you'd meet it as badly as that. The French are officious, of course : and that shortens my life. But sometimes they're very good. And now come and dine with us. What have you done with Cicely all this time ? "

" Cicely," said Toby, " is due in seven days. I've wired to her to meet me in San Sebastian—that should be safe by then. I suppose she's still alive. You see, she's visiting cousins—fine, deep-chested brutes, with enormous hands, that ' take a dip ' before breakfast and ' never feel so fit ' as after thirty-six holes in the driving rain. So I thought I'd give them a miss. Brief life is here our portion, so why make it briefer, still ? "

Toby was like a tonic. I think I laughed more that evening than I had laughed for years.

Two days later we dined beside The Rock.

And within the week I was back at Maintenance.

With my arms about my darling—

" Jenny," I said, " there was a time, my sweet, when I'd every reason to think that I'd never see you again."

" I know," she said. " On a Friday. The thirty-first of July. I couldn't sit still that day and I couldn't sleep that night. And then very early next morning, I knew you were safe. And now tell me everything."

And so I did. And I gave her Mona's note-book, as Mona had bade me do.

When she had studied the letter—

" I'd love to know her," said Jenny. " We feel the same about things."

CHAPTER XI

A LADY LEAVES TOWN

SEVEN months had gone by, and Jenny and I were in Town. We had had to come up for a wedding, and should have stayed with Mansel in Cleveland Row : but he was away. So we had stayed at the Savoy. And now we were about to be gone.

We had lunched at half-past twelve, for we wished to be home for tea, and Maintenance was roughly a hundred miles away.

I had paid our bill and our luggage was in the Rolls, which was waiting, with Bell at the wheel, upon the Embankment side.

I finished my coffee and rose.

" Ready, my darling ? "

" Yes."

" Then I'll get my coat."

Q

I crossed the floor to the cloak-room . . .

As I was coming back, I almost collided with Mona, who had just descended the steps.

She looked away at once, but I caught her arm.

" Why, Mona ! "

And then I saw the stricken look in her face.

" Keep clear of me, Richard. Any moment now I'm going to be under arrest."

I drew her arm through mine and held it tight.

" No, you're not," I said. " You're going to get into the Rolls."

I beckoned to Jenny and urged her away from the steps.

As Jenny came up—

" This is Mona," I said, " of whom I have told you so much."

" Oh, I'm so glad," cried Jenny.

" She's in a hurry, my sweet, so we'll talk in the car."

" Richard," cried Mona, " it's hopeless. I——"

" It damned well will be," said I, " if you won't do as I say."

Mona gave the ghost of a laugh.

" All right. I'll go quietly," she said. " But wait till you know the truth."

" Where are you staying ? " I said.

She named an hotel that stands in Kensington Gore.

" We'll drive there first. You can talk as we go along."

In less than a minute, I think, we were all in the Rolls ; and Bell was driving as fast as ever he dared.

Mona was speaking jerkily, with Jenny's arm about her and Jenny's hand upon hers.

" I'd meant to lunch in the grill-room. As I came in, I saw a man called Gonzales, a Portuguese. And he saw me.

" It was the damnedest misfortune. I think he's the only man who could send me down. Nearly a year ago,

I—met him in Portugal. Only for a moment, of course : but he never forgets a face. He's a very big banker— Gonzales. And thirty thousand pounds is a lot of money to lose."

" Go on, Mona," I said.

" I don't think he thought I saw him : I gave no sign. I took my seat at a table . . . At once he rose and went to the telephone . . . The moment his back was turned, I left the room. And then I ran into you."

" You're wanted in Portugal ? "

" Yes."

" Extradition," I said. " I wish I knew the law."

" He'll get all he wants from the Yard. He's a very big man."

" Won't a warrant have to be issued ? "

" They can detain me, Richard, at any time."

" If you're recognized—yes."

" She must come to Maintenance, Richard."

" Never," cried Mona. " Never. I'm not going to foul your nest."

" It isn't that," said I. " But Maintenance isn't safe. I can't shut the servants' mouths, and if she was seen leaving with us, the police will be there tonight. And now let me think, you two."

" I knew he'd say that," said Jenny.

" So did I," said Mona. " But I'm up against it, Jenny. Richard, you know I am. This isn't France."

" You're telling me," said I. " All the more important that you should let me think."

If Gonzales was known to the Yard and could speak with a big enough man, Mona Lelong's position was grave indeed. Unless she could leave the country, she would be laid by the heels in forty-eight hours. Yet, before I could get her to Dover, the port would be watched. Croydon was out of the question—criminals fancy the air. And if she could board some liner, long before she could land, the wireless would pick her up. And then I thought of the s.s. *Harvest Moon*.

I had seen her name in the papers. The ship was about to sail on a luxury cruise. And I knew Geoffrey Majoribanks—who was a powerful man on the Black Moon line.

It seemed the only chance. The police might rule her out, for luxury liners bring back their human freight. If Mona went aboard at Southampton, to Southampton she would have to return—unless she could disappear at one of the ports of call.

As the Rolls came to rest—

" By what name does Gonzales know you ? "

" Christine Lefevre," said Mona.

" I see. Now you're going to pack and be ready in half an hour. We shall be back by then."

" I'm going to help her," said Jenny.

" What could be better ? " said I. " And no rot this time, Mona. You're going to be in the hall when I come back."

" Very well," said Mona, dully. " I oughtn't to let you do this, but I don't know what else to do."

I saw them out of the Rolls. Then I took the seat beside Bell and told him to drive to Pall Mall.

*   *   *   *   *

" My dear old fellow," said Geoffrey, " you're just four weeks too late. The *Harvest Moon* sails tomorrow, but she's been full up for a month. It's a very popular cruise—Gibraltar, Naples, Corfu and the Isles of Greece."

" Room for a little one," said I. " She's badly in need of a change—and a very great friend of ours."

Geoffrey fingered his chin.

Then he picked up a telephone.

" Send me Mr. Collins," he said . . .

Mr. Collins raised his eyebrows.

" There's Seventy-two, Mr. Majoribanks."

" And nothing else."

" Not a berth, let alone a cabin."

Geoffrey turned to me.

" Cabin Seventy-two is one that we seldom sell. It is
' a director's cabin ' : but, as it's so late in the day, I think
I can take the risk. It's a very nice, two-berth cabin.
To a friend of yours, say, a hundred and twenty pounds."

I took my cheque-book out.

" I'm very grateful, Geoffrey."

" That's all right. What's her name ? "

" Miss Mona Lelong, of Rydal. We'll take her down
to the ship. What time does she sail ? "

" Half-past four. They'll let her aboard at two."

Five minutes later the ticket was in my hands.

" Well, goodbye, Geoffrey. And thank you very
much."

" That's all right, old fellow. Give Jenny my love."

*   *   *   *   *

Much less than three hours later, the Rolls slipped out
of Winchester and on to the Lyndhurst road.

Mona's nerve had come back, but her eyes were
strained.

" Soon be there now," I said.   " Is everything clear ? "

" Yes, my dear. You lunch with me tomorrow at one
o'clock. I am all packed and ready before you come.
And at two o'clock we leave for Southampton docks."

" Swear you won't—let me down."

" I swear I won't. But I feel very badly about it. If
you get involved, I'll never forgive myself."

I turned to Jenny.

" That from Mona—who saved your husband's life."

Jenny set her cheek against Mona's.

" You saved two lives," she said.

Then the two of them talked together, while I sat back

in my corner and tried very hard to foresee what the next few hours would bring forth.

It was not quite five o'clock when we set Mona down at the door of *The Grand Hotel*. And the stable clock struck six, as we came to Maintenance.

* * * * *

We had dined, as we always do, at half-past eight, and now we were sitting together before the library fire.

"Will it be all right, Richard?"

"I hope it will, my beauty. If I can get her aboard, we're halfway home."

"Only halfway?"

I nodded.

"She'll be in danger as long as she's on the ship. Once she lands at Naples, she's out of the jurisdiction."

"When will she get to Naples?"

"Not for ten days," I said.

There was a little silence.

Then—

"And if the police come here?"

"I think I can fob them off. Once she's gone, they can sit on the mat all day. But I must have tomorrow off. I hope if they see me go hunting, they'll leave it there."

"When's Jonathan coming back?"

"I've no idea, my sweet. I wish I had."

"He couldn't have done any more."

"He's quicker than I am, Jenny."

"Perhaps he is: but he couldn't have done any more."

Here Bell came in with a salver.

I picked up the card.

DETECTIVE INSPECTOR GOALBY.

C.I.D.

"Thank God it's not Falcon," I said. "All right.

I'll see him here, Bell. Jenny, my sweet, you sit in the drawing-room."

Jenny stooped and kissed me and left the room.

A moment later the visitor was announced.

I got to my feet.

" Good evening, Inspector. What can I do for you ? "

" I'm looking for a lady, sir. I think she's a friend of yours."

I frowned.

" When you say ' looking,' " said I . . .

Goalby nodded abruptly.

" I've a warrant for her arrest."

I opened my eyes.

" What's the charge ? " said I.

" Uttering forged bank-notes—to the sterling value of thirty thousand pounds."

" Good God," said I. " You must want her very much."

" A Portuguese banker does, sir."

" I see. Well, please get this. Friends of mine do not utter forged bank-notes. If they did, they wouldn't be friends of mine."

Goalby seemed taken aback. When he spoke again, his manner was much less assured.

" Perhaps I should have said ' an acquaintance of yours.' "

" That's better," I said. " I knock about quite a lot and I meet all sorts and kinds. Still, I can't think of anyone——"

" At the Savoy, sir. Today. You took her off in your car."

" What, Miss de Winton ? " I said.

" That may be one of her names."

" A tall, dark girl, with a very striking face."

" That would be her, sir. Dressed in a blue costume and wearing a mink fur coat. Where did you drive her to ? "

I motioned him to a chair and took my seat on the kerb.

" I think you're wrong," I said, " but here we go. I drove her straight to the Ritz—at her own request. I was going that way myself, when I ran into her in the hall. It seemed she had a luncheon appointment, which she was most anxious to keep. This was at the Ritz. Without thinking what she was doing, she had driven to the Savoy. Only when she looked round the grill-room, did she remember that she should have gone to the Ritz. And she hadn't a penny left—in her purse, I mean. She'd given her last half-crown to the taxi that brought her there. And so she fell upon me."

" That was the tale she told you ? "

" It was perfectly credible. And I had no reason to think that she wasn't telling the truth."

" How well do you know her, Mr. Chandos ? "

" Not very well. I met her at Biarritz last summer. Danced with her once or twice."

" Christian name ? "

" I didn't use it. I think she was called Elise."

" And you set her down at the Ritz. At which entrance, please ? "

That meant he was going to see Bell. Well, let him. My servant knew what to say.

" The Piccadilly entrance," I said.

" And then ? "

" We drove down here," I said.

" May I know what time you arrived ? "

" I really couldn't tell you," I said. " Later than we had intended, for one of our tires gave in, and we had to change a wheel."

" That wouldn't take long, Mr. Chandos—not today."

" As a matter of hard fact, it took us forty minutes: we couldn't shift the hub-cap—it hadn't been off for years."

A car cannot talk, but the Rolls would bear me out. She was washed by now, but one of her tires was flat.

Goalby stared at his note-book.

" It's a wicked case, Mr. Chandos ; and we are very anxious to help the Portuguese. And there are other aspects. For more than five years now, batches of beautiful notes have been uttered all over the place. It seems likely—extremely likely—that if we get Miss de Winton, the issue will cease. I'm sure you wouldn't allow any personal sympathy——"

" Miss de Winton," I said, " is nothing to me. I'm always sorry to see a lady go down ; but I shouldn't risk my freedom to help a casual acquaintance, because I met her at Biarritz and danced with her once or twice."

" She's a woman, Mr. Chandos. From all I'm told, a highly attractive girl."

" That's perfectly true. And I should swear that the banker had made a mistake, if I didn't know for a fact that more than one topnotcher is really a crook."

Goalby got to his feet.

" Well, that's all for tonight, Mr. Chandos. I may have to ask you to let me see you again."

" When ever you please," said I.

" Tomorrow, perhaps ? "

" Tomorrow evening with pleasure. Tomorrow's a hunting day."

Goalby looked at me very hard.

" I see. May I see your chauffeur ? "

" Of course."

I stepped to the bell.

" I'll see him alone, if I may, sir."

" By all means." Bell entered the room. " The Inspector wants to ask you some questions. Take him into the morning-room."

" Very good, sir."

I turned to Goalby.

" Will you want me again tonight ? "

" Not tonight, sir, thank you."

" Good night," I said.

I brought Jenny back, and the two of us sat in silence, till Bell re-entered the room.

I raised my eyebrows.

" He's gone, sir."

" He's not very satisfied, Bell."

" Not altogether, sir. He's spending the night at *The Crown*. Asked where the meet was tomorrow : so I told him Gallowstree Hill." This was quite true. But the Blackmore Vale is not the only hunt. Other hounds were to meet at Flourish, which lay some thirty-five miles from Gallowstree Hill. " He asked what time you'd leave, sir : and I said I thought about ten."

" So I shall," said I. " D'you think we can count on Walter ? "

" I think so, sir. He'll leave at half-past six."

" Very well," I said. " We can't do anything more."

I told Jenny all that had happened, and when we had talked for a little, we went to bed.

Had I had a little longer, I could, I think, have made a better plan : but the devil was driving hard, so I had to make my bricks of what straw there was.

At half-past six a groom would leave for Flourish, leading Romford and riding my second horse. He would put them up at a little inn that I knew, until I arrived in the Rolls at eleven o'clock. *But if I did not come, he would keep them stabled till four and then bring them home.* At ten o'clock, I should leave in the Rolls, in hunting dress. Bell would be driving me. In a barn near Flourish, I should change. And from there we should make for Lyndhurst as fast as ever we could. Once Mona was safe aboard, we should return to the barn, where I should change again. Then I should foul my boots and return to Maintenance.

The plan was far from brilliant, but, as I have said, it was the best I could make. And at least the Rolls was faster than Goalby's car.

*   *   *   *   *

It was three o'clock, and Mona and I were aboard the *Harvest Moon*. As once before, we were sitting alone in her cabin. . . .

All seemed to have gone very well. After all, the police are human, and four other ships were sailing that afternoon.

I glanced at my watch.

" I ought to be going, my lady. Only ten days to Naples—and then you're safe."

Mona bit her lip.

" Only ten days," she said.

I took her hand in mine.

" I know. It'll seem a lifetime. I'd come with you, if I could. But keep your heart up, Mona. We've been through worse than this."

" Supposing . . . the worst should happen."

" Wire me at once," I said. " It won't matter then. And I will get hold of Mansel, as soon as ever I can. But nothing will happen, Mona. Send me a letter from Florence to Brooks's Club."

" And you ? "

" I'll write to Florence, I promise. You'll find a letter there. Sure you're all right for money ? "

" Indeed I am. I'm full of travellers' cheques. How much do I owe you, Richard ? In cash, I mean ? "

" Let that go for the moment. We'll settle another time. And now I must go, my dear."

We both stood up and I put my arms about her and she put hers round my neck.

" God bless you, Richard," she quavered. " God bless you and Jenny for what you've done."

" Don't be silly, Mona. We're three of a kind."

I think I shall always see the smile that swept into her face.

Then she put up her lips and kissed me, as once she had done before.

* * * * *

Dusk was in, when we came to Maintenance.

As the Rolls slid up the avenue—

" The Inspector's there, sir," said Bell. " I can see his car."

" Damn the man," said I. And then, " It can't be helped."

As Bell brought the Rolls to rest, Inspector Goalby moved to the foot of the steps. And, as I got out, he looked me up and down.

" Had a good day, Mr. Chandos ? "

" Not too bad," I said.

" Are you quite sure that you have been hunting ? "

" What do you mean ? "

" This. I attended the meet at Gallowstree Hill."

" Well, what of that ? "

" I—didn't see you, Mr. Chandos."

" That's not surprising," I said. " You attended a meet of the Blackmore Vale. I often hunt with them, but today I was hunting with the Beaufort. Hounds met at Flourish. That must be thirty-five miles from Gallowstree Hill."

Goalby's eyes were burning.

" I'm afraid it's my fault, sir," said Bell. " I thought you were going to hunt with the Blackmore Vale."

I looked at Goalby.

" You should have asked me," I said.

Goalby turned on his heel and got into his car.

* * * * *

Eight days had gone by—eight very worrying days. Jenny and I could think of nothing but Mona . . . Mona alone in the midst of that jovial throng—four hundred carefree souls, all of them bent on pleasure, laughing and making merry and bidding her join in their mirth. And she would smile and comply—for the look of the thing . . . with the sinister aerial above her, that terror by day and by night.

On the eighth day we went hunting—without much heart. But the meet was at Gallant's Folly, less than a mile from our gates.

In fact, the day did us good : and Jenny was chattering gaily, as we rode home in the dusk.

I followed her into the hall, and Bell came forward at once to take my things.

" Chief Inspector Falcon is at *The Crown*, sir."

" Oh, hell ! " said I. " Has he been here ? "

" Not yet, sir."

I passed on thoughtfully.

Falcon was late in the field, but I knew he was a very good man. Mansel thought much of him and had told me so. Still, though it meant more lies, I did not see what he could do. I had taken care to find out exactly how hounds had run on the day of the meet at Flourish, and Walter knew where I had mounted my second horse. Though Falcon might know something, at least he did not yet know where Mona was, for, if he did, he would not be wasting his time in the Wiltshire countryside. And charm he never so wisely, he should learn nothing from me. Still, I was far from easy. Falcon was very clever, and I am at my worst in a battle of wits.

He did not come that evening : but I knew very well he would come the following day.

And so he did.

It was a lovely morning, clean out of the basket of Spring. We had breakfasted betimes, and Jenny was in the meadows and I was sitting on the terrace, reading the morning paper, which reached us at half-past eight.

Towards the foot of the page, a paragraph caught my eye.

SUDDEN DEATH OF A PORTUGUESE BANKER

Senhor Vasco Gonzales, the eminent banker, who was on a visit to London, collapsed last night, when dining at the Portuguese Embassy in Belgrave Square. Senhor Gonzales expired, before medical aid arrived.

For a moment I stared upon the statement.

Then I knew such a sense of relief as did not, I fear, accord with the death of an honest man.

We had won the match. Mona Lelong was saved. There could be no proceedings, for the only man who knew her could not be called. Had she been taken before the ship had sailed, Gonzales would have testified at Bow Street, and that would have been the end : for, though he had died the next day, she would have been extradited to Portugal. But now she was saved.

I was just going down to tell Jenny, when Bell appeared to say that Falcon was in the hall.

"Wait thirty seconds," I said, "and then show him into the library."

With that, I entered the room, whose windows were wide. Then I sat down at my table and took up paper and pen.

"Chief Inspector Falcon, sir."

I rose to my feet.

"Good morning, Chief Inspector. D'you mind if I finish this letter, before we talk ? "

"Of course I don't, Mr. Chandos."

"Then sit down and take the paper."

"Thank you. I will. It hadn't arrived when I left."

Writing idly, I watched him—with the tail of my eye.

And then I saw him start—and stare at the paragraph.

I let another minute go by. Then I rose and left the table, to move to the fire.

Falcon folded the paper and got to his feet.

With a pleasant smile, he looked me full in the eyes.

" You win, Mr. Chandos," he said. " You're a very good friend, but it seems there's a better one, still."

" Death makes no mistakes," said I.

" From what I hear, I don't think you made very many. Goalby, of course, should be broken for going to Gallowstree Hill."

" Where would you have gone ? "

" Where you went, Mr. Chandos." He put out his hand. " Goodbye."

" Goodbye," I said. " I'm sorry I spoked your wheel. But not very long ago she saved my life."

" In that case, honours are even. If she had been extradited, she wouldn't have lived very long."

* * * * *

And that is the end of my tale.

We often hear from Mona. I cannot say where she lives : but I know she is not unhappy ; for no one whose heart was heavy could write the charming sketches that lighten *The* ——. That great gentleman, Jonathan Mansel, becomes our most welcome guest at least four times in the year. John and Audrey Bagot spend Christmas at Maintenance. And Carson and Rowley are nearly as much at home there as Bell himself. But I often think of the days when Gedge and Brevet were rampant and we were badly placed—when I was lying in Arx, and Mansel and Bagot were kicking against the pricks. And then I remember Mona : for, as I must have shown, but for that gallant lady, this tale would not have been told.

THE END